Descending From The Moon

Book 1 of
Brother To Jackals

by
Steven Popkes

Descending From
The Moon

Steven Popkes

Cover design by Wendy Zimmerman
Cover illustration © 2025 by Wendy Zimmerman

Published by Walking Rock Publications in
association with
Book View Café
304 S. Jones Blvd, Suite #2906
Las Vegas NV 89107
www.bookviewcafe.com
ISBN: 978-1-63632-326-8

Also By Steven Popkes

Novels

Caliban Landing
Slow Lightning
Welcome to Witchlandia
God's Country
Jackie's Boy
Danse Mécanique
House of Birds
Nuthatch County
Smilodon Country

Collections

Simple Things: Collected Stories
Tom Kelley's Ghost: Collected Stories
Winters Are Hard: Collected Stories
Looking Up, Looking Down

Novellas

The Long Frame
A New World

This one is completely for Wendy, who had faith in it far beyond my own.

Table of Contents

"I have become a brother to jackals, a companion to owls."

    —Job 30:29, New International Version

Prologue

"Animals are not brethren, they are not underlings. They are other nations, caught with ourselves in the net of life and time."
—Henry Beston

Mister Coyotee

Disclaimer: **Mister Coyotee is an animated system interviewing representations of actual human people. Resemblances to individuals, living or dead, are not coincidental at all. Resemblance of Mister Coyotee to an actual coyote, real or mythical, is marginal at best. The guests of the show may or may not be simulated, in whole or in part, at our discretion.**

M.Coyotee: We're going to be serious tonight in honor of the twentieth anniversary of the Restoration of the United States. While this is not a recognized holiday, it is an opportunity for a moment of reflection.

My two guests tonight are Doctor Willa Rogers, historian from Columbia University in New York, and Doctor Michael Brandt, historian from Harvard University in Cambridge.

My question to my guests seems a simple one: it has been twenty years since the Restoration. It has been close to seventy years since the beginning of the Die-Back. Where are we today?

W.Rogers: I'm not sure that's where we should begin. After all, Mike and I can't even agree when the Die-Back began and when it ended.

M.Brandt: Oh, please.

W.Rogers: I'm serious. Did the Die-Back begin with the first plagues, fifty years or so before the Restoration? Did it start with the Year of the Tsunamis—forever known as YOTT?

(Both laugh.)

Did it begin ten years after the first plagues with the disbanding of Congress and the Chu abdication?

M.Brandt: Clearly, the Die-*Back* had to begin when people actually *died*.

W.Rogers: The Year of the Tsunamis killed millions of people.

M. Brandt: Yes, it did. And I am not going to disparage the pain and suffering it caused. But out of eight billion people, the tsunamis didn't kill a measurable fraction. The *real* Die-Back—when the plagues started taking ten or twenty percent of the population *per year*—didn't begin until five years later.

W.Rogers: Agreed. But the rebuilding physical and social movement that began with the tsunamis was the environment in which the plagues began.

M.Brandt: So what? The plagues began in a social structure. What a surprise!

W.Rogers: You don't think that had an effect?

M.Brandt: I do not. I think the effect of wiping out the vast majority of humanity in barely a generation swamped any influence from the contemporaneous social structures. Therefore, *I* start the Die-Back fifty years before the Restoration.

W.Rogers: That's where we differ. I think not only did the social reforms influence how the Die-Back proceeded but had an effect on the Restoration.

M.Brandt: You're talking about the Big Five Amendments: 34: National Referendum. 35 and 36, the two voting reform amendments. 37, likeness and privacy. 38, nationalized disaster response. I think you can make a case for nationalized disaster response having an effect on the Die-Back itself but not for the other four. They *do* affect the Restoration, of course. But tracing a line from the beginning of the Die-Back to now isn't justified. Saying the amendments had an effect *then* and have an effect *now*, therefore they must have had an effect *between* then and now is just wishful thinking.

W.Rogers: You don't think the Chu abdication had any effect on the Die-Back?

M.Brandt: Only as an indication that all of the efforts to stop the Die-Back—including nationalized disaster relief—had failed.

M.Coyotee: You can't agree on when the Die-Back began. You also said you didn't agree when the Die-Back ended.

W.Rogers: The plagues died down fifteen years or so before the Restoration. Was that the end of the Die-Back? But those fifteen years were hard enough without having people dying of plagues. They were dying from things like starvation and lack of medical care.

M. Brandt: I think here Willa and I are closer to agreement. I do hold to a strict historical interpretation of the Die-Back timeframe: it began when the plagues began and it ended when the plagues fell back to pre-Die-Back levels. But that doesn't mean I'm blind to those years between the Die-Back and the Restoration. People were still dying from the knock-on effects of the Die-Back—

W.Rogers: Dying from lack of government, mostly.

M. Brandt: Dying from lack of supplies, *I* think.

Words matter. Some historians have said that the two great wars of the twentieth century—World War I and World War II—should be considered the same war. That neglects the twenty-one years between them. Twenty-one years that included a great depression, technological advancements, and huge political changes.

This is true here. A strict interpretation of when something began and ended is necessary to understand properly what came before and what came after.

W.Rogers: I disagree. *I* think that we are impressing boundaries and labels on things that were not so boundaried and labeled at the time. The Die-Back starting point might be apparent to my worthy colleague from Harvard but it wasn't so clear to those living *at the time*. To them, it was a wave of disasters the scale of which would not be clear for decades. That said, they had already lived through a significant disaster just a few years before. *That* disaster drove their response to *this* disaster.

M.Coyotee: And we're back to arguing the beginning instead of the end.

W.Rogers: These things matter.

M.Brandt: Of course, they *matter*. But they matter mostly to you and me. These are academic discussions.

W.Rogers: Academia was *lost* until after the Restoration. Harvard reopened fifteen years ago. Columbia reopened ten years ago.

M.Brandt: These things don't much matter to the people now, twenty years after the *end* of the Die-Back.

W.Rogers: Has the Die-Back even actually ended?

As Mike said, those who lived through the last seventy years are not monolithic. Some lived through the entire span of it regardless of where we place that date. They suffered excruciating trauma. Some were born in the latter days of the Die-Back leading into the Restoration. The world they were born into had already been destroyed. They saw that destruction as normal. The Restoration was a relief. Some have been born since the Restoration was declared. They live in increasingly better times.

But all of them—and us—live in the shadow of the Die-Back.

I don't think the Die-Back is done with us yet.

M.Coyotee: Let's table *this* discussion and say for argument's sake that the Die-Back began seventy years ago and came to an end with the Restoration, twenty years ago.

This is a presidential election year—the fifth since the Restoration and the first one with an incumbent seeking reelection. It's also the first such election where the full complement of voters born in the year of the Restoration are eligible to vote.

So: on this anniversary, where are we?

M.Brandt: Traumatized.

W.Rogers: Hopeful.

M.Coyotee: Explain. Willa?

W.Rogers: All of the legal and social changes before the disbanding of Congress are still in place, plus some new ones that came just before and after the Restoration. The remaining one percent—

M.Brandt: Or less.

W.Rogers: —of the population is trying to make sense of things. They've moved towards cities—

M.Brandt: Because of the Accords.

W.Rogers: Because of the robot industrial base that has been made accessible to them *because* of the

Accords.

M.Brandt: Which nobody likes.

W.Rogers: It's hard to like mechanisms that were shooting
             citizens to protect rotting crops. The Accords
             changed that.

M.Brandt: But if there are robots and a robot industrial
             base, why are we so limited? We have
             magnificent trains. Why don't we have
             airplanes?

W.Rogers: Exactly. We have an autonomous, industrial
             base supplying goods at essentially no cost.
             Why can't we create—*overnight*—the same
             culture we had before the Die-Back happened?

M.Brandt: Is that so unreasonable a question?

W.Rogers: So far, the robots have been rebuilding
             housing, reconstructing water, sewage, power,
             and network infrastructure, and supplying
             food. So, in this time frame, *yes:* it's an
             unreasonable question.

M.Brandt: My point isn't that the prospect of getting
             everything for Christmas may or may not be
             reasonable. My point is that the question, *itself,*
             should come as no surprise. People want
             airplanes. They get biotech—of which they are
             just as suspicious. Most consider the Die-Back
             an example of biological warfare.

W.Rogers: Not state-supported warfare. More like
             biological terrorism by uncounted non-state
             groups.

M.Brandt: That makes no difference to them.

W.Rogers: So, you're saying that not trusting the robots
             and not trusting the biotech—both of which are
             making the Restoration even *possible*—is
             natural?

M.Brandt: Exactly.

W.Rogers: That's irrational.

M.Brandt: That's human.

M.Coyotee: I think we understand why Dr. Brandt said "traumatized." But we didn't hear why Dr. Rogers said "hopeful."

W.Rogers: Each year since the Restoration we've had to contend with one crisis or another just to achieve normal operation. Now we have reliable water. Reliable power. The last Shuman election was uneventful—no one blowing up polling stations. No network worms consuming votes. Just casting votes and counting them—comfortable normalcy. Hence, hopeful.

M.Brandt: I disagree with my worthy colleague. I agree we've been distracted by crises for the last twenty years and those have largely been addressed. We have normal business. We have normal leisure. But we also have new concerns. New religions. New issues poking up their heads. We still have our repressed traumas and fears to be faced—as Willa pointed out, we have half the population considering the Die-Back as a morality play and the other suffering from PTSD because of it. It's a seethe of free-floating anxiety from a thousand sources. Eventually, it's going to crystallize around something.

W.Rogers: What?

M.Brandt: I have no idea.

M.Coyotee: Nor do we. But when we do, you know we will talk about it here. Wherever you are, viewers, good evening or good morning, and from Mister Coyotee, good night.

Three Years Before

‹ Marcus ›

The solarium had an indoor pool, but few of the apes did more than occasionally wade in the water. The pool lay, blue and inviting, in the center of the vast, enclosed concrete span. Only a young chimp and an orang played in the shallow end.

Around the pool, there were dozens of apes enjoying a warm winter afternoon nap. Most of them were gorillas and orangs, with a scattering of chimps.

Marcus Joan Marcus, an old silver-backed gorilla, slept in a favored spot on the top of the thirty-meter board. Normally, the orangs occupied this spot, but today he had luckily found it empty and claimed it. Marcus had a melanin dysfunction causing a white splotch on his left shoulder. It itched continually. Marcus scratched in his sleep.

Now, he dreamed.

He kept trying to dream easily, peacefully of a lake, glinting in the sunlight, the mountains purple behind the water. But his manmind wouldn't leave him alone. It kept populating the image with boats, birds, a man fishing, the sound of the wind. In his sleep, Marcus kept blinking the clutter away. It kept coming back. He brushed his hand against his face, waving it away in irritation, and the contact woke him. He scratched his shoulder.

Above him, sitting on the railing, a young orang watched him. For a moment, Marcus kept seeing lake and canoers and he couldn't figure out what this young orang was doing here. Then, he came fully awake and sat up. He looked outside the solarium and saw the light snow on the ground, the white buildings, the beach, and beyond the whitecapped marbled shallows, a towering reef of trees, shielding them all from the cold Atlantic Ocean farther away.

"Are you awake, Marcus?" said the orang. "Did you dream?"

"Nothing of consequence." Marcus rubbed his face. Then, Marcus realized that given the young orang's lesser status, he would not be here without a mission. He stared at him balefully. "Pontiac, how long have you been waiting for me to wake up?" he said irritably. The damned orangs were so formal—if something was going on, why the hell didn't Pontiac just nudge him?

"About an hour, I think. Maxwell sent me."

Marcus stretched his back and stood up. It hurt to stand up straight but Marcus managed it as often as he could. The other apes respected you more when you stood like a human. "What about?"

"He sent me to fetch you. To come to the chimp building. It's about Pearl. He said specifically to tell you it was about Pearl."

"Pearl?" Marcus looked down at Pontiac witheringly. "And you waited an hour? May you be culled." He swung down to the patio and lumbered between the sleeping apes out into the main lobby. Then, he took the first outside door and started to climb the nearest cable towards the roof. Many of the apes did not like the cold but Marcus enjoyed it. A brisk wind made him shiver delightedly.

In his mind, Marcus could see LeRoy shaking his finger at him, his all too human face wrinkled in concern. He could almost hear LeRoy admonishing him: *Pneumonia, damn it. You're going to get pneumonia.*

Marcus laughed. "Christ, LeRoy. Don't get your

ass in an uproar." LeRoy made a clumsy deity but he was all they had and Marcus loved him for it.

The shoals were gunmetal gray and through the trees, he could see the foam breaking. There was a storm coming in from the north. Closer, on the island itself, the trees were winter bare of leaves with a light snow on the ground. The different ape trails were marked by trodden ice and their clearings by mud.

The island was small as islands go. It had been a resort off the Georgia coast in the late twentieth and early twenty-first century, but nine hurricanes in two years, followed by a series of catastrophic tsunamis and the resulting deep economic depression, had battered the buildings and sent the tourists home scared. Even then, the parent corporation had held on until bankrupt. The island had been sold to LeRoy's LifeWorks as a research station after that. For over seventy years it had been the apes' home.

Marcus trotted over to the edge of the roof. The resort had been adapted to the apes long ago. Every corner and edge had thick iron climbing bars jutting out as well as strong cables running up and down the walls. It gave a crabbed, spidery look to the buildings. In good weather, the apes chose the overhand route as often as not and it made the buildings look alive with them. It was so much a part of his landscape Marcus didn't think about it.

Maxwell's message nagged at him. Something about Pearl. Pearl, who didn't seem to have a mind and manmind, but one spirit and soul. Except for fifth-generations such as Pearl and Lethias, every ape had struggled with this dichotomy since the beginning. *The best of us*, thought Marcus. Our hope.

Overhand and down to the roof below this one, down that one also, and across the top of the walkway. He met two other apes and greeted them briefly and anonymously in sign. He knew them.

There was no ape on the island that he, and every other ape, did not know. The community was too small. But he was not constrained by any protocol to talk to these particular apes, and so he did not waste time. Strange, he thought. It's been what, eighty years since the first of the Old Men were born? Marcus himself was nearly fifty. Protocol affects even the fifth-generation apes. Curious how much custom has grown.

At the end of the walkway, he dropped down to the frozen grass next to Maxwell's room. He entered it through the window. Maxwell wasn't there. Absently, Marcus brushed the melting snow from his body as he thought. Small, faint hoots escaped him until he noticed them. Then, he made himself stop and stood up straight. Think, Marcus. Think. He sent Pontiac after you. Either the message wasn't urgent—he did send an orang, after all. Or he sent the first ape he found. If it's something important, it's got to be something he doesn't want to bring up with LeRoy. At least, not without backing. The chimps were nothing if not political.

Marcus passed through Maxwell's room and walked up the corridor towards Pearl's. He could smell her in the wind. Damn. Damn. He raced now on all fours, knowing there was nothing he could do.

Outside Pearl's room, a half-dozen suitors sat in abject misery. The smell of Pearl's season was thick in the air. One of the chimps had lost himself and was hooting and displaying an erection. Marcus looked away in mild distaste. Chimps were so *public* with everything.

Inside, Maxwell sat huddled against the wall moaning, reaching out his hand to Pearl.

Pearl was dressed in a gingham dress, wearing a shawl and heels. The shoes must have cut her feet terribly, but she gave no sign as she walked over to

Marcus to shake his hand. Pearl smiled at Marcus. "It's good to see you."

"Hi, Pearl. It's good to see you, too." Damn. Double damn. "Look, Pearl. I've got to talk to Maxwell. Can I borrow him for a little while?"

"Of course."

"Marcus—" began Maxwell.

"Come *on!*" Marcus grabbed Maxwell by the arm and dragged him out of the apartment, then let him go. Maxwell followed him outside to one of the balconies. It was occupied by chimps. Marcus pointed inside. "We need this. Please go."

The chimps looked first at Marcus, then at Maxwell, then moved slowly inside.

Maxwell wrung his hands. "Marcus, what am I going to do?"

Marcus sighed. "She's got Joan's Disease. You know that. What do we always do when an ape goes human? We send her to LeRoy. Maybe this one he can cure. Call him up. Or I'll do it for you. He'll probably talk to her himself. That'll make her want to go. You've seen it before."

"It was so sudden—"

"No, it wasn't." Marcus stretched his arms above his head until his back popped. The cost of respect. It made you more like a man. And we all, he thought bitterly, have an investment in being like men. "It's been growing for months."

"How did you know? Why didn't you tell—"

"I didn't know. You're not thinking. I know the signs—Joan was my mother, remember? Did you see the way she walked in those heels? She must have been practicing every day for months. Call LeRoy or let me call him for you. There's nothing else to be done."

Maxwell turned away and looked out over the ocean. "Yeah, I know." He shivered, then looked back and gazed straight back at Marcus so that he had to turn away. "Why our best? Pearl is our best."

"I don't know," said Marcus thickly. "Let's go call LeRoy. Jesus."

They returned to Maxwell's room, past the chimps in the corridor. The chimp with an erection struck Pearl's door once, cracking it down the middle. He cried her name and ran down the hall to the balcony Marcus and Maxwell had left. They heard the slam of the sliding door and the crackling sound as he caught a climbing cable and was gone. Maxwell did not notice but Marcus saw him reach the roof's corner, stop, and begin desperately masturbating. We all lose, Marcus thought, bitterly.

On the north end of the island was the ferry terminal, a small trauma center, and a helipad. Any problem too great to be handled here was taken directly to the mainland, to LifeWorks headquarters in Charleston. To LeRoy Parkin.

Maxwell spoke a few minutes then rang off. "That's it," he said softly. "Quinote is on the next train down. He'll be on the ferry to meet us."

"Good," said Marcus, realizing the kindness. The ferry was automated. Without Quinote, there would have been no one to accompany her back to Charleston.

"The best of us, Marcus. She's the best of us."

Marcus held Maxwell for a long minute, then groomed him. Marcus did not like grooming much, and he especially disliked grooming anyone other than someone from his own band. But Maxwell needed it right then so Marcus gritted his teeth and did the best job he could. Then, they waited until a horn announced the ferry's approach. Then, the two of them made their way to the dock.

Lethias met them there. Lethias' music and Pearl's painting had made the two of them the shining stars of the fifth generation. He sat heavily next to Marcus and stared into space.

Marcus glanced at him and Lethias looked back. It was as if they could read each other's minds: *if it could happen to her, it could happen to any of us. It could happen to me.*

In the steady, frozen drizzle, orangs, gorillas, and chimps milled around the ferry dock quietly. As the apes moved, strands of ice hanging from their hair, grown long in the cold, clinked together and broke. The faint sound lingered in the still morning like that of fine china breaking. Even the baboons, those first modified and thereby strange and darkly sinister to the apes, had come to wait on the beach next to the landing: silent, still, fur-covered sculpture in the cold spray.

The ferry came silently into its slip. Automated systems made themselves fast to the pier, opened the gate, and waited. Montague Quinote limped out and waited on the pier, his withered arm held to his chest.

The apes signed to one another and some spoke. The baboons were graven images, taking no notice of anyone else. Yet, they were all waiting for Pearl to appear, baboons included. It was a moment of sad unity for the island community.

Marcus and Maxwell returned with Pearl. She walked carefully, but strongly, in her heels, her back straight and her head erect. She wore her gingham dress and jacket like a gown, carrying her handbag high and holding her small hat down on her head so it wouldn't fly away. Her smile was small and formal and so close to human Marcus wanted to cry.

Pearl went on board with Quinote and stood in the stern of the ferry as it sped across the water back to the mainland. She gave a short, bright wave to them all as she left. The small crowd was as silent as the baboons until she was out of sight. Then, with whispering and the slight sounds of lumbering bodies, they dispersed back into the compound, to the warmth, to the other apes, to each other. Only the baboons were left on the beach.

Two hours later, LeRoy Parkin himself called Marcus. Pearl had never made it to Charleston. Quinote had left her on deck for just a moment and she disappeared into the fog. Upon searching, Quinote found only her clothes, folded carefully on the deck. Next to them, arranged precisely adjacent to one another, lay her small, pointed, high-heeled shoes.

That night, no one ape could have known the thoughts of any other ape for none spoke, either in sign or in words. Still, a kind of vigil developed next to the ferry docks, where the apes stood silent, not watching one another, but only staring at the sand, the buildings, the shoals, and the trees. A single arcing thought drew them together, an image looming in their minds from beyond the shadowed trees and across the sea: the mainland.

Two Years Before

LeRoy Parkin had a long face with a thin sharp nose; his lips were thick and his cheekbones high. Long ago, when his wife, Cindy, had been alive, she'd drawn his attention to his resemblance to a bust of Akhnaton in a traveling exhibition. Cindy had laughed for a good minute. The bust had been made of malachite and the resemblance had been marred by the difference between the green of the stone and LeRoy's own blue-black skin. He'd said he didn't understand and she'd informed him that he had no sense of humor.

Gone better than sixty years and I still miss her.

"Get me some tea," LeRoy muttered. There was no answer. "Get me some tea!"

"Christ! Get a life," the teapot muttered as it shook itself. The teapot had been built from a pangolin to resemble a stylized boar: short, stubby bristles surrounding the spout. The resemblance was not exact. There was a ring in its left ear, a tattoo on its right shoulder, and one of the tusks was made of steel. It bared its teeth briefly towards LeRoy, then shrugged, raised itself on small legs, scuttled to the corner of the desk, and plugged itself in.

"Remember when pangolins were endangered? They were poached near to extinction? I hear they're doing great back in Africa and Viet Nam. Nothing like no humans to poach for seventy years. Do we have to use them to make teapots?"

"That's the Old World," said Amanda. "We're up to

our ass in pangolins in the New World."

"At least, that one's not our fault."

"In Brazil—"

"Okay, *mostly* not our fault. Next in the queue is Widnergog on the Caterpillar project."

"Boss—" Amanda's face appeared on the screen. As an automated proxy, Amanda was flawless. She was the best investment he ever made. Pity she never let him forget it.

"Just get him, will you?"

"You've been like this every month for the last year. Whenever the Council of Old Men—"

"*Goddamn*, I hate that name!"

"Gathering of the Most Prestigious Apes on the Island in Order to Discuss What to Do About the Pearl Problem," said Amanda sweetly. "Is that better?"

"That's worse."

"You sweat bullets every time they meet. It's been a year. They'll figure out what to do eventually and they'll tell you. Don't get your panties in a bunch about it."

LeRoy shook his head wearily. "Just get Widnergog," he said. "Grant me a small distraction."

Widnergog was a small thin man. LeRoy remembered that the name was a corruption of some unintelligible Finn name but couldn't recall what it was.

"Good afternoon, Doctor Parkin."

"Hi, Friedrich." LeRoy leaned back in his chair. "How's the weather in Richmond?" Absently, LeRoy reached for the cup.

"Wait," cried the teapot, bestirring itself.

LeRoy looked at it, annoyed.

"F'Christ' sake," said the teapot wearily. "It's too fuckin' hot. You're going to burn your lily-livered, weak, capitalistic, right-wing, pustule-on-the-backside-of-an-oppressed-proletariat lips." It waved at him. "But what the hell? Go wild. Burn them bloody pink."

"They're *my* lips." LeRoy glared at it, then at Amanda, and put the cup back. He turned back to Widnergog.

The scientist had stopped, mouth open. He closed it and cleared his throat. "My word. Is that a... *biological* teapot?"

"It was a gift."

"From a *friend?*"

"Sometimes I wonder. What's the problem?"

LeRoy waited patiently. LeRoy had weathered the Die-Back out on the island but Widnergog was old enough to have been born in the middle of it. When things had stabilized, Widnergog managed to claw his way up through a recovering Yale. LeRoy would never ask him about how he had survived the Die-Back—one didn't. There were still too many neglected wounds. Widnergog had been safely ensconced in academia before he'd been recruited for LifeWorks. Listening to him required patience. As LeRoy waited, the scientist considered the project, in detail, at length, and with long, sonorous, alpha-wave-inducing sentences.

To cut to the chase: Caterpillar wanted smarter construction equipment.

Caterpillar had very smart equipment, networked together, under the control of a team of humans. Even before the Die-Back people found that robots did not do well without continuing human interaction. They drifted. Robots—even intelligent robots—operate within defined paradigms. Those paradigms remained constant but the world shifted under them. The Die-Back left robots to their own devices and over time the robots were left with imperfect mappings between the real world and what they expected of the real world. The *simplest* response was to stop working. Most had done just that and left rusted hulks on the landscape. But not all robots were gifted with a simple response. Some agribots had ended up using anti-tank weaponry against competing farms while letting nearby villages starve. This history gave human beings pause, relegating robots to construction in unoccupied areas in the dead of night. As long as humans didn't see them, they didn't have to acknowledge they were there. Robot construction being free didn't hurt.

During the Die-Back humans had to figure out how the robot mind might be massaged to bend the rules—the Accords. But the history before the Accords was remembered. While the surviving agribots and fisherbots had been essential to recover from the Die-Back, they were not loved.

This suited Caterpillar just fine: they were perfectly willing to be the visible face of construction while being supported by free robot labor. Caterpillar *wasn't* free but that was just fine with them.

That said, while humans were pretty terrible at the activities of construction, being neither strong nor accurate, they were uniquely suited to handle decisions involving the activities of construction. They were also quite capable on their own of building large buildings to ruin complex ecosystems, dams making huge lakes bereft of fish, and nuclear power plants in all the wrong places. Thus arose the current paradigm: smart machines advising humans while humans gave smart machines direction.

Regardless of Caterpillar's opinions and economic model, the current arrangement worked fine as long as the human operator wasn't overloaded. Most operators could handle three or four pieces of equipment simultaneously. Some exceptionally talented individuals could handle as many as seven. In circumstances where a high number of unique decisions—such as an emergency or the recovery from some kind of a mistake—an operator might be able to handle only one. In extreme cases, more than one operator might be needed for a single piece of equipment.

When this happened, most humans switched to manual or just walked out of the operations shed over to the site and did it themselves. Caterpillar found it embarrassing when three or four pieces of multimillion-dollar construction equipment went *bzzz* while a human went out and handled the situation with a shovel.

Nobody trusted robots and nobody could do without them.

But Caterpillar, and other companies, still held to their dream: to cut the human out of the loop entirely. Biological mechanisms might provide the answer. The irony that they were attempting to replace one biological organism with a different biological organism that might someday be just as difficult to deal with escaped them.

"But we're having random problems with the neurological systems," admitted Widnergog. "Sometimes the equipment operates perfectly—nearly self-directing within the paradigms. Then, the neurological systems go..." He paused a moment. "Crazy," he said distastefully.

LeRoy raised his eyebrows. "Do we need a little magic?"

"Please, Doctor Parkin."

"Sorry." LeRoy rolled his eyes. Christ. It wasn't so long since LeRoy was out of the lab. Widnergog had no excuse for trifling word play. "Extracorporeal physics? Cori Phenomena?"

"It's hard to tell—"

"It sounds like one of *those* situations. 'Inexplicable, random behavior ascribed to sophisticated neurological systems'—that's a quote from *your* book. Do you need a physicist to come down there and diagnose the computer-organismal linkage through psychic means?"

Widnergog looked as if his teeth hurt. "It would help, I think—"

"Now the hard question: why did you set up a meeting with me? Have you talked to Monty?"

"Doctor Quinote—"

"He *is* the Consulting Scientist on this project, after all."

"He—"

"In fact," LeRoy leaned towards Widnergog's image. "This is the sort of thing on which he is supposed to consult, is he not?"

Widnergog sputtered for a moment.

"Sideline him, Amanda." LeRoy thought for a moment as he watched Widnergog converse with something he thought was LeRoy. "How did this jerk get past you? And what's Monty doing with him?"

Amanda appeared in a window next to the scientist. "He asked for an appointment and you have a standard policy of talking with any lead scientist. As for Monty: this is one of four approaches he and Sims are attempting for the same class of problems— *reproducible* Cori behavior in isolated neurological control systems."

"He doesn't expect success from Widnergog?"

"Monty has set this up as a win if Widnergog is successful within the Caterpillar requirements without invoking Cori Phenomena. But it's also a win even if Widnergog fails and accidentally creates a Cori Phenomena laboratory model. Monty is trying to take the human out of the equation just as much as Widnergog is. Just in a different way and for different reasons."

"What are the four approaches?"

"Widnergog's using networked mole rat brains.

Jorenson is using dogs. Bryant is using goats. Frederson is going completely non-mammalian and has been trying to adapt the brains of tuna."

"How's Frederson doing?"

"Poorly. He can't take advantage of any of the mammalian work so he has to start from scratch."

"Anybody trying cephalopods?"

"Not yet," said Amanda, sweetly. "Do you want me to set up an R&D fund for it?"

LeRoy shook his head. "Idle thinking."

"Monty is giving Widnergog's lab what he thinks are appropriate resources to solve the problem."

"How does this fool's approach stack up against the others?"

"Too soon to tell."

"Make nice noises to Widnergog for a minute."

"Commencing Operation Nice: you will appear to him like his lost father. That is, if he liked his father."

"Right." LeRoy thought for a minute. "Put a call into Monty's proxy and ask if I can bring in Sims on a quick contract. Let's give Widnergog enough rope and let him either hang himself or build the next better widget. If he hangs himself—well, the pangolin project could always use another warm body."

There was a quiet minute where LeRoy watched Widnergog continue to speak soundlessly. *Pangolins.* Old World animals that had no business in the new world. Someone had clearly brought them here and let them loose—likely as a solution to the fire ant infestation in the southwest. No one knew. But during the Die-Back without humans killing them they had been successful and had spread down into South America. They were a nuisance everywhere. Using them to help rebuild the Amazon rainforest had seemed such a good idea at the time.

"Monty's proxy says go ahead if it will make you feel as if you're still in control."

LeRoy grinned. "Patch me in." He waited for Amanda's cue. "Okay. I'll see if I can get Sims to give you a call. That should help. Okay?"

Widnergog looked relieved and nettled at the same time. "I think this is perhaps beneath Doctor—"

"Don't worry about it. Give me an update by the end of the week."

Widnergog began to speak again. LeRoy looked up at Amanda's display and the scientist's voice cut off.

"Handle him the rest of the way, will you?"

Amanda nodded. "Done, Boss. The usual good employee/employer relationship will be maintained under my expert control—"

"Save it." LeRoy thought about Cindy, lost friends, and the Council of Old Men. He reached for the tea again, stopped. He watched the pot suspiciously. It was silent. He picked up the cup and sipped. The damned thing did make good tea.

‹ Sims ›

The world's leading authority on extracorporeal physics—named after its creator, Ethan Cori—Carrol Sims stepped off the Boston train and stood for a moment in the swirl of people. He did not especially like or dislike crowds. They were, to him, like molecules trembling and careening against each other. Standing there, he was reminded of Brown's first view of the motion of molecules against microscopic pollen grains. He wondered if he were the pollen or the molecule: was he buffet-*ee* or buffet-*er*?

It was a familiar notion but only quasi-scientific. In the world of physics since Albert Einstein, all roles were relative to the frame of reference of the participants. Since Ethan Cori, they had further become contextually dependent.

At some point before the twenty-first century, graduate student Ethan Cori had what some might call a psychic experience. He'd never told Sims the nature of the experience except it had been undeniable and unexplainable according to current physical models. It had become Cori's obsession to extend physical models to include that experience. When the Die-Back became unmistakable, LeRoy had brought his wife, Cindy, Ethan Cori, the whole division, and their families to weather it on the island. Only Carrol Sims, Montague Quinote, LeRoy Parkin, Jim Secondson, and Bill Springbuck had survived.

Sims missed those long walks with Cori along the Atlantic. Sims knew exactly how smart he was. It wasn't arrogance—he didn't go out of his way to rub other people's noses in it. But he'd spent a good portion of his life waiting for others to catch up. Sims had often had to struggle to keep up with Cori. He missed that.

Widnergog had wanted Sims to discuss the project from a distance. Sims had made non-committal noises to him, hung up, and booked a seat on the next train south. He knew places to stay in Richmond. Sims didn't like telecommuting: he preferred to see things for himself, to observe up close and personal. That said, he didn't travel unless he had to. The island was where the apes lived. Cambridge was where Monty lived. Sims considered both home.

On the train, he spread out Widnergog's experimental data across the active surface of the table. He studied them as he drummed his fingers on the table. Then, he called back to his lab. "Joanne?"

Joanne's angular face appeared in a window next to the layouts. "Yes?"

"Busy?"

"I'm looking over Widnergog's experimental layouts." She snorted. "Not so much."

"Did you read my mind?"

"It wouldn't have been hard." Joanne gave him a lopsided grin. "What do you think?"

"I'm not sure."

"Come on! What's not to love about using mole rat brains?"

No one wanted to dumb down Caterpillar's intelligent machines. The problem was they wanted the level of flexibility of a human without a human involved. In other words, they wanted to set the system in place to build a skyscraper and have the system figure out all that was needed, handle deviations and changes, adapt to changing part inventory and weather, and have a skyscraper in place when they returned rather than a bent forty-five-degree spiral. Widnergog had proposed a biological system to act as a mediator. This wasn't entirely novel—biological systems had millions of years to develop modeling capabilities that were not easily perturbed by changing conditions. Mole Rat Brains were as good as anything else.

Widnergog had developed domains of machine interfaces to an AI that was, in turn, supported by a network of MRBs. The AI/MRB conversation drove an incoming request towards a workable decision. The AI presented alternatives and the MRB decided which ones were crazy and decided among them.

If a domain couldn't come to a decision, it tossed it up to a supervisor domain called a Site Boss. Each Site Boss had its own network of MRBs. If the Site Boss System couldn't come to a decision, then humans would be called in. It all seemed workable.

Until it wasn't.

"Did you look at the logs?" asked Sims.

"Yeah. Suddenly, the Site Boss started handing down decrees and altering the thrust of the project. The subsidiary domains accepted the new rules and the whole demonstration project took off in a new direction." Joanne looked cross.

"Recognize the new target project?" Sims asked.

"Well, *I* didn't. But it didn't take long to find the image on the network. What do you think the mole rat brains want with the Notre Dame Cathedral?"

"I have no idea." Sims said.

"'Unexplainable behavior ascribable to sophisticated neurological systems,' indeed," said Joanne.

"You read Widnergog's book?"

"Sure. Did you calculate the computation indices yet?"

"No." Sims pointed at her. "But I can tell *you* did. What did you find?"

"Each MRB segment is a tiny fraction of the complexity of a human brain. Networked together and with an apex point, they start to approximate about .01 Hawking. Widnergog didn't create a human brain equivalent—not even close—but somehow, he crossed the threshold into possible Cori Phenomena."

".01 Hawking," mused Sims. 1.0 Hawking represented the average parallel computation ability of an average human being. .01 Hawking was quite impressive. "Where do you think the cathedral came from?"

Joanne shook her head. "I have no idea. More importantly, how does any networked cognition system develop enough *gestalt* sophistication to develop a point-of-view? POV is an essential component of the Cori Field Equations. Complexity and computation aren't enough by themselves."

"I don't know." Sims thought for a minute. "You handle Widnergog's problem. Figure out how to dampen the cumulative interaction that seems to underlie the issue. I'll try to figure out if and where the Cori behavior is coming from."

"You got it, Boss. Maybe I'll find out if MRBs lean

towards Catholicism." She rang off.

Joanne had seen to the heart of the problem: the POV variable in the equations. If the MRB system was acting like an actual perceiving brain, its very perception changed the nature of its circumstances—that was core to the Cori Field Equations in their original formulation and stayed true through Sims' matrix mechanics derivations. However, the field equations represented point-of-view as a singular, scalar value. A constant.

Damn, she was good. Whistling, Sims got to work.

For the networked MRB system to exhibit Cori behavior, it *had* to have point-of-view. But the MRBs were too simple for that. Only in the networked form did they represent enough sophistication to qualify. But they were *still* separate systems and would not be expected to be capable of point-of-view.

Oh, goodness, thought Sims. Cori's understanding of POV was wrong: it wasn't singular. It was a descriptive function in and of itself. Cori had developed *special* field equations for the condition that POV was indivisible and unitary. Cori had not developed *general* equations that would encompass POV as a field.

Interesting. One of the problems with extracorporeal physics was scale. In nuclear physics, for example, fission could happen at the atomic level but scale up into an atomic inferno. But Cori Phenomena didn't scale up properly. Cori's original POV constant had been large but experimentation had reduced it to a tiny value—still demonstrable but unexpectedly small. Cori's equations allowed micromanipulation without damaging the underlying material. Imagine a laser able to manipulate atoms without imparting excess energy to those atoms. LeRoy's branch of the biotech industry was based on using those techniques to manipulate embryos.

But if POV wasn't a constant, then the effects of Cori phenomena could scale to the value of the field.

Sims' mind whirled. What could create a point-of-view field, then? Parts of a brain interacting together? A brain acting as a whole? A population of individuals?

He could see it. Points of view acting discreetly, entangling with other points of view, breaking into points of view components, components interacting with other components to form new points of view. All affecting the underlying automata of reality with those automata affecting them in return.

Sims began to write down some ideas on how to attack POV as a derivable function. He grinned.

This was going to be *fun*.

Book 1: Descending from the Moon

Glendower: I can call spirits from the vasty deep.

Hotspur: Why, so can I, or so can any man; But will they come when you do call for them?

   —Henry IV, Part 1

Mister Coyotee

Excerpt from the Mr. Coyotee Show, subscribed service:

Disclaimer: **Mister Coyotee is an animated system interviewing representations of actual human people. Resemblances to individuals, living or dead, are not coincidental at all. Resemblance of Mister Coyotee to an actual coyote, real or mythical, is marginal at best. The guests of the show may or may not be simulated, in whole or in part, at our discretion.**

M.Coyotee: Tonight, we have as our guest, Fernandina Isobanna. Ms. Isobanna is the spokesperson of the One People anti-biotech coalition in the Pacific Northwest. One People is behind the Oregon Initiative. Welcome to the show.

F.Isobanna: Thank you. It's a pleasure to be here. I have to correct you a wee bit.

M.Coyotee: Please do.

F.Isobanna: We are not anti-biotech. Biotech is essential to modern civilization. We're against unregulated biotech.

M.Coyotee: What does that mean?

F.Isobanna: We want to ban biotech that violates common sense, family values, religious imperatives, and fundamental esthetics.

M.Coyotee: That's very broad.

F.Isobanna: Thank you.

M.Coyotee: The Oregon Initiative must be very complex.

F.Isobanna: It was, originally. The first version was sixty-five pages excluding footnotes and graphics. But our legal team and scholars boiled it down to its very essence.

M.Coyotee: Which is?

F.Isobanna: Banning any biotech that we don't like.

M.Coyotee: Is that the text of the Initiative?

F.Isobanna: Oh, of course not. You have to be more subtle than that to get on the ballot. We were intentionally vague with just enough specificity to get past judicial review.

<Claps hands.>

And we succeeded!

M.Coyotee: That you did. It's on the spring ballot, correct?

F.Isobanna: Exactly. Spring ballots have historically low turnout—even lower than primaries. This gives us a better chance to pack the vote.

M.Coyotee: Would Monsanto's slug technology be covered under this bill?

F.Isobanna: Of course. Slugs are icky.

M.Coyotee: They are very useful in reclaiming old landfills and repairing old buildings.

F.Isobanna: But icky. They violate essential esthetics.

M.Coyotee: I expect you would use this to outlaw foves.

F.Isobanna: Does anybody really know what foves are?

M.Coyotee: Modified higher animals into useful new species with the ability to reproduce. None exist as yet—

F.Isobanna: But that doesn't say much, does it? After all, that could be anything. What's a species?

M.Coyotee: To my knowledge, it's a group of animals reproductively isolated from one another.

F.Isobanna: The dog is *Canis familiaris.* Is it a separate species? It can interbreed with wolves.

M.Coyotee: I think it's termed a wolf sub-species—

F.Isobanna: Or coyotes and wolves—no one ever argues *they're* the same species. And different species of baboons can produce viable, hybrid offspring.

M.Coyotee: With some difficulty—

F.Isobanna: Or chickadees.

M.Coyotee: Chickadees?

F.Isobanna: Different species of chickadees hybridize at the edges of their range.

M.Coyotee: I don't understand your point.

F.Isobanna: My point is that the concept of *species* is fluid. So. the concept of *foves* should also be fluid.

M.Coyotee: Chickadees are not made by human beings.

F.Isobanna: Piffle. Once a species is created—by evolution, God, or man—it's created. Take pangolins.

M.Coyotee: Please.

F.Isobanna: They're part of the Amazon Restoration Project. And *they're* breeding like mad. Pangolins could be foves. Slugs could be foves. Anything I define to be foves are by that definition foves. And I define foves to be any biotech I don't like.

M.Coyotee: Monsanto's slugs can't reproduce. They have to be cloned.

F.Isobanna: That's what *they* say. But people and corporations that disagree with us must be lying, right? I mean you wouldn't want your sister to marry one, right?

M.Coyotee: Marry a slug?

F.Isobanna: See? The very idea is repulsive.

M.Coyotee: And before our subscribers think we're repulsive, it's time to close. That's our show, subscribers. Wherever you are, good evening or good morning, and from Mister Coyotee, good night.

Chapter 1.1

Marcus had fallen asleep. His great, silverbacked body twitched and frowned. He tended to dwarf the other apes. In the meeting room, Whitefingers, Crazylegs, and the other gorilla leaders gave him room as he slept. His temper when suddenly awakened was famously foul.

In sleep, Marcus dreamed in quick, explosive flashes. Remembering his grandfather, Big Black Jack (confused emotions towards him as authoritarian male, gentle friend, impressions of size, sleeping next to his huge, warm, inarticulate bulk) gave way to remembering his first coupling with Jefferson (Joy! Now he had his own female. Now he had his own band. No longer Marcus Joan Jackson, he was Marcus Joan Marcus! A band of his own. Children. Females. Jefferson crying out under him. Warm fur. Skin. Warm. Warm.)

Then, the dreams went pale and he was alone, floating in a sea of green grass under a warm sun. Vegetative. Content.

A voice came to him: *only the senile dream like this. Nothing coherent. Only bits and snatches. True dreaming spoke to you. True dreaming shows you what you need to be shown.*

Marcus frowned and half awoke, tried to roll away from the voice. Gorilla proverb: manmind talks, who should listen? You're so disgusted with me, then give me a dream. Bless me or leave me alone. Give me something I can use or shut up.

The voice faded into a dull hum and Marcus relaxed, tasted buttercups and lemon, felt Jefferson snuggling next to him. Faded further into warmth and light. Warm. Warm.

Then, he began to dream in earnest.

Marcus awoke suddenly, staring at the ceiling. Whitefingers sat nearest him. Marcus glanced in his direction, but Whitefingers stared resolutely at Maxwell the chimp, and edged subtly, but deliberately, away. Whitefingers showed his own melanin dysfunction in his hands.

Marcus sat up and scratched his shoulder, glanced at the white patch in irritation. He studied his foot intently, picked at a toenail, listening to Maxwell to see what he had missed. It had been over a year since he had taken any significant interest in these meetings. *Pearl's meetings*, he thought darkly. *We wouldn't be having these meetings if it weren't for Pearl.*

Three years ago, it had seemed imperative to do something *now*, to make sure the horror could never happen again. Pearl had driven them nearly crazy with grief. They had to do *something*. They had formed the Council of Old Men to try to figure something out. But three years had passed. Three years of the chimps making proposals no one else could agree with. Of the orangs speaking of waiting and inaction finds the way and how stones knew how to fall. Of the gorillas falling asleep. All of them worried that this would be the year another chimp, orang, or gorilla would fall into Joan's Disease and be sent to the mainland to waste away and die.

Productive, Marcus thought. Very productive.

"Look," said Maxwell slowly as if speaking to children. "It's very simple."

The tone flamed a dull, familiar resentment in Marcus. The chimps always felt they were held back by the others.

"It's always simple when a chimp says it," said Whitefingers. He laughed. "Come on, Max. Say something new. We've been hearing you do nothing but talk for three years."

"You want more than talk? Like what you did when your son got caught four years before Pearl?" Maxwell pointed at Whitefingers. "Did you take Ricardo down to the dock? Did you at least tell somebody something was wrong with him? No. You hid him in a cave on the south corner of the island. Marcus had to hold you down while Crazylegs pulled him out."

Whitefingers' face relaxed. A dangerous sign. "He was my only son, Max."

Maxwell ignored him. "At least, *we* have a *plan*."

Whitefingers got up slowly. "I got a plan, too. I plan to wrap your legs around your ears."

"Sit down, Whitey," said Marcus. "Let's hear him out—again."

Whitefingers sat down and looked morose.

Maxwell ignored them both and continued. "This island used to be a resort. Then, the hurricanes and the Year of the Tsunamis happened. Since the Die-Back and the Restoration, a new leisure class has been developing. Better building codes and techniques. There hasn't been a hurricane disaster since the Restoration or a tsunami of any magnitude since the Die-Back. *Now* the market is prime again. If we sell this place, we'll have enough to move."

The chimps cheered him.

Lao-Tzu, the orang leader, looked up at Maxwell. "A small question: who has title?"

"LeRoy. I have assurances he will act on our behalf."

How did they talk like that? wondered Marcus. The chimps were facile, the orangs elegant. Both groups always made Marcus feel slow.

"Yeah, Max," said Whitefingers dryly, seemingly calm again. "We sell the place. What's next?"

"Ah. Now we have *money!* Now we can buy a *home!*" Maxwell clapped his hands.

"We have a home," rumbled Marcus, scratching his ankle. "Where else should we go?" Getting old, he thought. Can barely see my toes anymore. Wonder if LeRoy can get me fitted for glasses. Like to see Jefferson's face clearly again. Like as not regret it, too. She's older than I am. He chuckled. Have to remember to tell her that one.

"Don't laugh," said Maxwell sharply.

Marcus looked up at him. "Don't get pissy. Answer the question."

Maxwell turned back to his graphs and charts. "Cigars have recently grown in popularity—it's a sign of luxurious living. People are taking luxury seriously now. We have investigated getting a farm in Connecticut. Since the Restoration, cigar tobacco is being grown there again. Our needs are simple. With the proceeds from the tobacco crop, we can be self-sufficient."

He stopped and reached out to the other chimps. Silently, they touched him in return. "We chimps feel that we should embrace human beings. We believe that Joan's Disease isn't a disease at all, but an artifact of our isolation living here. We don't know people, so we imitate them—what else are we to do? So: we need to move to the mainland and trade with people. Touch them." Maxwell reached behind and his hand was grasped by Serina, Pearl's sister. Maxwell's sister, too. She stroked him as the room fell silent.

Reassurance. Chimps always need reassurance.

Hell, thought Marcus sourly. If it had happened to your sister, you'd need reassurance, too, thinking each minute that you had it inside of you. It's our Original Sin. *In Adam's fall, we lost all.* Marcus rubbed his face. Damned manmind again. Just once he'd like to have a thought without all those noisy echoes of association.

"You think Joan's disease is in their heads?" asked Whitefingers quietly. "Ricardo wasted away in front of me in that cave. He had seizures. You think that was all in their heads?" He rolled onto his legs and knuckles. "Do you, Max?" he said quietly. His neck was corded with anger.

Lao-Tzu shook his head slightly. Marcus noticed and stole a glance at him. He liked Lao-Tzu's color, a kind of golden red. He was pretty to look at. Any decision had to be unanimous; the Council of Old Men had all agreed to that in the very beginning. If Lao-Tzu accepted an idea, the other orangs would follow: the orangs were more autocratic than the other apes, though they did less with it.

"To deny the physical aspect of Joan's Disease is to deny reality," said Lao-Tzu, nodding towards Whitefingers. Marcus reached over and patted Whitefingers' thigh. *Settle down.*

Whitefingers slapped his hand away but he sat down.

"We have noticed," the orang continued. "The chimps get Joan's Disease the most often. The gorillas contract it less than the chimps. The orangs rarely succumb. The baboons, never. Consider this. Perhaps Joan's Disease appears most among those apes closest to man. Perhaps it is a genetic flaw."

When is tact not tact? thought Marcus sourly. *When an orang does it.*

"No!" cried Maxwell. "There is *no* flaw!"

"Excuse me," said Lao-Tzu gently. "Of course not. But you are closest to men. Walking so close to the edge of the abyss, is it so strange some of you fall over?"

"Some abyss," muttered Marcus, then he spoke more loudly. "This is where Pearl has gotten us? With Maxwell—smart as he is—trying to sell us on making cigars in Connecticut? Are we that desperate?"

He stood up fully erect and both chimps and orangs quieted. The other gorilla males were careful not to look directly at him. "I think we try to become humans because we don't know who we are. None of us knows any better than anybody else, but we *think* we do: chimps, gorillas, and orangs. Baboons *know* they aren't human. The rest of us are confused—"

"I know I am not a man, Marcus," said Lao-Tzu dryly.

They will always be able to outmaneuver me. Marcus felt suddenly old and tired. What was the point? For a moment, he lost his train of thought, then regained it. "I know that. But I know you're also trying to understand human beings just as hard as Maxwell is. Maxwell studies money. You study Confucius. It's still *human*. Who else have we got to watch? Who else can we pattern ourselves after? Whales? Cockroaches? We're as distant from human beings as we are from wild apes. If there were wild apes here, we might use them but there aren't any. Only humans."

"We don't want to leave the island. It's our home." Lao-Tzu was watching him carefully now.

Think like a human. Isn't that how we were built? That's how you do these things. Catch at the man part of them. Think like a human. "You don't want to leave the island because some humans like to stay at home and stare into their navels and you identify with them. The chimps want to leave because some humans are adventuresome."

"And the gorillas don't want to do anything because some humans are lazy," said Maxwell sarcastically.

Marcus laughed. "Right. And boy, do we identify with *them*."

Whitefingers nodded. "Especially Marcus."

The other gorillas snorted with laughter.

"I'm lazy. Maybe I'm even asleep now," said Marcus. "But awake or asleep, I'm damned if I'm going to move my family on a chimp whim to some place no ape has ever lived before. I'd be crazy."

"Don't have to be crazy to feel that way," said Manuel. The gorilla looked at Marcus when he said it. The other gorillas muttered assent.

"I had a dream," began Marcus.

‹ 2: LeRoy, 3/5 ›

LeRoy Parkin was having a bad day and he was damned if he was going to admit it.

He sat watching the main display unit in his office, hunched forward in his chair, back and kidneys aching and swearing to himself. I'm too old for this. I was too old for this fifty years ago.

His Akhnaton face was now creased by tension into a dour black mask. His long dark fingers pointed to one section of the screen, then another, arresting motion here, changing dialogue there. The whole ad made him unhappy. As he edited portions of it trying to make it more appealing, it made him more unhappy.

"Goddamn it," he muttered. "Is it too much to ask that an advertising agency actually *do* something you want them to do?"

The second display unit on his desk lit up and Amanda's face appeared on it.

"What's the problem?" she asked.

"Bob's goddamned online ad. It's right there. You can see it. It is oh, so, proper."

"LeRoy, they sent it to you on spec. It's just the result of a two-hour meeting. It's not like you had the specifications graven in tablets dropped over there by Holy Messenger."

"This is supposed to articulate the new vision of the company—*my* company. 'Fove technology is the wave of the future; it will revolutionize the industry,' and like rhetoric. But, look at that actor," he said. "He's all chin. He's *boring.*"

LeRoy leaned his head in his hands and thought for a moment. "Maybe the best way is to play us as mavericks. That's what we are, right? Risk-takers. Foves are modified animals that can breed true. They are new species. Fove technology is risky. It's interesting. It breaks from the pack. *We* broke from the pack when we restarted LifeWorks after the Die-Back. We were the first large-scale industry to stake our business in a reclaimed city. All that other nonsense. We don't want to be lumped in with our competitors—Eli Lilly didn't restart in Indianapolis until we showed them the way. J&J *never* went back to New Jersey. They restarted in nice, safe Connecticut. Monsanto was reconstituted in Maryland and *never* returned to Missouri. Let *them* be the unexciting, successful, gray business-suit people. They would use foves for personalized bank tellers. For waiters. But if you want something really fantastic, come to LifeWorks."

Amanda cued in applause. LeRoy refused to be drawn in.

"You missed your calling," she said. "You should be in show business. Or politics."

LeRoy pointed to the screen. "That stuff is too damned expensive to waste. Make a letter out of what I said, would you? Then, let me see it."

Amanda morphed her face into the familiar white face and blue eyes of Mister Coyotee.

"Howdy, Bob. This is LeRoy Parkin, Chief Executive Officer of LifeWorks." The coyote nodded his head so that his ears flapped. "Just saw your proposal. I think—"

"Amanda!"

"—I think, you understand—that it's just too conservative. Do you remember the word conservative? Say yes, if you do. The world—by that I mean the *whole* world—has to think we're mavericks. We're risk-takers."

LeRoy leaned forward until he was a hand length from Mr. Coyotee's face.

"That's right, Bob," said the miniature coyote. "Risk takers. We don't want to be lumped in with our competitors."

He couldn't help it. He laughed and tears came to his eyes. "Okay. Okay, dammit. You got me. Bang: I'm dead. Murdered by very own corporate hell proxy."

The coyote looked deeply into LeRoy's eyes. "Do you remember the word 'lighten up'? Say yes, if you do."

He placed his forefinger to his temple like a gun. LeRoy thought for a long minute. "Send it."

Amanda's face replaced Mr. Coyotee's. "You're not serious."

"The hell I'm not. It's a great idea. It'll give Bob something to chew on—if it doesn't make him laugh, it'll make him eat his liver trying to figure me out." LeRoy laughed again. "Tell him he should use the Brazilian project."

Amanda shook her head. "Boss, we've *blown* that one."

"Hell, we did! Okay, we did." He held his hands out, palm down, as if he were quieting a crowd. "Goddamn pangolins were supposed to die on cue. They were never supposed to interbreed. And if they did, our modifications were supposed to be recessive or lethal—failed on all counts. But we *are* going to get the repair contract. It shows again we're not afraid to take risks, not afraid to fix them—and with the way it turned out, everybody's going to end up a winner." She started to speak and he waved her silent. "I know, I know. If we're lucky. If we're *very* lucky. But that's what makes a success story. Besides, the design team tells me they've got it licked."

"They better. Frankly, I'd rather be ass-deep in crocodiles than ass-deep in pangolins. They smell better."

"You don't have a nose. Or ass." LeRoy leaned back. "Let's see Luthor's status on the Life Bank legislation."

"You aren't the least bit interested in the Life Bank right now."

"It's important!"

"It is. It's just not important enough."

"Since when do you tell me what to do?"

"Since you had me built. It's about time you figured out I am the power behind the throne." Amanda shook her head on the screen. "Your interest lies about eighty kilometers west and seventy-five kilometers south from here. In a secret fove project you've been running for eighty years, on a little island facing the Atlantic—"

"Damn you, Amanda. Shut up."

Amanda fell silent.

LeRoy closed his eyes and rubbed his nose, so thin it was like a protruding, aching bone. He wondered where that nose came from—some white ancestor, probably. Not from his father, an immigrant from Somalia during that country's troubles. It must have come from his mother. She'd always been closed-mouthed about her family. Both parents died decades ago from AIDS, long before the Die-Back. But since then, most people he had known were dead—

the fundamental problem when you've lived long past your time. The Die-Back had not spared LeRoy's family and friends. The number of human friends he had left could be counted on one hand.

He rubbed his nose some more, thinking of the skin stretching against the bone. I can find out where it came from, he thought. The timing sequences that generate faces are pretty well-known now. I'd have to check and see if the racial variations have all been worked out.

His interest died and he thought again of his parents, dying. First his father, thin and gray, then his mother, dying of the same thinness, the same gray color. As the life faded from them, they grew to look alike. LeRoy had had AIDS but he'd kept himself alive long enough until HIV research caught up with him. He'd bounced from one treatment to another until he'd returned to HIV research and developed the next class of treatment. That had been LifeWorks' chief product in the early years.

Of course, there was no cure short of full DNA repair. That wasn't possible then and not possible in an adult now.

When it was clear things were falling apart, he and Cindy had closed LifeWorks and taken the ape team to the islands. Forty people had moved to the island to be safe. Seven that counted, as far as LeRoy was concerned: He, Cindy, Monty, Sims, Jim Secondson, Bill Springbuck, Ethan Cori. Nobody called it the Die-Back then. Names were given after the fact. Ethan had died first, succumbing to a rampant pneumonia carried by dandelion seeds. Cindy had died next of one of the many nameless wasting diseases that seemed to just float through the air. Five had survived. Some would consider LeRoy lucky that he'd lost only two of the people he loved. LeRoy did not.

Living on the island gave them a lot of time on their hands. It was just work on the apes and keep each other alive. That work kept LeRoy coherent closing in on a hundred-forty years. He still had no end in sight. He wasn't sure if that was a good thing or a bad thing.

LeRoy stood and looked out the window. That was a long time ago. Four of the five of them had returned to Charleston. Monty had moved back to Boston as soon as travel was feasible. Jim and Bill had moved back to Arizona and founded the Hopi Development Corporation in Second Mesa. LeRoy had reopened LifeWorks. Most of the Charleston he'd known was now underwater. Everybody and everything was gone. LifeWorks lived on. Only Sims still lived on the island—mostly. He traveled for contracts.

In the mild April weather, the sailboats were blowing across the bay.

LeRoy still missed Cindy.

"I want to be over there," LeRoy said softly. "I want to be with them every month."

"I thought we agreed—" began Amanda.

"*You* said no. *You* argued it. *I* acquiesced. Not the same thing."

The teapot shook itself and muttered in its sleep. "Oh, Porky."

"You said I should butt out—those were your words, remember? This was something they had to do on their own. They couldn't think clearly if their creator-father figure was hanging over them." LeRoy turned and looked at her face on the screen. "And I said *okay*."

"I didn't want you to get morose. You wanted them to be independent after Pearl."

LeRoy suddenly realized Amanda's pale face looked like Cindy's. He wondered if this was a gradual development or if Amanda had done this years ago and he'd never noticed.

Amanda continued. "If you're worried about the island, call Lethias. He'll talk to you."

The teapot roused itself. "Excuse me," said the teapot.

LeRoy shook his head. "What's the difference? Go there or phone them. Isn't it the same thing?"

Amanda looked frustrated. "You need to ask them, not tell them, what to do."

"Bloody hell! Do you want some more tea?" cried the teapot. "It's getting cold. Sorry to interrupt, your ill-gotten-wealthiness."

"No, thank you," LeRoy said coldly. "Amanda, I don't like that teapot."

"Good. You're not supposed to."

"Okay," it replied, picked up the cup, and dragged it to the corner of his desk, leaving a dribbling trail of cold tea. LeRoy blotted the tea with a tissue.

"Aren't these... gifts getting a little much?" asked LeRoy, staring at the teapot. "This one is really unpleasant."

"Nope. You'll thank me some day, old and bent, but still with a spring in your spirit and a twinkle in your eye. 'Amanda', you'll say to me, 'you kept me from stagnating all those years. Just think—"

"Spare me."

"Fine," she said. "Then call the island."

LeRoy looked out the window down into downtown Charleston. He could see the Atlantic Ocean from here and the weather was clear and windy. The sailboats had their spinnakers out. "I'm a stupid old man. I'd just get in their way."

Amanda snorted at him. "Okay. You can't actually talk with somebody that's bothering you. Okay. Then, call somebody else. Somebody human. Call Monty. It so happens..."

Her face disappeared and Monty's face came into

focus. A Hopi face, dark as a brick. For a moment, LeRoy didn't know him. Everybody ages differently, he thought. Monty never seemed to age at all.

"Hey, old man," Monty grinned at him. "Amanda tells me you're brooding again."

"Why aren't you?"

Monty shrugged. "Too busy having fun, I guess. Y'know, I've been dating a student—"

"That could be fatal."

Together, they finished: "If she dies, she dies."

"To think," mused Monty. "I was thinking you were becoming such a depressed old man."

"That's the second time today somebody called me old."

"Don't be self-pitying. You're not young enough."

LeRoy stabbed a finger at Monty. "If you're so smart, give me something useful: figure out what's causing Joan's Disease." LeRoy shook his head, feeling suddenly guilty. Monty had been in it with him from the beginning. He had been working for years trying to isolate the problem. Only breeding away from it had helped. "Sorry. That was uncalled for. It's just... Hell, Monty: every few years, no matter what we do. Progressive dementia. Death by suicide or just wasting away."

"Not since Pearl. Not for three years. That's progress." Monty spread his hands. One opened normally. The other opened as small and perfect as an orchid. LeRoy had always found it oddly endearing.

"We'll find it eventually," continued Monty. "Look, in five generations we have intelligent apes that have back troubles, club feet, arthritis, and a tendency to some forms of incurable and degenerative psychosis. We could have a lot worse. We could have leukemia. We could have scoliosis leading to brain damage as it crushed the human cortex we so cleverly laid on their spine. We could have lost half of them. We could have lost *all* of them. Be thankful for what you've got."

"Damned cold comfort, that." LeRoy bit his thumbnail. "They're going to do something one of these days. Maybe today. I feel something's going to happen."

Monty nodded. "That they will. Let Pearl go, LeRoy. They have."

LeRoy shook his head. "They never did." Sometimes, between the boats, he could see the old ships ghosting in between them, bringing from Africa, spices, tea, and slaves. Today, there were no dark shapes on the water and the sails looked like limp flags. "That's why Pearl is so important to them. They never let go of anybody."

‹ 3: Marcus, 3/5 ›

"A dream!" screamed Maxwell. "Who cares about a fucking dream?"

"Was there fucking in the dream?" asked Crazylegs with sudden interest.

"Shut up," said Marcus. All of the apes grew silent and listening. Even Maxwell, beating the floor with his fists in frustration, beat the floor quietly.

Okay. You've got their attention. Nothing gets their attention like a dream—it's manmind and apemind talking together. You know what you think, but what if the dream won't hold them? Lao-Tzu'll have to help.

"The dream went like this," he said slowly.

"There was a family of gorillas in the forest: Big Black Jack, Corina, another female named Maria, and a young white male named Snow.

"Now, Snow's mother was dead. She'd been a First like Big Black Jack and couldn't talk. Corina was a second. You remember her. Like Corina, Maria in the

dream was a second. Corina liked Snow, even though
he wasn't her kid. Maria didn't have any kids of her
own, so she was taking it out on Snow, beating him
up all the time. Finally, Big Black Jack pushed Snow
out of the band to keep the peace and Corina helped
him leave. Snow ran away from them, into the forest,
feeling very low and lonely.

"After a long time walking, he came upon this little
house. Inside the house were seven men. Normal-
sized men, but to Snow they were little. So, he stayed
with them. Snow stayed with them for so long he
forgot he was a gorilla. He just thought of himself as
a big, hairy man.

"Meanwhile, back in the band, Big Black Jack had
taken a dislike to Maria. Nobody knew why, of course.
Jack couldn't talk and didn't like to sign. He just kept
pushing Maria away and wouldn't sit next to her. She
came in season and Jack ignored her.

"This drove her crazy. She figured it was all
Snow's fault. She went looking for him and found him
in the men's house. The humans weren't there—out
doing man things, I suppose. She waited until Snow
came out and then she killed him.

"The men came back and she hid in the woods.
The men mourned Snow and tried to fix him, but they
couldn't. They began to cry and rush about like men
do when they're upset.

"Corina had an idea what was going to happen, so
she roused Jack and made him come with her as she
went after Maria. Jack was slow. Since he didn't really
understand what was happening, he followed her.
They found Snow's body. Jack saw Snow dead and
went over to him. Corina went over to where Maria
was hiding and said to her, 'if you don't run off right
now, I'll get Jack to kill you.'

"Maria left.

"Corina joined Jack at the body and they held

Snow, holding him like you would a little baby. The men all surrounded them, but they were shadowy and I couldn't see them clearly. Jack and Corina held him for a long time. After a while, Snow began to breathe again. And pretty soon, he was brought back to life, better than before." He looked around at them. "That's it. That's the dream." He sat down.

Maxwell laughed once suddenly. "That's a long dream for five minutes of nap-time. It's Snow White and the Seven Dwarves. Jesus!"

"Hush", said Lao-Tzu.

"Why should I? It's just a fairy tale."

"Hush," said Lao-Tzu again. "'In dreaming there is seeing' This is what Joan said back in Charleston before we came here. Before we lost her. In dreaming, is there seeing? Marcus has dreamed a broken fairy tale. It is the story of Snow White, but that is not all it is. Shall I try to interpret it?"

"Please," said Marcus. He suddenly felt a sudden hope. If Marcus didn't have the orangs, he had no one.

Lao-Tzu was silent for a long time. "The white ape is our future. That much is obvious. Big Black Jack is our past. Corina and Maria are our present. With our conflicts, we send our future away from us, out into the world of men where it may become lost and know not its name. This is not a bad thing, in and of itself. Yet, we send our hate and our fears after our future to kill it. We are so afraid." He looked at the ground. "We are so very afraid. But there is hope in the dream. Hope that we can succeed. With our past and the best aspects of our present, we can bring our future to life." He said nothing for a long time, looking at each of them in turn. "We orangs change our mind. Clearly, it is necessary to somehow contact the world of men."

Maxwell stood up. "Good. Then, we can leave!"

"That, I don't know. I only said we should make contact with them."

Maxwell shrugged. "It's the same."

Lao-Tzu shook his head. "It is not."

Marcus sighed heavily. "Not so fast. There's more," he said in a rumble.

"I had thought there might be." Lao-Tzu nodded.

"In the dream, Snow's face was that of Lethias."

Lao-Tzu clapped his hands and laughed. "Of course. We shall send him and him alone."

"Lethias!" Maxwell leaped in the air and slapped the floor with both hands and feet. "What can one ape learn? What can one ape know?"

Lao-Tzu, still chuckling, answered: "That, Maxwell, is what we are going to find out."

‹ 4: LeRoy, 3/5 ›

In an urge to distraction, LeRoy had stalked through his offices, canceling appointments and forcing decisions back on his subordinates until he was standing in front of the LifeWorks building on Market Street. He walked towards where the waterfront used to be, now submerged into the Cooper River. A block more and he entered the Charleston Royal Tennis Club.

The Club was young as royal tennis clubs go: just a little over a century. The Boston Tennis and Racquet Club was over two hundred years old. Henry VII had built Hampton Court's site in 1530. Royal tennis was the original tennis from which all European racquet sports derived.

LeRoy's club had been built during royal tennis' rebirth, before the hurricanes and the Year of the Tsunamis. LeRoy had been one of the first members. Like everything else, it had been abandoned during the Die-Back. But, unlike most of Charleston, the rising waters had not managed to destroy it. LeRoy had helped reopen it when LifeWorks had returned.

The Club was busy. Flora Flores approached him—she ran a company specializing in biotech gourmet foods. She shook his hand and introduced her doubles partner, Herman Winebitter, the manager of VirungaLand.

"Glad to meet you," LeRoy said. "Interested in a game?"

"Sure," said Flores. "Get yourself a partner."

As he left, LeRoy overheard Winebitter. "Isn't he a bit old for this?"

"No," said Flores. "You were saying about the loose apes?"

"Yes. There are several scattered sightings over the Appalachian Corridor but we can't get any help finding them."

Damn right, I'm not too old, LeRoy thought. It's in the brain more than the body, anyway. Besides, with Amanda watching my every move I'm not much different from a man of sixty. He remembered the last bit of conversation: free apes in Appalachia. A possible contract? LeRoy grinned to himself. If Lethias went there, would anyone notice?

In the dimness of the bar, LeRoy found a young man nursing a drink.

"Hey, there," LeRoy said.

The young man looked up with a start. "Excuse me?"

"New here, right? We need a doubles partner on the court. Want to play?"

The young man looked at him dubiously. "Royal tennis?"

LeRoy felt himself grin. These young guys. "Yeah. Think of us as a charity case."

Two hours later, the young man—named Carl, he found out—spoke shortly and retired again to the bar.

"Touchy. Friend of yours?" said Flores.

"Never met him before today. He'll get better when he's older."

As they showered and changed, Winebitter lamented he would never understand the game.

"Sure, you will," said LeRoy. "You just have to think like the monks who invented it."

Winebitter looked at him, confused. "Monks?"

"Sure." LeRoy toweled himself and realized he felt good for the first time in days. "In the middle-ages, the best young men in Europe gathered in the monasteries, studying scriptures and other things people study in monasteries. They got bored. One day, they make up a game—maybe one of them has an old fishing float they could use as a ball. That's where the covered cork ball comes from. They'd play in the courtyard, right? It's got a shed roof on three sides of it—that's where the roof in our court comes from. The fourth side is the flat side of the church. But there's a bend in the wall. That's the *tambour.*" He grew excited, thinking about the creation of the game centuries ago, imagining shivering, young men standing in the morning cold, throwing themselves into the creation of the game with the same enthusiasm with which they'd go to war. "Then, to make things interesting, there's a window into the Abbott's study. We put that behind the service side— you hit a ball in there, the Abbott gets all pissed off and you get a point. That's the *dedans.* At the other end, there's a little vent window that opens into the kitchen. You knock a ball in there and it clatters around the pots and pans and the cook gets all mad. That's the *grille* and why the *grille* has a bell. Get another point—" He stopped when he saw Winebitter's face; the same rapt expression one would have listening to a madman or a priest. LeRoy turned his attention to tying his shoes.

"You're really into this game, eh?" Winebitter

shrugged.

"It takes my mind off my troubles."

"It's not helping me. I'd be happier if VirungaLand were doing better."

"I overheard you were having difficulty with escaped apes. Are the loose apes what's giving you trouble?"

Winebitter sighed. "Not really. They're more of a nuisance than anything else. Nobody in the Appalachian Corridor considers them a threat, least of all me. It's just lost revenue and lost breeding. Other things are more of an actual problem: cougars, tigers, bees, and God knows what else has taken root out there since the Die-Back."

"Could be worse. You could be trying to make it out west with the mastodons and the saber tooth cats. Or the komodos in Tennessee. Or the cobras in Georgia."

"No thanks. I hate snakes." Winebitter shuddered. "My point is it takes a lot of money to make VirungaLand safe for the apes *and* the tourists. Then, there are the tour guides and the vet bills. But you know what's the biggest cost?"

LeRoy didn't care. Now that it was apparent there wasn't a contract forthcoming, he wondered how he could get rid of Winebitter without being rude.

Winebitter didn't wait for an answer. He stood up and began pacing. "I'll tell you. It's that damned Total Cost Tax—who the Hell is the government to tell me the ultimate cost of my business? Who cares about some acres of swamp land and scrub? There's plenty of it out in the Corridor. It's not like my little business is making any dent in any of it."

LeRoy stared at him. From the way he stood and the way he'd played, LeRoy guessed Winebitter was 30. It was hard to tell these days. Regardless, LeRoy *knew* he had to have been born towards the end of the Die-Back when the worst of it was over.

The Total Cost Tax had been enacted before the Die-Back, after the Year of the Tsunamis when everything felt fragile. While the tsunamis did not result from climate change as much a geologic instability, the hurricanes, famines, and wars *did*. The sense of fragility had been palpable. It had been one of the first things reinstated with the Restoration.

The Tax was the *mildest* of the pre-Die-Back reforms. At the time, they had seemed the only wall that might keep the human race intact. Of course, no one then knew the Die-Back was coming.

The Die-Back reinforced that feeling. Losing almost every friend, neighbor, parent, sibling, child, celebrity, politician, businessman, caretaker, and doctor had the effect of taking mild environmental activists and hardening them into radicals. No one could prove the Die-Back came from humans tearing the environment apart, but that didn't change what they knew in their hearts.

Now, with the Die-Back twenty years safely in the past and the United States restored, only fossils like LeRoy seemed to take those reforms seriously. He wondered if the American Civil War veterans had ultimately felt the same way.

"That's not what the tax is all about," said LeRoy quietly as he finished getting dressed. "If the government has to clean up the mess people leave, somebody's got to pay for it. Taxes are the only way to get the money. Make VirungaLand operate cleaner—it'll drive the TCT down."

"I've got it as clean as I can. Any more and the price of admission would go up—and it's at the limit now. People won't pay any more to watch a bunch of apes." He stared at one shoe morosely. "It's a little better now that we have our own rail spur. More business. Malcolm Luther helped us with that." He seemed to puff up with pride at mentioning the Senator.

"Good for you."

"It wasn't me that did it: I consulted my oracle." From under his T-shirt, Winebitter pulled a small leather bag attached to a string. "I bought it from a certified Roma. I paid top dollar."

LeRoy looked at him. "I'm sure you did."

Satisfied but still appearing depressed, Winebitter dropped the bag back beneath his shirt. "You get what you pay for. Can't be too careful. I asked my oracle how to vote this fall, but she said the answers were hazy and I'd have to ask again later. I can't vote for Shuman. I've been hearing she's going to drive the Tax even higher—more and more emphasis on biotechnology. More on foves, too, I guess—whatever the hell they are. Christ, it's all part of the problem— look at Brazil. Shuman is the favorite in the Corridor but she's lost touch everywhere else. I don't think I could possibly vote for the Red Republicans. And the Green Republicans are a joke."

LeRoy felt a cold wave move through him, shook it off. "Look, maybe I can give you a hand." He gave Winebitter his card.

Winebitter read it, looked up at him with a confused expression. On his face, it appeared comfortable.

LeRoy sat next to him on the bench. "Most of the animals in the corridor are natural enough. They've just taken advantage of the Die-Back. The foreign animals are the ones you need to look out for. The komodos came in illegally as part of the pet trade and escaped. The tigers were traced to a breeding group from the National Zoo. The bees have been here since they came up from Brazil, long before the Die-Back. I know some techniques we could apply that might help you out."

"You think so?" Winebitter stared at the card in his hand. For him, it seemed that dubious was as common an expression as confused. He turned away, still holding the card, and walked into the shower.

LeRoy sighed. The card was waterproof. He dressed and left quickly and walked down Market Street towards the water, trying to get rid of the agitation from his conversation with Winebitter. It was late afternoon and the wind had died. The spring heat was stifling.

Damn. Oh, for the world of his birth. Wasn't it a simple life? That world had been freer, less regimented. Nobody believed in ghosts or spirits or magic talismans. Physicists only worked with particles and waves and disregarded faces that appeared on eggshells. Biotechnology was limited to what one could do with viruses and raw chemistry. It was Ethan Cori who had let the genie out into the world, who turned the micromanipulation of genes and embryonics into something a person could touch, transformed physicists into magicians, and brought superstition out of the closet where it belonged.

The same forces that Cori had used to describe "non-deterministic phenomena" had allowed LeRoy to engineer biological forms. Cori's work provided the ability to make accurate, real-time microscopic observations and manipulations through the action of the human mind. LeRoy, the biological engineer, had been created by Cori as surely as radiologists had been created by Roentgen through his discovery of X-rays.

LeRoy found himself on the edge of the Phillip Street Water Treatment Canal. Upstream, the Canal was covered and under the street, anaerobically processing raw sewage. But a block north, the covering disappeared, turning whatever remained into vegetation and flowers. Looking down into the water, LeRoy saw a single dolphin guarding his small herd of manatees, consuming the excess and turning vegetation back into meat again. LeRoy sat on the bench next to the water. The manatees munched contentedly on the water hyacinth. The constant sound of their eating was soothing. He leaned back against the bench, listening to them and the people walking on the street behind him. The murmur of voices blended with the sound of the manatees and he finally began to relax.

The dolphin watched him carefully.

"Hey, boy," he called. The dolphin ignored him and remained watchful. The manatees were brought in every summer from Miami. He'd heard that when the dolphins shepherded them up and down the coast, they carried guns to protect them from the ichthyosaurs. But it was probably a rumor. LeRoy wasn't sure what a gun that a dolphin could use might look like. Or what kind of gun would take out an ichthyosaur.

LeRoy liked the green, floating plants in the water and the smell of the clean air next to the Canal. The Canal died back some in the winter, but for the last decade, like a spring migration, the manatees and their dolphin keepers came back to Charleston.

A lizard crawled out of his shirt pocket. "Yah!" LeRoy leaped to his feet, cried, and tossed it on the ground, heart pounding.

"Ouch," growled the lizard and righted itself, dusted itself off. "Grow up. I'm not going to bite."

"Amanda is going to be the death of me. I know it." LeRoy sat back down on the bench and felt his heart ease.

"I'm a handheld. You got a call." The lizard lit a cigarette. "You going to take it or do I have time for a smoke?"

"I'll take it."

"Damn," said the lizard calmly and hopped up on the bench next to LeRoy. He stubbed out the cigarette, then rolled up into a ball. Small metallic appendages grew out of his back. "That smarts," it muttered.

Amanda appeared in the air before him. "I've got a call for you."

"Could I have a real handheld?"

"We can talk about that later. It's Maxwell."

Her face faded and dissolved into the chimp's. "Hello, sir."

"Just LeRoy, Max." LeRoy rubbed his face. It was going to be bad. He could feel it.

"LeRoy." Maxwell shook his head. "We had the monthly meeting today. And we decided something. For once."

Very bad. "What?"

"We want to send a gorilla to the mainland. To be with people."

"You want to bring an ape out here." LeRoy buried his face in his hands. "I thought I was kidding."

"What?"

"Nothing. Male? Female? Old? Young? Why a gorilla?"

Maxwell squirmed. "A male. Average sized. Fifth generation." He paused. "We chose a gorilla because the orangs and the chimps couldn't agree on each other."

"Jesus." Just what he needed. "You want to integrate a two-meter, two-hundred-kilo silverback gorilla into society?" LeRoy pounded his fist against the dock railing. "This is where Pearl's death brought you?"

Maxwell looked down and LeRoy felt a rush of guilt. Wonderful. I am such a great father to my children.

"We think it's a good idea. Marcus had a dream..."

Maxwell began to hoot softly.

"It's all right, Max. I'm getting mean and cranky in my old age. It was Marcus' idea? Marcus? The old bastard." LeRoy tapped his fingers against the railing. "Who would have thought he had it in him? I would have thought a plan would have come from you chimps."

"We *had* one. It was our idea to buy a cigar farm in Connecticut with the profits from selling the island. But Marcus and Lao-Tzu came up with this—"

Cigar making? Now, *that* was a silly idea. He'd have to make sure the apes accessed better reading materials. Starting a business was the right idea but *cigars?* "Lao-Tzu? Him, too? Hm. Where is Marcus now?"

Maxwell shrugged. "Who knows? He said he was going to check the other constituency."

LeRoy thought for a long minute. Who would that be? "And which ape is going to take the plunge? I am not agreeing to this for a minute, you understand. I am just curious."

"That's the other thing," said Maxwell. "We chose Lethias to go."

"Lethias?" Not Lethias. Not the best of the gorillas. The best of all of them, even Max, since Pearl died. The implanted human cortex and the original wild ape brain were always negotiating over dominance. Since, Pearl, Lethias had come closest to integrating the two. A magnificent pianist. I had higher hopes for him than for Pearl. No one had any doubts about the chimps—it was like enhancing our cousins. But who knew about the gorillas? The gorillas and the orangs had so much further to go.

LeRoy shook his head. Any ape coming out here is going to get eaten alive. He's going to be a martyr for the cause. How could it be otherwise? Lethias is my friend. I can't do that to him.

"Where is Lethias?" said LeRoy.

"I don't know." Maxwell looked miserable. "I think he went looking for Marcus."

"Have him call me when you see him. Soon. Get Marcus to call me too." If Max had been human, LeRoy would have thought he was about to cry. "Lighten up, Max. It'll be okay."

He consoled Maxwell for a few minutes, then switched off.

The handheld unrolled back into a lizard. It stretched on the bench and rubbed its back. "I should get double pay for this."

"Shut up. You don't get paid."

"How do you know?"

"Shut up." LeRoy closed his eyes. Lethias was too precious to leave the island. It was time he took a hand in this directly. It's for the good of the project. Right, he answered. Right, you hypocritical old man.

The lizard relit his cigarette. "Where to now, Boss?"

"Back to the office. I've got work to do."

‹ 5: Lethias, 3/5 ›

Lethias lay in his room trying to sleep. His corn-shuck mattress made noises as he turned on one side, then the other. The sounds soothed him. The late afternoon shadows made the room less regular, less square. He stretched his long gorilla arms until his back popped.

He could feel something about to happen like an approaching storm, a deep electricity that clung to everything, making his eyes smart and his fingertips tingle. Lethias could almost smell it: wet, dusty, sharp. Doubting himself, he had come to his own room and tried to sleep. And this, too, had caused doubt. Was this how Pearl began to change? First, feeling more comfortable by herself than in the close company of the other chimps. Then, perhaps, feeling oddly naked without clothes—but secret, mind you. It was nobody's business but her own, after all. And finally, forcing her broad feet into those ridiculously tiny shoes, stumbling in them. All the while thinking, I'm just trying them out. Or, how can they wear those shoes? Or, at last, on me, they look good.

Until she paid them no mind at all.

Pearl was chimp, Lethias gorilla. But both of them were fifth generation—the generation when hand/eye coordination had finally caught up with cognition. Pearl had painted. Lethias played the piano. Both of them were gifted. When Pearl had left the island, Lethias thought he would die of grief and fear. *Was this what was waiting for him?*

The thoughts of Pearl opened a black well inside of him and he thrashed again on his pallet. To look down into the cold water and leap—sinking immediately, for no ape could float. Had LeRoy cared for her? Had he said a prayer for her?

Lethias had tried but there had been no words, only a deep grieving ache that came from deep in his gorilla heart.

He closed his eyes and tried to imagine himself on the side of the Virunga Plateau, hoping to make himself dream, looking down on the ancestral gorilla homeland with only gorilla eyes. Watching that vast green descent into mist, thinking with never an English word. Deepening twilight drew him down and down until finally, he relaxed and slept. He dreamed he saw Pearl smiling at him.

And awoke again, immediately, when he heard the door open.

He looked to the door and saw only a dark shape and in the span between dream and waking thought for a moment it was Pearl. His dreams of her had called her back and he almost cried out from relief.

You are not dead. Come to me. Come.

But a moment later, Lethias saw the shadow was far too large for Pearl and he could smell a she-gorilla, excited, afraid, and in season. The light from the window caught her face. It was pale from the melanin dysfunction that no one understood but randomly appeared across all of the modified apes. There were three bright red tattooed lines down across the chin—Catherine. No one he knew well. But there was no one on the island he did not know. He did not move and she came over to him and knelt next to him. The smell of her made his fingers itch.

She rested a hand on his chest. "I wanted you before you went away," Catherine said softly. He barely heard her as she touched him and he drew her to him. Yes! He cried out: *yes! Yes!*

Afterward, they lay nestled like moist spoons. His mind was a deep, warm river, drowsy and content.

Catherine pulled away and sat up, watching him.

Lethias tried to pull her back but she would only hold his hands.

He pulled loose and touched the red tattoo. "Why?"

She shook her head and didn't answer. One more mystery.

Then, Lethias remembered what she had said.

"Where am I going?" he said sleepily.

"Away." She stood up and he could see serene determination written on her face. "You will come back to me. Remember that: you will come back to me." To emphasize it, she signed it to him twice more, then she left.

Lethias shrugged, losing himself again in a vegetative warmth.

Going away? his manmind said. Going where? Going when?

He sat up, fully awake. Something had happened.

Damn it. The Old Men had finally decided something.

Lethias rubbed his face with his hands. Christ. Damn. Damn. Damn.

Outside his room, Lethias could find out nothing from the buzz of conversation on the balcony and below him from the pool. He walked over towards the Grumpus Room, where the Old Men habitually met. There, he found Jefferson carefully twisting thread together into rope. She smiled at him.

"What are you doing?" Lethias asked curiously.

==Making rope.== she signed. It was a signature of many of the second generation that they did not use their voices as much as later generations. Whether this was from practice or habit learned from being raised by the inarticulate first generation, Lethias did not know.

"Whatever for?"

Jefferson shrugged and grinned at him. ==Seeing if I can.==

"There's some kind of bother among the apes over by the pool like something's happening," began Lethias. "I came over to check it out."

==Nothing happening here. They're all gone. You can listen if you want.== She gestured to the closed door and grinned. Lethias grinned back. *When half the conversations were in sign.* Right. She always made him smile. Jefferson had taken him in as her own child when Constantine, his mother, had left the island thinking she was a human woman named Amelia Earhart. Another casualty of Joan's Disease.

"So, you don't know what might have happened?"

Jefferson shook her head. ==Got no idea.==

Great. Either something's happened and she's not telling, or something's happened and she doesn't know. Maybe she doesn't know—she *was* a female, after all. Females had their own doings. Catherine, for example, said Lethias was going somewhere. Where?

"Bless me," Lethias said to Jefferson softly.

She kissed him briefly on the head and he left her.

Up three floors to the roof: he looked out towards the sea. March had brought early summer and Lethias could see apes moving in the forest. Let's see, he mused. Let's stick with the idea Jefferson doesn't know. If not her, who could tell me? Not the orangs— he thought briefly of his friend, Grendel. No: in political matters, orangs were hierarchical. If he spoke with them, it would have to be through Lao-Tzu. And I'm just not up to talking to him right now. He grinned and felt pleasantly heavy in his loins. Maybe later, when I don't feel quite so good.

Maybe Maxwell would know?

Sister Hanna was waiting for him inside the chimp compound.

"I saw you come," she said excitedly. "I know you have news. You know you do. You're going to tell us, aren't you? Aren't you? What is it? What's going on? I could tell from the roof that something was going on. People were dancing around the pool, jumping up and down. Turning cartwheels. What's happened? Are you the dream emissary from the lost Great First Generation who cannot speak? Will we be able to ask them questions? Will you be he who can answer for them?"

"Peace!" cried Lethias. He picked her up and shook her gently. "You are impossible. I am no emissary. I have no news. Is Maxwell around?"

Hanna drummed on his chest with her feet. "Put me down! Lethias! Put me down! Now. When I have children, I will have them beat you with sticks!"

He shook her again. "Maxwell. Where is he?"

"I lied to you about people jumping up and down. I *lied* to you. I'm glad I lied to you. Do you understand me?"

"Maxwell!" he said menacingly.

"You can't see him. He said if you came around here, I was to beat you and throw you out. There! I lied to you *again!* See? See?"

He looked past her up the corridor. "*Maxwell!*" he roared.

Sister Hanna hammered on his head, then began to pull on his ears. He closed his eyes and held her away so she couldn't reach them. She kicked at him.

"I'm here," he heard Maxwell say.

Lethias set Sister Hanna down.

"Well," she said curtseying first to Maxwell, then to Lethias. "Now that I have brought him, you will, of course, excuse me." Then, she ran down the corridor.

Lethias sighed and smiled at Maxwell. "Joan's Disease isn't the only crazy we get. What's her problem?"

Maxwell shrugged. "I don't know. Maybe she thinks she's Florence Nightingale."

"Right."

Maxwell seemed smaller somehow, shrunken. Now, that he had found him, Lethias felt at a loss to speak with him.

"Hey," he said finally. "I got a name."

"No kidding?" asked Maxwell absently.

"With Catherine. Now, I'm Lethias Constantine Lethias. I'll let you continue to call me Lethias. Out of the goodness of my heart."

"I'll remember that."

And silence fell again.

"Look, Max," Lethias began. "Something's going on—"

"You better talk to Marcus."

"Damn!" exploded Lethias and slammed his fist into the wall. The building boomed and Maxwell, startled, fell into a crouch. "Sorry," said Lethias. "It's just—where is he?"

"I don't know."

"Damn," Lethias said again, but softly this time.

Maxwell shrugged and looked stricken. "I have to go. Marcus said he wanted to talk to the other constituency. Whatever that is." He turned and ran down the corridor.

"Okay," Lethias called after him. "I know where they are."

‹ 6: LeRoy, 3/5 ›

"What the hell do you want?" LeRoy snarled at Monty. "I'm not brooding *now.*"

He'd returned to his office to wait for Lethias to call. He'd been back for perhaps twenty minutes when Monty's face appeared above his desk.

Unperturbed, Monty just smiled. "Oh, I just thought I'd call and see how you were getting on and all. One must always stay in contact with one's friends."

"I just talked to you this morning."

"Time means nothing to a friendship as deep as ours."

"You want to know how I'm doing? I'm doing terrible." LeRoy slammed his hand down on the desk. "The Old Men want to send an ape out into the world. A gorilla. "

"How does Lethias feel about it?"

"I don't—wait a minute. Did Amanda call you? Amanda!"

Over the desk, Amanda's face appeared next to Monty's. She looked down on LeRoy archly. "I have not called anyone on your behalf, Doctor Parkin." Her face winked out.

"She's angry," Monty said seriously. "I have a sense about these things."

"Oh, shut up. How did you know?"

"I know many things. I have been empowered by

the Sun Spirit—"

"Spare me!" LeRoy glared at him.

"Marcus told me," Monty admitted. "He called me before he called you."

"Damn you to hell, anyway." LeRoy buried his face in his hands. "What am I going to do?"

"Put up with a house guest. "

"Be serious."

"I am. You know my opinion: they should never leave the island. Ever. But they're thinking beings and thinking beings cannot be contained. If we can't keep them there, letting one out for a little bit is better than all of them. You won't have to put up with it for long. Lethias will come out for a bit and go back and they will be satisfied."

"The Sun Spirit told you, I suppose."

"I go by many names—"

"Wait a minute," said LeRoy, suddenly grinning. "Ever since VirungaLand got started there have been apes living in the Appalachian Corridor. Lethias could pass pretty easily out there."

Monty shook his head. "The apes want Lethias to interact with people. The Corridor is pretty sparse—"

"You have been talking with Lethias!"

"No. Just Marcus. I figured the rest out myself."

"Anyway, you're right. The best place for him is Boston."

Monty stared at him. "What did you say?"

"It's obvious," chortled LeRoy. "Boston is far away from LifeWorks—your connection is ten years cold. We can't have anybody connecting Lethias with LifeWorks. Now, you're a mere consultant, not an employee or a stockholder." LeRoy rubbed his hands. "It's a connection but not an *obvious* connection."

"I *am* a stockholder."

"Private stock. Nobody knows. Besides, Charleston is too puritanical. People think the human form is God given."

"What about New York?"

"Too provincial. Boston's much more sophisticated. There are a lot of cosmetically altered people up there. Lethias can pass without conversion. You've already got some characters up there already. Like Ranquiz."

"Look, LeRoy—Carmine shouldn't have been flying over Cambridge. I talked to him—"

"What's this about his flying over Cambridge?"

Monty waved his good hand. "Don't worry about it. The cops were just bored. There's not enough happening. You know how a person gets elected to Cambridge city council? He goes out and gets fifty people to write down his name. Now, this is no small feat, I concede, given the literacy rate in the home of Harvard and MIT. But that means almost anybody can get elected. So, the police chief goes to the council and says, 'we got this transformed jerk flying over the city', while his men run around the room yelling, 'The sky is falling! The sky is falling!' Pretty soon the council is following them around and baying at the moon. After that, they vote on the matter at hand."

"Sounds like this year's presidential election."

"Oh, no. The presidential election is *much* less sophisticated."

LeRoy rubbed his face. "Human biodesign. And how I ever let you talk me into that I'll never know."

"*Cosmetic* human biodesign was the single biggest single money-maker we ever had. We needed the money. It was a shame we had to shut it down."

"We should have shut it down sooner." LeRoy shook his head. "Carmine could have been a normal, exceptionally rich, child."

Monty shook his head, eyes glinting dramatically. "An exceptionally screwed-up kid. Now, he's a fairly normal kid that looks like a bat. His father is happy with him and because of that Carmine is a lot better adjusted than most. Who's to say?"

"Exactly," said LeRoy. He waved away the argument. "It doesn't matter: there are a lot of wealthy, biologically modified kids in Boston and Cambridge. Lethias will fit right in—no one will ever know he's the exception."

Monty threw up his hand. "Are we going to matriculate him?"

"Absolutely," LeRoy nodded his head vigorously. "As soon as you can forge papers for him."

"*Forgery!* Not only are we bringing an ape into the civilized world, we're going to *lie* about it! *And* set ourselves up for scandal. *And* break the law."

"Who cares? We've been keeping the apes a secret for eighty years."

"On an island in the middle of the Atlantic."

"They were in Charleston before that." LeRoy held up his palm. "And the south Atlantic coast is not Borneo."

"Come on, LeRoy. I've been out of this kind of business too damned long."

LeRoy laughed. "That's right. Too damned long. Welcome back to the family."

‹ 7: Lethias, 3/5 ›

It was over an hour walking along the north beach before Lethias found the baboons. There were well over a hundred on this beach alone. There were more baboons than all of the other ape species combined. *No one breeds like a baboon,* went the saying. They were crowded together sitting still at the edge of the ocean. He could hear some of the children playing in the brush out of sight, but here there were only adults. He couldn't quite get over the feeling they were waiting for something. Baboons *always* seemed as if they were waiting for something. The sensation was no easier to overcome by its being familiar.

As he approached them, he also felt, as usual, a little dread. The baboons made him nervous. He looked at them closely. They showed the changes most obviously with their rounder cranium, more hunched-over posture, and pronounced bulge on their spine. The baboons looked like a first draft. The heads of other apes were similar to their wild brethren; it was the expansion of their spinal column that had increased their intelligence and perception.

(Lethias had a sudden memory of a conversation with LeRoy: "Had to change the backbone anyway," cackled LeRoy once. "I didn't want to change your profile, just what was behind it.")

Or maybe it was that the baboons had always been part of each other: they had been the subjects of the preliminary experiments to see what was possible, but they could never be brought as far as the apes. They had no collective guilt from Joan and never suffered from Joan's Disease. Or maybe it was the way the baboon's eyes always looked flat and empty. The way they would sit completely still and move suddenly and purposefully as if they had been contemplating what they would do long enough to be planned out. The baboons were much smaller than gorillas, but somehow, Lethias could never convince himself he was the physical equal of any of them.

Lethias shook his head. Others he knew covered over their fear by saying they were still animals. Lethias could never dismiss them quite so easily.

As he neared the baboons, he felt their sudden attention even though they showed no sign. He stopped and waited. One of the old males casually sat up straight and yawned, made an idle sign to a female. She spat on the ground and left the band, walking towards Lethias. Was that spit a sign of disgust? Acquiescence? Lethias did not know. The baboons had their own sign, mutated much farther from the same Ameslan root than the apes'. Unless it was their intention, no one but another baboon understood them.

The female stopped in front of him. ==You want something?== she signed shortly.

==I came to visit. Can I help fish?== He had always heard it was best with the baboons to offer to help.

She slapped one hand on the back of the other. ==Laughter.== Gorillas don't know how to fish.== She turned back to the band and Lethias followed her.

Lethias could see individuals that he knew slightly and nodded to them. Inside the band, he saw a large dark form lying down. *Christ on a stick!* he muttered to himself.

Marcus lay on his side, watching the Atlantic. Lethias sat next to him and touched his shoulder. Marcus made a *let me think* sign and Lethias left him alone. The old male that had dispatched the female walked nonchalantly over to him and squatted down.

==Ape comes to talk?== the old male signed.

Lethias didn't know if the male referred to him or Marcus. He made the signs hesitantly. ==I came to talk.==

==Not fish? <Laughter.>==

==Not fish. To ask.==

The old male nodded. ==Him, too.== He pointed to Marcus with his foot.

==What was asked?==

The old male looked at Lethias for a long time. Lethias had to turn away to break his gaze. What were these animals? What had Parkin and Quinote created?

The old male touched his arm to get his attention. ==I am Runs-From-Water. == he signed.

Lethias did not move for a full minute. A baboon had offered an ape his name. He had heard of this happening four times in his lifetime. Once to Big Black Jack to end a conflict. Once to Joan herself for reasons only she had ever known. Twice to Corinne: the first time to enable her to argue with LeRoy about the direction of the breeding project and the second for her to accept the compromise she and LeRoy reached. Each time it was to someone special, someone important. To be offered this seemed to mean no lies could be told, all things were to be shared. It was a relationship the apes found obscure and a little frightening. Lethias looked at the sand then back at Runs-From-Water. What to say? What to say?

==I have no name.== Lethias signed slowly. He couldn't insult Runs-From-Water with a spoken name the baboon could never pronounce. Lethias had no sign name, not like this. His own name was signed out in three letters: L, th, and S. Some of the old apes had sign names, true sign names, but that custom had declined as later generations were more capable of speech.

Runs-From-Water did not move immediately. ==I name you Comes-At-Noon.==

==I thank you.==

Lethias noticed Marcus had sat up and had been watching them.

Lethias looked at Marcus. "What do I do now?"

Marcus nodded. ==Walk with me.==

Lethias turned back to Runs-From-Water. ==I must go.==

Runs-From-Water nodded. A wave curled up the beach near his feet and he looked at it with distaste.

"I have no baboon name," Marcus said meditatively. "Nobody does—or, at least, nobody ever admitted to it. I've never even heard of one being offered." He looked at Lethias. "Did you know, I asked him if he thought one of the baboons should go to visit the humans in their own land? He replied that the one who should go is Comes-At-Noon." Marcus picked up a shell and looked at it. "I had no idea what he meant. Did you tell them you were coming today?"

"No. I heard something had happened and went investigating. This was my last try before I gave up."

Marcus nodded again. "They have their own ways of finding out things," he said shortly. He leaned back and watched the water then crooked his finger in the listen-to-me gesture. "I'll lay it out for you, kid. When Pearl died, we didn't know what to do but we had to do something. Whatever it was we had to do, we thought we had to do it fast. It's been three years and people pretty much have come to their points of view. The orangs want to stay, the chimps want to leave, and the gorillas want to be left alone." Marcus scratched his belly and looked at his nails speculatively. "Put it another way, the chimps want to get as close to humans as possible, the orangs want to get away as far as possible, and the gorillas don't think humans are all that important."

Two baboons watched them a moment, then looked idly back out to sea.

Marcus shook his head slowly and Lethias remembered when he, Maxwell, and Pearl were young. They had hidden a public viewer in the basement of the main hotel and managed to hook into the public network looking for the old flat-screen version of King-Kong. Marcus reminded Lethias of Kong's slow dignity.

"It doesn't matter, I guess. But this creeping paralysis has to break. And Lethias?" Marcus stared straight into Lethias' face. "We still don't know what to do."

Lethias looked away, embarrassed. "Okay. What

does that have to do with me?"

Marcus turned away again and stared at the dock for a long time; he turned back to Lethias. "We want you to go to the mainland."

Lethias felt a shock of excitement and fear. Go to the mainland where the humans were? "To talk with LeRoy?"

Marcus shook his head again, that quiet, strong movement. "No. We want you to go to live with humans. On your own."

Lethias felt a moment of panic. "You're casting me out."

"Of course not. At least, not in the way you mean. We want you to go and live there for a while. Say, a year or two."

"I don't understand." Lethias shook his head. "What good is that going to do?"

Marcus shrugged. "We don't know."

Silence fell between them and Lethias could hear the gulls flying over, heard the waves breaking. The sea still smelled winter cold, though this was now March. Go to the mainland. He was going to go. Catherine had been right.

"The only thing I do know," rumbled Marcus, "is that when you come back, we'll know what to do. I had a dream." Marcus told Lethias the dream and Lao-Tzu's interpretation.

"I don't know that it has such a fancy meaning," Marcus said after a long pause. "I think it really means that if we send somebody—probably anybody—out there, that by what happens to them we'll know what to do."

"I *am* a sacrifice, then," Lethias burst out.

Marcus didn't reply immediately. He buried his hands in the sand and made small piles on his feet. "Maybe. I don't know. It could be the first ape we send out there is going to die. Or maybe he'll come back so different we'll decide we don't want any part of humans—and then where'll we be? Or maybe he'll come back and say it's not that bad."

"But, why me?"

Marcus looked at him and grinned. "You're the best we got, kid. Don't you know we always sacrifice our best?"

"Shut up. You're scaring me."

Marcus grunted. "Good," he said and turned back to the sea.

Runs-From-Water sidled over to them and made the sign: ==Notice me.==

==I see you,== signed Marcus in turn.

==You are going to leave.== Runs-From-Water signed to Lethias. ==You must get a wife.== Finished, the baboon walked away back towards the sea.

"Yeah," muttered Marcus. "He's right. We got to get you a woman, kid. What the hell else would you have to come back to?"

Lethias grinned. "Already got one. Catherine came for me a little while ago. I figured she must have learned it from you or somebody else and just couldn't wait."

Marcus gave him an unfathomable look and didn't respond.

Lethias began to get uneasy. "How else could she know?"

"She was in season," said Marcus idly.

"So?" asked Lethias uncertainly.

"She comes into season the same day you leave? I got news for you, kid. Nobody told anybody about this." Marcus shook his head. "There's a lot of weird things going on. My dream. Catherine coming in season. The baboons knowing things before I tell them." Marcus slapped Lethias' arm.

"And now me leaving," said Lethias bitterly. "Cast out."

"It's not like that. I said—"

"So just by me going, you all will know what to do? How will you do that? Like magic?"

Marcus grinned at him. "That's right, kid. Like magic."

‹ 8: LeRoy, 3/5 ›

LeRoy heard a bell and Amanda appeared looking down on him.

"Yes," he said quietly.

"Lethias is on the line."

LeRoy looked up into Lethias' great black eyes and saw the confusion and the uncertainty. It was as if a hole had opened in his heart. "Hello," he said.

"You wanted me, sir," Lethias said.

"Oh, stop that. I have to take that from Maxwell and the others but I'm damned if I'll take it from you."

Lethias tilted his head to one side and grinned. "You like Lord and Master, better, maybe?"

He must have learned that from Monty. "That's enough. I understand you want to come out."

Lethias lost his grin and nodded quickly. "I've talked it over with Marcus and the others. They want me to go."

"What do you want?"

Lethias looked down and shrugged. "I want to go. I've always wanted to see Charleston."

LeRoy smiled at him. "Well, you're going to see precious little of it this time. You're going to Boston. If we've got to accommodate this insane idea, we'd best do it in the best place. Charleston's not wild enough to support someone like you. What do you think about that?"

"It's never been a possibility."

"Think about it. Tell me what you think when I see you. You can take the ferry over when you're ready."

"I'm going?"

There was a wealth of faith in those words. Suddenly, LeRoy knew he could stop them now. Keep them on the island—safe—as long as he wished. They trusted him.

"Of course, you're going," LeRoy said gruffly. "You want to, don't you?"

"I think so."

He leaned towards Lethias. "Think hard, son. Think real hard about it." And disconnected.

Think about *that*.

‹ 9: Lethias, 3/10 ›

Lethias stood on the stern deck of the ferry. It was a dull, gray foggy morning, and the sun was a sickly creamsicle orange as it shone down on them. Along the dock, he could see every ape he knew, and that was every ape on the island. The baboons stood farther off and he could see Runs-From-Water watching him. He grinned and waved to them. Several of the baboons waved back. He remembered the night before when Jefferson had taken him aside.

==Remember,== she had signed. ==When you need to, you will dream of home.==

In his excitement, Lethias couldn't imagine needing to.

There was silence for a long minute. Then, Marcus began hooting, joined in by the other gorilla males. Soon, they were beating their chest and jumping up and down, calling after him like thunder. The male chimps and orangutans joined in, the shrill screams and deep bass cries blending in with the gorilla thunder.

Lethias leaned back and listened, arms outstretched, bathing in that long cry of hope joining them all.

Soon, it faded and the ferry slipped silently into

the water. The island was lost in the fog.

Restless, Lethias prowled over the boat, from tip to stern. Two big men armed with tranquilizer pistols watched him carefully. After Pearl, no ape would ever again be left alone on the deck of the ferry. The rest of the crew was down below. Quinote was not aboard as he had been with Pearl. This meant a lot to Lethias. He would not let Marcus, LeRoy, and the rest, down. But his excitement had faded and was replaced by a nagging misgiving. He didn't know what it was.

He finally stood on the forward deck, leaning against the railing and watching the water. He could feel the guards behind him. He ignored them. He felt sad. The fog showed no signs of burning off. The air was cold and damp.

Little shoes, he thought. They'd found only her clothes, folded neatly, and next to them those ridiculous, little shoes.

He sprang back from the railing as if burned, hooting softly to himself. He leaped in the air and cried out, beat his chest, and shouted against the fog, the sea, the cold, the trip itself, with the full-throated cry of a gorilla. The men watched him, guns loose in their hands, but did nothing. The cries poured out across the gray water.

All the time, inside, he cried out to himself: *It's not going to happen to me! It's not going to happen to me!*

Chapter 1.2

‹ 1: Tamar, 3/11 ›

Tamar Longren listened to the signature theme as Mister Coyotee finished speaking with Ferdinand Isobanna.

Isobanna's features contrasted sharply with the cartoon face of Mister Coyotee. Tamar felt something light land on her shoulder. Annoyed, she shooed Jackie, her photographer/guard-wasp, back into the air. It flew around her head and landed again on her shoulder.

"Damn it." Jackie was hungry. Tamar rummaged around in her desk and found a food pellet. Jackie flew over to it and began munching on it contentedly. Marilyn, the other wasp, buzzed them, then landed under a light on top of the cabinets. She spread her wings to get as much nourishment as she could from the light. Tamar knew it wasn't enough and that as soon as Jackie finished, Marilyn would be eating. For the moment, Marilyn just sulked.

The guard wasps were far bigger than normal—closer in size to murder hornets. But *Vespa mandarinia* was unsuitable for Tamar's purposes. The queen/drone/worker paradigm was too strong. Individuals withered and died without a hive to back them up. Reviews of guard hornets made from *V. mandarinia* also mentioned that they were prone to die from overheating. The LifeWorks' product line was based on *Sphex pensylvanicus*: a large, solitary wasp more amenable to individual applications that didn't overheat. That was what the LifeWorks brochure had said, anyway.

The brochure had also said the *Guardian* product line was the first introduction of fove technology into the consumer marketplace. Tamar had her doubts about that. The whole idea of foves consisted of the complete redesign of a whole organism towards a specific goal that was reproductively self-contained. I.e., a new *species*. Releasing reproductive wasps into the wild didn't seem likely. Tamar decided the whole concept of "fove" was being turned into marketingspeak.

Monsanto's slug technology was certainly a redesign of slugs and Tamar would be willing to bet deep in the production factory there were slug breeding colonies. It just made sense. From that point, the slugs were either breeding true—and representing actual foves—or were modified prior to sale. In either case, something inhibited purchased slugs from breeding. Tamar suspected the slugs were modified after they'd bred and one of the modifications was inhibiting reproduction. That, also, just made sense—as long as it worked.

Tamar leaned away from Mister Coyotee and stretched her back against the chair. Her face was dark and her eyes wide and almond-shaped, framed perfectly by her black hair. Her nails were done to match her hair. She held up her thumb in front of her and crossed it with her forefinger. A small spot of light appeared on her thumbnail and spread until she could see a small image of Tamar sitting at the desk. This was Marilyn's camera. "Let me see Jackie's." The next picture of Tamar bobbed and waved as Jackie ate. Good, they were both online. She touched up her hair.

"So that was what you were watching," Fred Reni, her producer, observed.

Tamar started, but he leaned forward against his

desk to watch Tamar's screen. "Good show, too. Yeah. He took Isobanna apart."

"I don't think so." Carrie looked over Tamar's shoulder. "Coyotee led Isobanna to do it to herself. I couldn't have directed him better than if I'd been directing Tamar." From across the room, Carrie's dog perked up at the sound of her voice and watched her intently. The movement spooked Jackie and she took off, flying in a slow figure-eight between Tamar and the dog. Marilyn came off the cabinet quickly and pounced on the food brick.

"Directing her to do what, may I ask?" Fred laughed.

"That is none of your business," replied Carrie.

"I agree. Even Tamar couldn't make it any better." Fred leaned back in his chair. "I liked Isobanna admitting the real reason behind the Oregon Initiative: 'Biodesign we don't like.' She looked ridiculous."

"*Everybody* looks ridiculous on that show."

"It's a nice simulation. Or live-action animation." Tamar froze the picture of Mister Coyotee looking over his shoulder towards the rear curtain. Isobanna looked uncomfortable. The production was seamless.

"No guest has ever admitted to being on the show," said Fred. "Saying they were simulated gives them deniability. A guest can say what they want because nobody believes it was really them."

"They could put somebody bonded on the show," said Carrie.

Fred snorted. "Yeah. That's a losing proposition. Either put up a simulation of someone bonded and watch every iteration destroyed or actually have a bonded guest discuss the experience revealing every little secret." Fred shook his head. "That will never happen."

"It would prove the interviews weren't a

simulation. Either the bonded images would be destroyed, showing the guests are real, or they would be marked, indicating the guests are simulations."

"The show's popularity thrives on that uncertainty. The certainty that it's real or the certainty it's simulation would damage the show's popularity."

Tamar looked at Mister Coyotee's sad face. "How do they get away with violating the 37th Amendment like that?" She pointed at Isobanna. "That's a clear likeness violation."

Fred shrugged. "They've never caught the producers."

"Nobody actually *knows* where this comes from?" Tamar considered Mister Coyotee across the net of the world, a silver bead replicating itself across the wires like so much rampant DNA.

Fred shrugged. "I heard some kids out of Tokyo University put it together and send it out on the net every couple of weeks."

"I don't believe it," said Carrie. "Look at the quality of the work. This isn't a student job."

Fred leaned forward and said in a low voice. "Some say it's the speech of the net itself. Others say it's the Voice of God." He grinned. "I like that: the Voice of God." He straightened. "It can't be any of those rumors. If they were true, the producers would be caught and the show expunged."

"Except the Voice of God part—or the net." Tamar expanded the face. Mister Coyotee looked out at her, a sad-eyed cartoon animal that looked like nothing more than the sort of hand-drawn animated figures from nearly two centuries ago.

"Aren't they the same thing?" Fred laughed. "There's a story going around that Shuman herself is going to be on the show."

"Do you think these are *always* simulations?"

asked Tamar quietly. "Or is it a mix?" I'd take the chance, to be broadcast across the net like that. She could almost feel it, all of the copies of her transmitted simultaneously.

"Simulations." Fred tapped his fingers on his desk for emphasis. "Who the hell would ever get roasted like that voluntarily?"

"Secondson wasn't roasted. Baked a little, maybe." Carrie leaned against Tamar's chair and casually rested her hand on Tamar's shoulder.

"Secondson is one of the founders of the Hopi Development Corporation. Maybe Mister Coyotee is a Hopi," said Tamar and leaned forward to turn off the image. Carrie's hand dropped to the back of Tamar's chair. "Maybe the show comes straight out of Second Mesa."

"Maybe." Carrie sighed and sat on Tamar's desk. "What are you doing for dinner tonight?"

"Studying more Mister Coyotee." Tamar watched the blank screen, thinking. "Working on a LifeWorks dateline. Parkin has been supporting the Life Banks bill." To herself, she muttered. "I'd like to be that good."

"Datelines are bo-*ring*. Blow it off," said Carrie with a sudden maniacal grin.

"Datelines are essential!" protested Fred.

Carrie ignored him. "We can go down into Boston and check out the restored Durgin Park. I feel the need for red meat."

Tamar looked up. Carrie's face was open and yearning. Tamar answered with a slow, but rueful, smile. It wouldn't do to make Carrie angry: one of the many inevitable complications of sleeping with your Boss. "Can't. I have to have the dateline ready tonight."

"When you two are finished with your mating rituals," drawled Fred. "Maybe we can get some more work done. Tam's right, Carrie. We need a little filler and the LifeWorks dateline is just about the right size. You do recall the name of the company?"

Carrie's disappointment showed in her eyes. Tamar knew she could expect a new present, soon. For a young, rich woman, Carrie was easily readable: she needed approval like farms needed irrigation.

"BioNews." Carrie stood up. "A struggling young newsnet trade service specializing in keeping track of the eternal struggle between Biogood and Bioevil."

Fred pointed a finger at her. "The Biodevil will get you if you don't watch out."

‹ 2: Monty, 3/11 ›

After LeRoy had told him Lethias was on his way, Monty canceled his dinner with Carmine Ranquiz. Dancing through their variations of the parent/child samba took too much bandwidth. Especially, since he was Carmine's doctor rather than his father.

Nor did he call Sims. He decided he would wait.

Most people found Sims and Monty's relationship confusing. When LeRoy closed LifeWorks at the beginning of the Die-Back, he had moved a whole division out to the island. By the time of the Restoration, only five of them were left: Montague Quinote, Carroll Sims, LeRoy himself, Bill Springbuck, and Jim Secondson. LeRoy had returned to Charleston to reopen LifeWorks. Bill and Jim had returned to Second Mesa. Monty had moved to Boston. Sims split his time between his appointment at Harvard and his lab on the island. By that point, he and Sims had lived together for decades and found it congenial to their nature. What was twenty more?

Today, Monty consulted in the Individual Medicine Lab with Izmodo and Blackbear on a new patient, Ainar Omarov, a two-year-old with defective lungs. Under Monty's direction, Richard Izmodo and

Steven Blackbear were helping Ainar grow a new lung.

The Lab's techniques were the same as they had first used in the LifeWorks lab back in Charleston and later refined on the island. Izmodo was the *dedo*. Steven Blackbear was the *ojo*. *Dedo* and *ojo*: manipulator and director. The mechanism Monty, LeRoy, and Sims had invented and the techniques Jim Secondson and Bill Springbuck had developed.

Secondson and Springbuck had taken those techniques back to found the Hopi Development Corporation. Both Izmodo and Blackbear had been trained there, then farmed out to Monty at exorbitant prices and ridiculous licensing arrangements.

Monty didn't mind. That had been the plan from the beginning. Besides, he had helped found the HDC, too.

Monty had seriously mixed feelings about the Die-Back. Without it, they would never have had the opportunity to delve so deep. Working on observing and manipulating the embryology of apes—nearly human, really—had prepared him for what he did when he left. Carmine was only one product of that effort.

Nor would the Individual Medicine Lab have existed without the Die-Back. For one reason, an enormous expenditure on only two or three patients a year made no sense when there were hundreds more needing similar effort. But those hundreds were gone. Human life had become infinitely more precious. Saving two or three had become worth it.

After the consult, Monty stayed through rounds on his neurological patients and then went out for late drinks with the bright young nurse who'd assisted him. Monty considered it a challenge to charm a woman far less than half his age and who was whole and upright, contrasted with his own withered left hand, limp, and twisted spine. When people asked him—and few people ever did—why in this day and age he retained these handicaps? He replied he'd been born with them and it was none of their business. If they pursued the matter, he didn't answer.

He'd not been born with a ceramic hip, plastic kneecap, or artificial kidney, either. But the answer remained: none of their business.

Ruth was a redhead with a figure like a slim pear: wide hips, little chest, and a gentle, forgiving sense of humor Monty very much enjoyed. Around midnight, he left her at her apartment in Cambridge, willing but dubious, and returned to the hospital. At his age, gallantry had become, if not a physiological truism, at least a chancy affair. Besides, he didn't need much in the way of sleep and there was always work to do.

Others might feel differently, he thought sourly as he took the train back. He pictured LeRoy playing royal tennis. Act your age, LeRoy. Don't be so normal. Eccentricity is the accepted province of the old.

Monty returned in plenty of time to give an early-morning neurology lecture. He'd been leading up to it for some weeks, setting up useful preconceptions, tearing them down, setting up new ones. Tonight's was on the reticular formation—his favorite. Though the lecture changed from year to year, he liked to have the same beginning: "For years, the reticular formation was considered the simple portion of the brain. Look at this slide; just a gray mass. As in many things, simplicity is an illusion. In this case, the illusion of technique. In fact, its organization is at the cellular level, a microscopic precision that can only be apparent when examined closely. In this way, it most resembles the human self." With such a nineteenth-century beginning, Sherrington and Ramón y Cajal would have been proud.

Then, it was time for his shift in the trauma center. Just in time for the mid-day rush. He threw himself into it with a will.

Four hours later, when his shift was over, he felt pleasantly exhausted. He returned to his office, pulled a pre-dinner Chianti out of his office refrigerator, and poured himself a glass. Lovely, he thought as he watched the hospital lights through the wine. He called Sims.

"Hello," croaked Sims, haggard and half-awake on the screen.

Monty checked Sims' location. "Carroll, you're home? I'd hoped to get the proxy. Why didn't you let it pick up?"

"I'm still in Charleston consulting for LeRoy. I had any legitimate calls forwarded. How that got me a call from *you*, I'm not sure. Probably a software bug. Where are you?"

"Still at the hospital."

"Enjoy your stay." He started to turn back to bed.

"Don't go yet. We're going to have a houseguest."

Sims stopped and turned back to him. Monty smiled at him.

"Who?"

"A friend."

"As long as she sleeps in your room, I don't have to worry about it. Good night."

"It's not a *she*. It's a *he*."

"As long as *he* sleeps—"

"And *he* won't be sleeping with me. It's Lethias."

It was very satisfying to watch Carroll's face: stupefied amazement, disbelief, pleasant surprise, suspicion, dismay.

"You're joking."

"Not at all."

"What's LeRoy going to do? Go public with the whole damned island?" Carroll ran his hands through his hair. "That is exactly his idea, wasn't it? I'll kill him."

Monty laughed. "Come now. We'll hide him in plain sight."

"It'll play hell with my grant if this gets out."

"It won't. But you should have some warning, right?"

"After I haven't slept in twenty hours."

"There was no way I could know that."

Sims grunted. "Why Boston?"

In the twilight, Monty held the wineglass, diffracting the lights across the river. They seemed to bubble and fume. "Maybe Coyote went there," he murmured.

"Beg pardon?"

Monty put down the glass to rub his withered hand. Sometimes after a long day, it ached. "Let us just say it's time for one of them to come out into the world and Lethias is that person. We'll need some identification. Some falsified records."

"We could do that." Carroll wore an innocent expression but his eyes twinkled. "But it would be wrong."

Monty laughed. "See you later tonight."

"No, you won't. Still in Charleston, remember? Probably in a few days."

Monty hung up and sipped his wine. Then he made a second call.

An old Hopi man answered.

Monty spoke without preamble. "It is as you said, my brother."

Jim Secondson snorted. "It was not a hard prediction. Bad luck comes in fours, like most things." He sneezed, which turned into a coughing fit. "Pardon. Had to smell out a dust devil today—damn things seem to multiply. Contracts are where you find them. Anyway, be careful and be secret. Things are happening."

"What kind of things, Jim?"

"Ripples in the water. Clouds across the sky. There was an Elvis sighting—first in ten years. Played Hell with his church in Memphis, I can tell you. A chicken gave birth to an egg shaped like a fish. Other unclear metaphors." The old man shook his head. "I can't follow the math."

"I could ask Sims for you," offered Monty.

Jim laughed. "He would insist on collecting them." Again, he shook his head. "We don't need any more silt in the water. Be discreet, brother. Be secret. Thank you for your bad tidings."

Jim disappeared.

Monty drank the rest of his wine and looked outside in the early summer night. Above the broad green swards on either side of the Charles, there were spring fireflies among the trees, winking on, winking off. Now that this had finally come to pass, he felt a great calm come over him as if he'd been waiting a long time for a dubious circumstance and it had now come to pass. Win, lose, or draw, waiting was over.

They had kept the apes secret for over eighty years. He wondered if Lethias, the apes, and the island could really stay secret.

Of course not, he chided himself. *What a silly thought.*

He turned out the light and started for home.

‹ 3: Wash, 3/11 ›

Washington Sunshine woke up when the westering sun struck him through the window. His dream of being chased by a *Pelagornis*, its toothed beak coming ever closer lingered for a moment. He woke, leaped out of bed, and stood in an easy combat stance, staring groggily around the room, searching for a giant, extinct, toothed bird.

"It's okay, Mister Sunshine. It's okay," said the soothing voice of Rocco, his apartment.

"I was being chased by a giant, extinct, toothed bird," he said, shaking his head. "Where am I?"

"You're in Brookline. In the Summit Avenue Legal Block. It's Monday, late in the afternoon." Behind Rocco's voice, Wash could hear the soothing strains of Mozart. "You came home this morning. You've been gone all weekend."

Slowly, the fog of sleep evaporated from the wide plains of his mind. He'd spent the weekend in Guatemala. The Mazetenango raid. For a moment, he relived the high-speed entry by glider, the silent touchdown, when he dispatched the suddenly lit glider to draw fire. Its explosion marked a failed assassination attempt on the prime minister who was in the hotel for a summit with the ambassador from Honduras.

Instead, Wash was already four floors down, dispersing gene-marked toxins. He made an unobserved Seven League Jump through the window into the dark street and walked nonchalantly away while the target, a minor health minister, slumped mid-coitus over his lover.

A nice, clean, professional, if unexciting, piece of work. Wash sighed. He was getting too old for this sort of job. No. Scratch that. *He* wasn't getting old. The *work* was getting old. The same thing over and over.

"Yeah," he muttered and shook his head to get the thickness out. "Damn drugs." He felt puffy and slow. "Get me some coffee."

"Coffee in your office."

After a quick shower, he still felt slow. He found the coffee and read Rocco's digested news. I-T? Something in Latvia? Anything in Europe would require a week at sea, the time the job required, then a return week at sea. Three weeks in the middle of the semester. Someday there will be commercial air travel again. He should call Kronkide and see if they needed something immediate and near country. Something America adjacent. Wash needed more tuition money.

American Poetry Review.

Carefully, he read the abstract. "Rocco! I got a better review this time!"

"What did they say, Mister Sunshine?"

"They said it wasn't completely dreary. And they said I read the news this time! That's better, isn't it?"

"I'm sure it is, Mister Sunshine. Would you like breakfast in the kitchen?"

He read the review twice before he was able to finish his coffee and settle down for breakfast. "Do I have anything to do this afternoon? I thought I'd work on some new poems."

"You have a class in the Banal Masters of the 1950s in an hour. It is a lecture class."

"Harvard," he muttered. "Why can't they have all their boring classes online like everybody else?"

Wash looked down at his plate and noticed the varicolored yellow and green mass. He stuck a fork in it and held it there. The material resisted being punctured by the fork for a few seconds, then gradually oozed up the silverware. When the tines were completely covered, he dropped the fork hastily. "What am I eating?"

"Do you like it, sir?"

"How do I know I like it until I know what it is?"

"I don't know, Mister Sunshine. Would you like it tomorrow morning?"

"What is it?"

"A new formulation for no-fat eggs. It's ecologically sound and morally pure."

"Yeah. What is it?"

"It's made from pangolins."

"The weird little animals with scales? Did this come out of the mess in Brazil?"

"Yes, sir."

Wash shook his head. He looked at his breakfast dubiously. "I thought I was a vegetarian."

"Not since last month. You're now an eclectic, ecologically sound nutritionist. Remember, vegetarians have been shown to have longer life spans but lower enjoyment per unit time. It was reported in the New England Journal of Medicine."

Wash looked back at the eggs. "Isn't that because of the kind of people who decide to become vegetarians?"

"I don't know, sir. The article didn't say."

"I should eat this?"

"Yes, sir."

Wash shrugged, closed his eyes, and finished it. "Let's not have this tomorrow. Let's never have this again."

"As you wish."

"Right." Wash checked the time on the wall. "I've got to go. Remind me to call Kronkide tomorrow." He placed the plates in the sink. "Any news in the building?"

"The Massachusetts Audubon Society has requested donations to help in its trademark suit against the National Audubon Society. The block has pledged a half percent levy. Security has been beefed up in case the New Hampshire Friends of the Bald Eagle refuse mediation."

Wash nodded.

"The annual Summit Ave Hawk Watch has been scheduled for next weekend. Armor is being provided. Two peregrines and a marsh hawk have been sighted from the building already. I signed you up for the field trip to Springfield, as I did last year."

"Great."

"The Pedersens are leaving the block. The Summit Ave Court found them Undesirable Tenants. Hal Pedersen said to thank you for the good word you put in for them. He says Jake sends his love."

"Damn. Where are they going?"

"I don't know. They haven't made anything public."

Wash drummed his fingers on the counter. He really liked Hal and Jake. What could have happened over the weekend? Damn. For a moment, he stared into the sink—the plates were gone. How did Rocco *do* that? "Are Hal and Jake in now?"

"Yes."

"Can I go over to see them?"

A brief pause. "They say you're welcome, but they're packing."

Damn. Hal and Jake were different from the rest of the block tenants. Hal was a nurse at Mount Auburn Hospital and an avid bird breeder. Jake worked for the Department of Reclamation Enforcement and hearing him talk about his work made Wash think of Mickey Spillane and Raymond Chandler. Not the usual members of the block. Hell, he could skip classes. There were some things more important than the Banal Masters of the 1950s.

"Tell them I'm coming over to say goodbye."

‹ 4: Carmine, 3/11 ›

Carmine Ranquiz, naked, stood preening on the roof of Widener Library, Harvard University. It was late afternoon and the evening wind had come up from the west, down the Charles River to the sea.

He was a little under a meter and a half tall. His skin was the translucent white of eggshell porcelain and his eyes, large in his face, were a deep blue. He had a quick smile, light brown hair, and fingers long and graceful as spiders.

When Carmine looked at his body in front of the mirror—something he did not do often—he thought his body resembled a small man wearing a long backpack. Once, a tall, blond lover had suggested that the arrangement on his back looked like butterflies' wings tied in square knots. That woman had never said if that was beautiful or ugly.

Carmine only thought of himself as beautiful when he was in the air.

His wings began at the base of his wrist and stayed connected to his body down to his ankles, resembling the flying membrane of bats. When extended, they spread out from his body some three and a half meters on each side, with long prehensile sections that drifted nearly six meters below his feet. Cross a moth and a pterodactyl, he thought sourly as he worked on them, and you have Carmine Ranquiz. Carmine was not the largest animal to fly—that honor belonged to *Quetzalcoatlus*, a creature with a twelve-meter wingspan that weighed more than two hundred kilos. Carmine had to console himself that he was merely the largest flying mammal to ever live with his paltry eight-meter wingspan and fifty-eight kilos weight.

At least, *Quetzalcoatlus* didn't have to assemble his wings every time he wanted to fly.

Each wing had to be unfolded and shaped. Long, flexible soft tissue became rods as hard as bone. Flaps were shaken, stiffened, and filled out to their proper size.

Strong muscles threaded from the leading edge of his wings to join at his side and back, down to his thighs, more muscles that roped over his shoulders down to his chest. These weren't enough. In addition, he had a bony protuberance on each wing which he pulled down with his arms. Even with that, he needed to take off in a headwind or dive down from a high place, catching the wind on his slightly furled wings until he rose high enough to open them all the way, riding the thermals and winds over the city. He envied extinct *Quetzalcoatlus*.

Carmine massaged one of the bones in the leading edge of his right wing and it gradually stiffened, tingling. As he worked, he sipped continuously from a large water bottle. Some of the tissues making up his wings were tumescent and he needed to be hydrated for them to swell properly. Later, when his wings relaxed, he would pee continuously for an hour. Carmine considered this a small price to pay for flight.

Carmine hadn't intended to go flying today. He'd meant to give the Cambridge police a little breather. They didn't like him flying. They didn't like him flying naked. And they *certainly* hadn't liked it when he buzzed them and flipped them off as they chased him along the river. Mustn't tickle them too much. They might get testy.

Damn Quinote, he thought. "'We have to cancel dinner,"' Carmine mimicked. "'I've got something important to do.' Well, *I'm* important, Doctor Quinote. 'Of course, you're important. Don't indulge in self-pity. It's unattractive in a young man.' And fuck you for that piece of information, thank you very much."

His wing shook out and caught the sunlight. The wing's flush gradually deepened until it glowed rose and pearl through his brown skin.

As he worked on the left wing, he began to recite the bones of his wing as he shaped it, grunting with the effort: "*Os* spinus *interior, os* spinus *exterior, os terminus, os* malum *superior, os* malum *inferior, os* acies *exterior, os* acies *interior, os tenaci.*" That's what he *said,* anyway. Between mutterings, he was *thinking*, fuck you, Doctor Quinote. *Fuck you, Doctor Quinote.*

Both wings were laid out, moving slightly in the breeze. He shaped his long ropy tail segments, carefully spread out the fan-shaped tips, and massaged them until they were firm.

Like one huge and complex erection.

Carmine knew the underlying physiology was considerably different, but the stroking and massaging to make limp things stiff was not lost on him.

Carmine stood up and cautiously spilled air out of his wings as he danced to the edge of the roof. Buildings were tricky things, filled with unexpected updrafts and sideslips.

"You're beautiful," came a woman's voice behind him. "Don't ever let anyone tell you different."

Carmine was so startled he nearly fell off the edge of the roof. He spilled air from one wing, caught it with the other. The resulting lift spun him up and down, now facing the roof's entrance door.

A dark woman was watching him. "Beautiful *and* talented. Such a combination."

"Who are you?"

"Joanne Biri," she said. "I saw you enter the building and followed."

"Why?"

"Because I know who you are, Carmine Ranquiz. More importantly, I know *what* you are. I have come to be present at a miracle."

Carmine shook his head. "I'm no miracle."

"Aren't you?" Joanne seemed to be laughing without making a sound.

He looked her up and down. He couldn't tell her heritage. Africa, of course. But not African American from her clipped English. Somalian, maybe? "Where are you from?"

"Georgia," Joanne said in a long drawl. Then, switched back to her clipped accent. "Does it matter?" She walked around him. "How can you remain here on the ground? You must fight flight every moment. It must take an act of will to walk the earth."

"It's not that bad."

She raised one eyebrow. "Isn't it?"

And Carmine saw how he snatched moments of flight from the nooks and crannies of his life. Fitting what he had been *built* for inside an earthbound existence.

"It is," he said.

"Then, go, Dear." Then, she did laugh. "Look back at me once from the air and bless me! Go and fly!"

He leaped out into space and spread his wings. They filled with air and he pulled hard: down, up, down. A west wind caught under his right wing like a caress and tipped him up. He kept the tilt, banking away from the wind, curving with it, and rising higher than the trees. Then, he turned back into the wind and he was suddenly flying, high over the campus. The wind blew across his arms and chest, down between his thighs, across his penis. Erect for real now, the wind touched him like fingers, like lips. The afternoon sun, the sky, the wind, made love to him.

He spun over the roof to see her and she waved with both hands. He waved and leaped in the air.

She was right. This was where he belonged.

Carmine looped around the campus chapel and laughed in sheer delight. Higher—a news drone flew alongside him, the small tube of a camera pointing out at him. He spread his wings and showed himself to the audience.

Carmine let go of his wing long enough to wave, banked under the drone, and flew south, over the river, over the green trees, the old three-deckers and Legal Blocks, the massive train yards and broken concrete platforms, over the recolonized colorful streets and the dark crumbling ones that remained abandoned. Over people, places, and things.

Carmine soared over Fenway Park and caught its thermal. It carried him as high as the lower towers and in sight of the Great Boston Tree. He was high enough to fly downtown but chose not to—he didn't like to fly between the buildings unless he had plenty of room to fall. He wasn't supposed to fly there at all. Sometimes, he did at night. Today, he flew high and watched the world unfurl below him.

See me now, Joanne! See me now!

The city hummed a deep throaty purr to him. He could smell it and feel the city's warm air buffeting him. Cities were best observed from on high, he thought. Almost anything was. Tired now, the sexual edge of flying gone dull, he fell off the edge of the thermal and banked back across Brookline. Time to head back. It was getting late and darkness was creeping in. Lights came on in Boston, Cambridge, and parts of Somerville, the outer suburbs dark and empty. In the core of the city, there was the illusion of population. Crowds walked up and down the streets. But the borders left by the Die-Back were stark: most of Massachusetts lived in the core. The rest of the state had been given over to the wild. Little of it registered with Carmine: this was the world he'd been born into.

Out of the dark and back across the reservoir, where there were still Brookline lights, over the long blocks of Brookline brownstones, the green paths and byways of inner Brookline and Brighton. Then, over the river. Carmine had to struggle upwind—the late afternoon breeze blew towards the sea and Carmine was flying upriver. He pushed himself higher, then came down towards Harvard in a long, shallow glide. He looked for Joanne but she was gone.

Instead, there were blue, uniformed men on the top of Widener—Cambridge policemen. One of these had a white hailer in his hand.

"You will come down here and be taken into custody," came the voice of one of the policemen.

Carmine grinned and circled Widener, flapped a few times to get some altitude. *Catch me if you can!* Then, he realized how tired he was. It would be hard going to fly anywhere else—he would have to get much higher and glide to the top of another building. The wind was against him now. At this time of day, the wind blowing between the buildings created a downdraft. It was not strong, but he was already tired.

"This is Harvard," Carmine cried down to them, circling. "You're out of your jurisdiction! Go get the Harvard cops."

"Come down here and be taken into custody," came the reply.

Unimaginative lot.

He circled Widener again. "Okay," he shouted. "Back off. I'm coming down." The policemen backed away from the edge of the building.

Carmine came in lower than the top of Widener and swooped up over the edge, saw the police unexpectedly rush towards him. He panicked and frantically beat his wings. One policeman grabbed his leg—Carmine screamed as he felt it break. The policeman let go and Carmine fell off the edge of the building. He ignored the pain in his leg and tried to right himself—beat his wings once, twice, and struck just as he felt himself catch the wind.

‹ 5: Wash, 3/11 ›

The door recognized Wash and passed him silently into the Pedersens' foyer. Wash hurried through into the living room. Hal, a tall thin man, was packing the spare bird cages of his cockatoo collection. The cockatoos, themselves, watched from their perches along the wall, muttering to themselves.

"We're going to miss that," Wash said awkwardly. "They're the pride of the block."

"*Was* the pride of the block." Hal jammed a large brass cage into a box furiously. There was a snapping sound. "Damn! Popped a strut." He straightened up and stared into the box, swearing quietly and repetitively. Abruptly, he turned towards Wash. "That's another one I can blame on Aunt Ida."

"Aunt Ida?"

"Ida Sung—president of the block governing committee. You don't—" Hal shook himself. "Come on. I need a cup of coffee. You really don't know who Aunt Ida is?"

Wash followed him into the kitchen. "No."

"Wash, if you don't pay more attention to life it is going to jump up and bite you right on your ass." Hal carefully brewed a deep black liquid. "Ida has been president of the block for ten years. Almost since she moved in."

Wash didn't know what to say for a minute. "How's Andy taking it?"

Hal stood up and looked exasperated. "Our beloved Andy believes that it is all for the best—he says *he* doesn't like Brookline. He says *he* doesn't like Boston. *He* says he wants to live in a *house*. Tomorrow is his last day at school—I think he's enjoying saying goodbye. Andy? He's happy as a clam. I don't know what I expected—he is a teenager after all." He turned back to the coffee machine. "Myself, I hate leaving here. My parents are from Brookline. So were their parents. They helped found the Winchester-Salem Legal Block just down the street. Held it all through the Die-Back."

Wash felt disoriented, like a swimmer in unexpected deep water. "You could get another place here—"

"I don't want another place," Hal said furiously. "*This* is my home." He put down the filter set. "I am not going to cry. I will not give her the satisfaction." He turned back to the sink. "We've been here eighteen years. The down payment was a wedding present from Jake's parents. They were so proud of us joining a legal block on our own." He finished making the coffee in silence. When he passed the cup and saucer to Wash, his hand was shaking and made them rattle.

"Where's Jake?" Wash sipped his coffee gingerly. Spicy, with a hint of nutmeg and cinnamon. He would miss this, too.

"He'd be sleeping it off if he had any sense!" came a roar behind them.

Jake stumbled in from the balcony. A big, florid man with red hair and beard, he seemed to fill the room. He was dressed only in boxer shorts and held in one hand a two-liter plastic bottle of Coke. Wash stared at it. Possession of plastic bottles had been a felony long before Wash was born—even before the Die-Back.

Jake followed his gaze and grinned wickedly. "That's right! I am not *eco*-logically *per*-fect. Goddamned Coke doesn't taste the same in goddamned glass bottles. Bought them in Guatemala. Not that I *had* to, understand. I had plenty of chances to keep contraband—a member of the Reclamation Police has many opportunities. *Had* many opportunities."

"Jake is, shall we say, under the weather." Hal chuckled bitterly and shook his head. "He was arrested for buying a six-pack of soda—"

"It's the ree-al thing," sang Jake.

"—and a package of Styrofoam cups."

"I'm a goddamned collector, goddamnit! I been collecting since I got on the force fifteen years ago." Jake clutched his bottle to his chest. "I've got a cupla' hunderd' thousan' bucks worth set up on display in the Museum of Fine Arts—I fucking *donated* it to them. How the hell did I know they weren't antiques? I didn't have time to cross-check them. Just whoosh, into jail."

"It was a sting operation," said Hal. "You would think they would have something better to do with their time. Apparently, there are illegal factories in other countries making these things for collectors and the FBI is trying to stop it here. Of course, Jake's now on suspension from the bureau."

"Suspension, Hell. They can't fucking fire me! I quit!"

Hal sighed. "You can guess the rest."

Wash could. Other blocks might have overlooked it, but the Summit Avenue Legal Block had formed from the same environmentalist group that had spearheaded the Total Cost Tax before the Die-Back. It was like having an Appalachian Corridor enclave in the heart of Brookline. The motion to relocate west, in fact, came up every few years. But nobody wanted to move to the outback. The relics of its history were all here. The Summit Avenue Bird Watching Society was world-famous—part of the block's attraction to Wash when he'd bought his apartment. Though the block had mellowed somewhat since the Die-Back and Restoration, the green feelings still ran deep.

"I was framed," muttered Jake darkly. He held up his bottle. "1990 Coke. Kept *cold*. Nothing tastes better with rum. That's the way it was. Thousands— millions of 'em. That's the ticket. *Damn* the conservationists. Full progress *ahead*."

"He's been like this ever since he was arrested. Ida found out about it and had our contract broken the same afternoon." Hal shook his head. "I am *not* going to cry."

Wash didn't know what to say. "Can I help? Do you have a place to stay? Do you have enough money?"

Hal gave a brittle laugh. "We have enough *money*. They had to buy us out. We don't even have to find a place to live—we're moving out onto Jake's family farm. It's sunny and very pretty, near the Appalachian Trail. In the country—" Hal threw the coffee filter set against the wall. "I was born in Brookline! I was raised here! This is my *home!*" He began crying. "I wasn't going to cry. I swore—"

Jake came up behind Hal and held him, steadying the both of them against the countertop. "It's all right." He turned his bleary eyes in Wash's direction. "You've been a good friend, Wash. It was nice of you to drop by. But maybe you ought to come back some other time."

"Right." Wash left hurriedly. He stood in the hallway feeling helpless and unsure of himself. "Can I speak with Rocco, please?" he said to the open air.

"Certainly, Mister Sunshine," said the hall.

"Sir?" asked Rocco.

"Write me up a letter, uh, protesting this... this *expulsion*." Wash looked at his hands. They were suddenly trembling with rage. It was a novel experience. Usually, the only rage he felt was induced when he was working. He wished momentarily that he could have Ida as a hit—she would have been protoplasm twenty minutes after he'd signed the contract. He shrugged such unprofessional thoughts aside and steadied himself. "Put it on paper."

"Paper, sir?"

"Yes. Let her read it on the skin of dead trees." He stalked down the stairs and out into the street.

Wash always found it difficult to stay angry and

outside the late afternoon sun leached his anger away. March had come in warm and unseasonably dry. The wind felt good on his skin. He looked for the block's driver. "Sam?" he called.

Sam Chedrikov was gardening in one of the twenty window boxes that adorned the outside of this portion of the Block. Regardless of his name, Sam was nearly pure Samoan from an enclave somewhere in California—two meters tall and nearly a hundred kilos of muscle. Wash envied him the texture of his skin.

"Hey, Mister Sunshine," Sam answered and laughed. "What can I do for you?"

"I need to get to Cambridge and I don't want to wait for the rail. Anybody going that way?"

"I can run you over. We're in the black on consumables this month." Sam frowned and plucked a small slug from the side of the van. "Wash-and-waxer, I think. Thought I gathered them all up this morning."

Wash looked back at the building. Along the base, he could see a couple of vague brick-red shapes. "There's a couple over there."

"No, Mister Sunshine. Those are the block slugs. They repair the walls and clean up the bricks. Sometimes they get on the van, though—I had to scrape half a meter of mortar off the bumper a couple of weeks ago. Monsanto delivered us a little mutant, I guess." Sam opened the door. Across the door, prominently labeled, read "I-T Personal Transportation Services."

"I saw Grimaldi's in the news again," Wash said as he stepped inside.

Sam sealed him in and entered the driver's compartment. "Brother Grimaldi is always helping our fellow workers," he said in a stern voice.

"I meant no disrespect to I-T."

"I'm sure you didn't." Sam relaxed somewhat as they pulled onto the narrow street. "Request to enter traffic."

"Where to?" came a liquid voice from the car.

"Harvard University."

"Request granted. Route determined."

The van pulled out onto the street and accelerated up to speed. Sam leaned back and turned to Wash. "She is a sweet car, isn't she?" He patted the dash affectionately.

Wash thought he might have offended Sam in some obscure way. He didn't want to apologize again so he cast about for some other topic of conversation. "Sam, don't you get bored telling the van where to go? I could do it—I could take the car by myself."

Sam laughed easily. "No. You're not allowed, Mister Sunshine. You don't own the van. You lease it, and me, from I-T. It's better that way. Less liability. Besides, I'm not here just as a driver."

"You're not?"

"No, indeed. I'm here as a medic. Or as protection. Or as counselor."

"Counselor?"

Sam nodded. "That's right. I'm a licensed therapist. You can tell me your troubles if you want to. Better than a bartender, eh?"

Wash looked outside in confusion. "I suppose."

"You don't spend enough time at home, Mister Sunshine." Sam waggled his finger at Wash. "You need to familiarize yourself with what goes on in the Block. I'm sure you got the stat sheet on me when I was assigned. Everybody on the block did."

"I suppose." Wash waved at Sam vaguely.

"You don't take much interest in such things, do you?" Sam shrugged. "Takes all kinds, I guess."

The ride progressed in silence for a few minutes. A winged shadow crossed over them. Reflexively,

Wash looked up through the sunroof.

"Follow it!" Wash cried.

"Follow what?" Sam looked around.

Wash pointed up at the great flying shape vaguely visible through the trees. "Up there! It's one of the new condors."

"Damned birds. We can't get out of traffic—there's a fifty-buck penalty."

"Hang the penalty. I'll cover it. Follow that bird!"

Sam slapped the clear button on the dash and took over manually. Nervously, he steered the van in the vague direction of the condor.

Wash leaned out the window, exhilarated. "It's turning towards Cambridge. Towards the bridge."

"Damned birds," muttered Sam.

The van followed the condor as it turned high in the sky and dropped towards Harvard Yard.

"Let me out here! I'll run the rest of the way."

"Good!" said Sam and stopped the van.

Wash jumped out of the van and ran through the gates into the yard. He thought he saw a winged shadow. Before him, he saw Cambridge police. Wash could hear a siren. He ran towards them. *They were hurting one of the condors.* The anger he'd felt for the Pedersens joined with outrage then and he leaped into the small crowd, knocking them back.

When he looked around, only downed and groaning policemen lay about him. There was no bird there. No sign of a bird. Only tracks and diminishing wail of an ambulance.

Wash looked at the policemen on the ground. "Shit," he said softly. This was going to be expensive.

‹ 6: Ida, 3/12 ›

Ida's knees creaked as she rose from the prayer rug. Sparkles of pain ran up and down her legs and she bent over to rub them. She sat back at her desk and tried to read the prescribed sections of the Qur'an and Bible but this morning the graceful Arabic loops and swirls had no more meaning for her than the markings of butterfly wings. The fine black type of Matthew's Gospel was no better. She leaned back in her chair and rubbed her eyes. Outside her office window, the Boston early light was burning through the morning clouds and unveiling the streets to her.

Ida Sung was a pale woman, nearly two meters tall and built broad and thick. She weighed well over a hundred and fifty kilos. Ida was built like a muscular wall—at one point, she had earned the nickname Wide Ida. No one said it to her face more than once. Her hair was black as an oil slick and short against the squareness of her head. The resemblance between her appearance and that of a fireplug was not lost on her. She had small, dark eyes and tiny, delicate, hands and feet that disappeared in comparison to the rest of her great gigantic body, giving the impression that she was the recipient of some kind of absurd transplant.

She was Director of the Northeast Section of the Division for Biological Affairs within the Department of the Interior. Her fiefdom occupied the middle three floors of the Frank Center, a miniature city that had subsumed Government Center and freed Boston to rename the area back to the original Scollay Square. Her office looked out on an expanse of brick and cypress trees. The feathery leaves waved in the wind and made her unhappy.

Like any bureaucracy in the Republic, her office spent a significant amount of time and money repaying campaign promises and political debts for the current administration. In the last election, Shuman had acknowledged the daring leap forward made by Boston in controlling and absorbing carbon dioxide by planting biologically tailored trees.

Everyone had to do their part in bringing down the excesses of the last century. Shuman had not mentioned that the City of Boston had done this on its own, without federal assistance. The city effort culminated in the Great Boston Tree, a gigantic, modified American elm more than three hundred meters tall growing in Copley Square. Shuman had promised federal help for the city by encouraging the rest of the country to follow Boston's lead, thereby paying back the Boston representatives for their support using only the cheap currency of prestige. The Great Boston Tree had been planted before the Die-Back and was better than seventy years old. Ida knew, more than most, the nutrient and water burden the Tree imposed on the city. It tickled her that the burden was accepted without criticism. She liked Boston.

Shuman's symbolic gesture involved a small, bricked, urban park on one edge of the Frank Center commemorating the Tree and other such efforts.

Ida had considered it quite a coup to get tailored cypress trees from a grower in Charleston, cutting that particular expense in half. Each tree had been engineered to grow quickly from a sapling to a full shade tree in three years.

Urban trees required open space around them for access to rain and fertilizer. The architectural design had called for porous, wrought iron mandalas surrounding each tree, each grate a work of original art symbolizing the Old and the New, with imagery from different religions. She was especially proud of the one displaying Hanif Robertson's revelation from which sprang her own faith, the Islamic-Baptist Union. Each tree grew through an opening in the middle of the grate.

Cypress trees, however, grow thick from the base of the trunk, tapering gracefully to a sharp point. This made them appear other-worldly, miniature, and beautiful. It also filled the opening in the grate in a single summer. She now had forty expensive— though, she reminded herself, less expensive than expected—trees that had grown to immobilize each of the individually commissioned grates. Two had split the grates that held them. Two more were withering as the growth pressure of the grates cut off the roots from the branches in a slow, inexorable amputation. One had grown around and absorbed the grate, gripping it tightly and raising it ten centimeters off the ground.

Ida took a private, bitter satisfaction the withering trees were in the Catholic and Shiite grates.

She was left with four choices: do nothing and watch as the trees found their own solutions (making the entire park effort ridiculous.) Cut away or expand the grates (the artists would certainly protest their work being ruined and probably get an injunction or some recompense. Expensive.) Cut down the trees and start over (much more expensive and politically catastrophic.) Attempt to re-engineer the trees in situ (much, much, *much* more expensive and probably not possible, but politically expedient.) None of them appealed to her. So far, the problem had not been reported in any reputable media but it was only a matter of time. Probably, she would have to turn to number four, taking a project that had started in the black and pushing it decisively into the red.

Ida sighed and turned back to the passages:

Qur'an, c.25, v.75: "These shall be rewarded with Paradise for their fortitude. They will be awarded the high place for as much as they were steadfast; and they will meet therein with welcome and the word of peace."

Matthew, c.5, v.11: "Blessed are ye, when men shall revile you, and persecute you, and shall say all manner of evil against you falsely, for my sake. Rejoice, and be exceeding glad: for great is your reward in heaven: for so persecuted they the prophets which were before you."

She read Matthew again. *Great is your reward in heaven.* That appealed to her right now. Ida wrote a memo to her assistant, Tom Ward, to begin soliciting quotes. She thought for a moment. It was Tom who had suggested the cypresses. She grinned and canceled the memo. Instead, she wrote a memo to Shuman's proxy—the president should know about her "gift", shouldn't she? It was *important* that Shuman be able to exercise her political commitments properly—and named Tom as head of the team to correct the problem. She sent it and a copy to Tom. Tom had been getting a bit frisky since he'd persuaded her to let Jake Pedersen go. Booting him out of the Summit Ave Legal Block was one thing. In retrospect, firing him might have been a step too far. Pedersen had been a terrific enforcer.

Ida sighed. Maybe she would be lucky and the trees would die before the contractor had been selected. Through God, all things were possible.

‹ 7: Tamar, 3/11 ›

Tamar stared at the LifeWorks quarterly figures. It was dinnertime. She rubbed her eyes. Her mouth felt ugly. The office was empty—she could go home, eat something, and continue. Tamar shook her head. That crossed the boundary between work and home. As long as she did her work *here*, she could keep her home life safe and protected. That she had violated that boundary a score of times didn't faze her. It was more guideline than rule.

She left the display and went to the bathroom. For a moment she looked in the mirror and checked herself: wide dark eyes limned with a darker line that

curled at the ends. As she watched, the curl shifted
slightly. It made her smile slightly—she liked the
effect of active makeup. Tamar wondered how the
effect would appear if—When, damn it. *When.*—she
appeared on the bonded net. Would people wait to see
the movement of the curl of her eyes? She had a
momentary vision of how she would appear: *Intro:—*
four thousand people died in yet another typhoon in
Bangladesh, today. Bonded reporter Tamar Longren
has the story:

Yes. I helped bury the dead today. I know the
feeling of a broken body in my hands. I know how to
lay the earth over a dead child—

Jackie lighted on her shoulder. Marilyn buzzed in
front of her face, aimed at the mirror to protect her. It
ruined the effect. Annoyed, she batted Marilyn out of
the way. In the medicine cabinet, she found a vial of
breath fresheners. She chewed the tablet and felt a
sudden warm mouthful of foam. There was a tickling
sensation as thousands of tiny animals—that was the
most specific term she would allow herself to
consider. She knew what they had been and refused
to think about it—hatched, consumed the various
plaques, food bits, and debris in her mouth, then died
happily. She spit into the sink and rinsed her mouth.
Where did the residue go? she thought. Don't think
about it.

Tamar would get on the bonded net eventually.
Through work and diligence, she thought wryly.
Through blood, sweat, tears, and toil. And luck. Lots
of luck. Tamar returned to her desk.

Or maybe she'd end up on Mister Coyotee.

Once again, the LifeWorks' dateline was about the
Amazon pangolins.

The Amazon rainforest had been devastated long
before Tamar had been born. By the Year of the
Tsunami, laterization—the leaching out of the acid

materials by rain—had taken the exposed farmland and in a generation had turned it to stone. The resulting starvation and three-way war between Brazil, Ecuador, and Peru had broken the national boundaries and the area had dissolved into tribes and small states. And that had happened *before* the Die-Back. When recovery began, the area was miserable and barren.

The Die-Back had been the best possible opportunity as far as the Amazon rainforest was concerned.

In the gradual reclamation following the Die-Back, the rainforest had been co-opted as a symbol of rebirth. Several attempts had been made at reforestation but had failed for lack of funds, will, or technology. Then, fifteen years ago—five years after LifeWorks reopened for business—a stronger effort was made. LifeWorks had started as just one of the contractors on the project. As the political climates shifted over time, it had become the prime contractor. The plan attacked the problem at the root: the laterized soil. The plan had been relatively simple, involving a small burrowing animal, the pangolin.

Pangolins had originally been solely an Old World mammal. Just before the Die-Back, some misguided individual had brought them into the southern states to combat fire ants. During the Die-Back, they had become established and spread south to include the Amazon as home.

LifeWorks had enhanced the pangolin's claws and given its skull given fine metallic teeth. The pangolin's diet had been broadened from ants and termites to include the soil for sustenance, supplemented by a LifeWorks-provided syrup.

Stories of the pangolins had been ubiquitous since Tamar had been a teenager: pangolins would get you if you stayed out all night. Two pangolins go into a bar. What do you get when you wrap a pangolin in electrician's tape?

Now there were millions of them, overrunning the forest they had been engineered to save. Question: Why did the President have a lover made from a pangolin? Answer: It was cheaper than the real thing.

Over time, Tamar had learned to hate the purple little beasts. Their small mouth, huge, burrowing claws, sick little teeth, skin covered over with overlapping plates each the size of her thumb. Unmodified pangolins didn't even *have* teeth—only the modified and the crossbreeds. But that wasn't the horror, or why they had captured the popular imagination to represent both the love and fear of biotechnology. No, the pangolin's ugliness lay in the fact of the steel and diamond glint in its idiot smile, its fetid phenolic smell, its jerky, programmed movements, its urge to find laterite soil, and, finally like rats and roaches, its complete resistance to dying when it was supposed to.

The pangolin was supposed to go out to the Amazon stone desert and chew on it, burrow in it, and break it apart. It did so and shat microbes and seeds amidst the shards. The microbes softened the soil and provided a rich medium for the seeds.

Each of the seeds was tailored from an original rainforest species preserved in LifeWorks' own storage bank. First came the moss, which the pangolins loved to eat. Churned in their gut, it changed the character of their feces and the second wave of seeds sprouted. And so forth and so on until the rainforest towered over them, large, green, silent. As the canopy grew and sunlight diminished on the jungle floor, the pangolins were supposed to die on cue of vitamin D deficiency and other weaknesses and never, *never,* successfully interbreed with native pangolins. Isolated, they were intended to be the first foves: a designed, brand new species.

But they did crossbreed, creating offspring that combined the LifeWorks changes and the robustness of the natives, violating their fove status. Evolution in action: pangolins that crossed and didn't have both characteristics died early. The remainder bred true.

The crossbreeds overran the jungle and prevented other animals from taking hold. The project had, to this point, been a LifeWorks success story. Suddenly, ten years after the project had really got going, just when it should have been nearing completion, it began to hemorrhage red ink. It was the kind of thing that nearly destroyed Corning and Replitech before the Die-Back. Parkin had been fighting a rear-guard action ever since, years of resisting stock takeovers, begging for government subsidies, and investment retrenchments. Bounties had been posted on the pangolins. Pesticides had been tried. What's the difference between a pangolin and a cockroach? You can kill a cockroach.

If any other biotech company had wanted the contract, Tamar was convinced LeRoy Parkin would have happily given it to them.

Tamar looked over everything she could find: freenet, certified programming, and bonded reporting.

The freenet was the natural child of social media, tested, broken, and reformed on the anvil of the Die-Back. *Assured* reporting had the lawful status of "news," with legal consequences for untruth. The Guild of Assured Reporting made sure that assured news was based on fact and brought legal consequences when it wasn't. Everything else on the freenet was considered opinion or fiction. The amount of salt taken with a freenet "report" was considerable. Not to say there weren't those who relied on it. Tamar Longren did, for one.

Assured reporting came in two flavors: bonded and certified. Certified programming consisted of mere governmental and corporate analysts: they had no independence. BioNews lived on the border of certified reporting. Trade journals like BioNews had much the same relationship and useful function to biotech companies as a snail in a sewage lagoon: necessary but offensive.

Bonded reporters—assured reporting's elite heroes and stars—were required to always broadcast the truth according to personal experience. The Guild decided the rules of bonded reporters, who would be elevated to that rank, who would be demoted if they transgressed, thereby assuring bonded integrity. In a network where anyone could be faked, any action be constructed artificially, assured reporting was valuable. That little owl on the edge of the bonded reporter's image was worth a lot.

That was Tamar's goal. Bonded reporters were brought up from the ranks by the Guild through dint of decades of work or magical inspiration. Sometimes, like striking lightning, a reporter might break a story so big, its genius alone could elevate her to lofty heights. In 2051, only a few years after voting by network was enabled by the 36th Amendment and on the hairy leading edge of the Die-Back, Dick Mattingly caused the impeachment of President Anthony Wing by uncovering the fraud by which Wing was elected. He was bonded a year later. Stephanie Gravano reported how the brain implants of Alex Chen, the Secretary of Defense, made him as crazy as a banana crossed with a beefsteak. Once Chen had been imprisoned, a settlement of the war between Washington and Beijing was accomplished in three weeks. Gravano was awarded her bond—and the Nobel Peace Prize—that fall.

Of course, that was generations ago. But the

recovered net still had inside it the bones of prior generations. Bonded reporting had begun before the Die-Back and continued now during the Restoration.

Tamar held close the hope it could happen to her.

The certified newsnet reports showed LifeWorks' stock drop over several years and listed the official statement, along with an analysis by an economics expert. All of the credentials and certifications were appended to the report. LifeWorks would be staying with the Brazilian Reforestation Project. Despite the problems, the multigovernmental contracts were a cash cow. The reforestation was a "project at risk," in that since no one had ever attempted such a thing, no one knew if it was truly possible. And so on.

The bonded reports showed a different picture: Arban Mondal, said that *he himself* had spoken with no *less* than a principal scientist at LifeWorks, a man of Swedish descent, and who could verify that the morale at LifeWorks was low. Mondal said his source was good in bed, too. On the freenet, unbonded and uncertified news crossed, uncrossed, and recrossed itself as people presented pictures, opinions, and outright fabrications for public view.

But the latest LifeWorks dateline wouldn't make her a star, even if there *were* hints of new wrinkles in the technology. Tamar could say fove techniques were in use. Who's to say they weren't? Well, any biologist since there was that unfortunate interbreeding with the rootstock. *Tamar Longren reporting: Foves among the pangolins, a new and romantic study.* She giggled, then made herself look fierce. Marilyn noticed and grew agitated, looking around for non-existent threats. More coffee and better thinking: that's the way to get bonded. Not made-up sensationalism. *Pangolins or not,* she thought. *What are the facts?* Don't look at the main story. Look at the edges—that's where you find gold.

Tamar cast a wider net, looking at the Brazilian Reclamation Project from the beginning.

Fifteen years ago, in the first third (*the first trimester? Does the embryology of an ecology resemble that of a child?*) of the Project, an enormous amount of money began funneling through cities like Sao Paolo, Rio, and Leticia. Like any large work of the public trust, there was corruption, malfeasance, pork—the ongoing cost of doing business. Papa Carlos Ranquiz had a hand in it all, from prostitution to payoffs, from illegal microbiology to perfectly legal murders, from the cocaine trade to the traffic in cosmetic surgery. It was the heyday of then illegal—but now legal—bodywork. The interim government of Brazil made no laws regarding biotechnology. There was little violence and most crimes were not crimes at all, but legislative gray areas open to indefinite legal dispute. From all over the world, the phrase, "You can get it in Brazil", became ubiquitous. LifeWorks was merely a Project subcontractor. It played no part in that freest of free markets.

Tamar was twenty when it all fell apart.

The interim government was replaced by the Verde political dynasty. The UN was brought in since no country wanted responsibility. LifeWorks sent in their Chief Technology Officer, Montague Quinote, to help bring the Wild West biotech under regulation and control. The needs of the modified humans came under control by the state. Papa Carlos retired, with his son, to Portugal. He took up mountain climbing and the growing of expensive and biologically idiosyncratic orchids. Except for a brief flurry of excitement about him when a servant kidnapped one of his prizewinning plants and attempted to marry it, Papa Carlos had effectively disappeared.

Tamar had watched, with an interest bordering on erotic, recordings of an aging Rupert Englemeyer—*He* *miraculously survived the Die-Back. Purchase the story **here!**—*reporting the bodywork stories on the bonded net. Ever the perfectionist, Rupert had had himself modified so that he could report first-hand what it felt like.

A window appeared in the display. It was a message from her home unit, busily combing the freenet for useful information, usually failing dismally. Tamar kept a number of freenet searches going just in case her own special opportunity happened to walk by.

It was a report concerning Carmine Ranquiz—the name clicked.

She checked to make certain. Sure enough, Carmine Ranquiz was the son of Papa Carlos Ranquiz and listed as a product of the same Brazilian biotech labs. He had been hurt flying—*flying?*—in Cambridge. Tamar looked at the pictures. Fuzzy—but something was *interesting* about Carmine Ranquiz. Something *modified.* Tamar knew the signs.

Papa Carlos' son was a junior at Harvard. How about that? She paid for an illicit confirmation against the hospital's files and winced when she found out what it would cost.

Hold on. The Brazilian Reclamation Project, and Papa Carlos' rise to power, happened fifteen years ago. His fall from grace ten years ago. Carmine was now nineteen—born four years before Papa Carlos' rise to power and a year and a half after the Restoration. Years before the Amazon project even began. The technology to make Carmine wasn't developed in a day. It had to pre-exist long before Carmine was born. Who had that technology at that time? LifeWorks, that's who.

Parkin had reopened LifeWorks at the very beginning of the Restoration. From where? Story was, he and his team had hidden in a safe place all through the Die-Back. Certainly, it was common knowledge that both Quinote and Parkin were born *before* the Die-Back. No one knew when, though. Private knowledge like that was protected by the 37th Amendment unless released by the owners. Neither Quinote nor Parkin would talk about it. Quinote had been LifeWorks' CTO during the Project. And he had been sent in by the UN to sort things out.

As the hospital confirmation came through, a predatory grin came over her features. Maybe Carmine had come to Harvard because of his education. Maybe it was purest chance that he'd come to the same hospital where served the same man who had cleaned out the labs in Brazil. Maybe, Papa Carlos had planned it—a special needs child had, of course, special needs. Needs that could only be satisfied by the best in the business. Or, maybe, Papa Carlos had thought if his only son had to go away to school, he should go to where there was a physician familiar with the case—knowledgeable about the original design, so to speak. Possibly, one of the original designers.

Quinote had always had a touch of the flamboyant and, thought Tamar as she looked at the hospital's specifications for young Carmine, this work was as flamboyant as hell. It *smelled* of him.

"Gotcha!" she chortled.

‹ 8: Monty, 3/11 ›

Monty often saw himself as a ridiculous figure, a sort of Hephaestus to LeRoy's Zeus. His limp and arm added to the illusion. It was a role that he did not resent any more than Hephaestus did for it gave him a freedom and enjoyment of life he rather suspected was denied LeRoy —or Zeus and Oberon, for that matter.

Thus, when the matter of Lethias came to him, it felt like Christmas might have felt to Puck. The first thought that came to him had been: *this ought to shake somebody up.*

He didn't feel that way about Carmine at all.

Carmine was unconscious when Monty barreled into the trauma center that early Thursday evening. Monty had called ahead and invoked Carmine's standing orders. He paged the Individual Medicine Lab to get ready and called Steven Blackbear and Richard Izmodo personally. Now, the boy was lying open-mouthed, unconscious, and splint-braced in improbable ways by the physician on call.

Monty saw the broken wings, the splinted leg and arm, and wanted to weep. Carmine had always seemed to be fighting a raging war between his desire and his capacity. Not for the first time, Monty had misgivings over the secret work he had done to make the poor boy. That Monty's involvement was only protected by Carmine's 37th Amendment privacy rights barely occurred to him.

Monty updated his instructions and had a quick conference with Boyer, the surgeon on duty. Monty would program the IBM 9000 Autosurgeon himself while Boyer did the actual opening and closing. They were both going to be working on Carmine into the wee hours. Monty left the trauma center with specific instructions on how to prep Carmine for surgery and scheduled the OR in three hours. He lied to Boyer and said it would take him three hours to set up the 9000.

Monty did not need the three hours. He always kept an up-to-date description of Carmine's subsystems, as he did all his pet projects. As he did for Lethias. No, he needed only twenty minutes to update the 9000 from his own databanks and the current hospital image of Carmine, forty minutes for a phone call to Papa Carlos, and the remaining two hours for a nap.

Lying on the couch in his office, staring out into the darkness outside his window, he found himself unable to rest. He kept thinking of the woman who had borne Carmine—Izbeka? Elzabeka? Something like that. No doubt he could just ask his office system and get the answer, but that seemed absurdly unfair. He should remember her name on his own.

It had been a tricky, technically exciting, ethically reprehensible project. Turn a perfectly healthy embryo into a flying adult. He and LeRoy had worked out the design themselves—with Sims' help, of course. Papa Carlos was patient and had waited for them.

Izbeka? That *sounded* right.

LifeWorks was in deep trouble over attempting a comeback. Two attempted takeovers in two years and the company deeply in debt. Papa Carlos insisted he was a *businessman* when he covered LifeWorks' note. But Carmine had been only one of their projects. How many children had there actually been? Over two hundred, at least. Two hundred "specials." It was amazing how many parents wanted odd things for their children. It was a kind of cultural Lamarckism: the parents passing whatever life lessons they thought they had learned to their children. Papa Carlos had been a client who was less... *personally involved* than most. LeRoy and Monty had been lucky not to be revealed when it all came out.

Carmine hated Monty and loved Papa Carlos. It was sort of like a Nazi hating Goering and loving Hitler, or a young Confederate soldier hating slavery and loving Jefferson Davis: perfectly plausible, consistent, and human.

Maybe it was Elzabeka, after all. The name of someone whose belly you pored over for nine months should stick more solidly in your mind.

Monty had few regrets: do what you must was his motto. But, still, here in the unrolling of the dark when there was no one in the room but himself and he could feel the pain of every tired old twist of his joke of a body, he wondered if Carmine was right to hate him.

The alarm chimed. It had been three hours: Carmine would be ready.

Monty sighed and rose to his feet.

It was time to cut.

‹ 9: Ida, 3/13 ›

That Thursday evening, the wind blew in from the west and cleared away any remaining clouds. The sunset tinged the blue with red and framed a full moon, rising as smooth as cream. Ida walked along Sudbury Street, beneath a sky like a carnival glass bowl. The thin voice of the Muezzin for Thursday night prayers seemed to come up from no particular place but echoed through the narrow cracks between the buildings, called from empty bricked corners, rose from under the docks. This is how the voice of God must sound, she thought. Not thunderous, but everywhere at once. Ida loved the walk to the Islamic Baptist Mosque.

The Islamic Baptist Union, Boston Chapter—called by those not of the faith, the Sufi-Baptists—occupied the entire block that began at the intersection of Friend and Causeway Streets, across from the Boston Gardens.

Friend Street was lined with chestnuts, the draped ceiling of their leaves freshening and cooling the air. The day had slipped into a lull. The commuters had already caught the train home and the evening partiers had not yet reached downtown. It was more or less quiet: there was no roar of people or machinery. Groups collected around the open shops and restaurants. Ida had a moment to breathe and look at the Union building.

Half the building was made of early 20th-century dirty brick, the top edge serrated like an old, Moorish castle. The other half was made of new concrete. Ida liked to think of the Union as being blended the same way the dogma of the Islamic Baptist Union was blended, differences preserved inside of the whole. Cut into the building's base were a fruit market, a bakery, four small and very crowded restaurants, and an occult shop, all sublet by the Union. The occult shop was closed. Like other shops of its kind, it kept banker's hours.

Though the street itself was empty, the remaining shops and restaurants were crowded with people, as though in the limbo between the time of work and play they wished for the comfort of one other. The crowd had escaped the confines of the building and spilled out onto the sidewalks and streets, stopping at an irregular but definite boundary. She listened as she passed to three men and a woman arguing politics. Occasionally, the argument drifted into Arabic or Hebrew. A man and a woman shared Ethiopian bread and spoke softly. He kissed her.

Here, she thought, was a distant illusion of the world before, purified of that world's sins. Ida was thirty-two. She had been born and raised on the coast in Salisbury, New Hampshire during the Die-Back's last days, when the final diseases were being wrestled to the ground by God and His Angels. There, you could feel His presence every day. She remembered when people began to quit dying. Children—Ida being one—managed to reach their teen years. The Union had been born from the Die-Back and Ida had been born in the Union. It comprised the entire town.

When the Union decided it was time for Salisbury to colonize Boston, Ida hadn't looked back. Look now

what they had become! In twenty years, they had
become one of the larger churches in one of the larger
cities on the East Coast. *Call to the way of your Lord
with wisdom.*

Their prayers had been answered.

A shadow passed over her and Ida looked up. High
above her she briefly saw between the leaves a dark
bird. For a moment, an ancient primate reflex against
avian predators awoke. She was startled, then
frightened. One of the condors, Ida supposed as she
calmed. Others joined her at the gate of the Mosque
portion of the Union building and she let them carry
her inside.

It was a large congregation. Tonight, a hundred or
so people had come. Dan Tamerlane and his wife
Hannah met her at the *hammam* in the outer
courtyard as she washed her hands and feet. They
surprised her and Ida felt cross with herself for being
startled. She had been coming to prayers with Dan
and his wife for three years. She had no business
being startled.

"Jack Braun didn't do so good in the New
Hampshire primary," said Dan as he bathed his
hands lightly, a symbolic gesture as if he'd just
urinated. Hannah ignored them both and scrubbed
her hands, then, with great attention, her feet.
Hannah rarely spoke in the Mosque.

As familiar as Dan and Hannah were, Ida
suddenly wished they'd go away. Irritation stuck in
her like a barb. Mostly it was Dan: his washing. The
vain way he looked up at the courtyard wall painting
of the Union founder, Hanif Robertson. Dan had
painted it for the *hammam* so they could always wash
their hands under his benevolent gaze. The way Dan
was always, *always*, talking. For Dan, prayers were
only periodic changes of conversational direction
when instead of talking to anybody present, he spoke

to God. Ida ignored him. Dan didn't seem to notice and Ida realized that she was acting the same way as Hannah. Anger burned deeply in her. Ida wondered if Hannah's silence showed constant rage.

"Yeah," Dan continued. "If Shuman doesn't mess up, she's a sure thing. Always a dangerous place to be. Not that she hasn't been at least an adequate president."

Ida shook her head. First being frightened of a bird and now this anger. She resolved to leave it behind here and wash it away. Hannah took her arm. Dan trailed them into the sanctuary.

Though the sanctuary was roofed, with the balconies leaning into the main area and the broad areas covered with rugs, it gave the impression of a medieval, Moorish courtyard open to the sky. This was intentional, intending to direct the faithful to open their hearts towards God. At one end of the hall was a large, plain cross. A spotlight shone on it, making it glow warmly. Melissa Adenour ascended to the pulpit, black hair tied back in a tight bun, pale face looking up to heaven, calling softly now, exhorting the faithful to pray to God, whose name is Allah, in His Aspect, whose name is Christ. When Adenour reached the pulpit itself, a ray of sunlight from the window lit her face, eyes closed in prayer.

Ida knelt and the fears, angers, and desperations fell from her. She began to pray. The shuffling drone of the same prayers all around her, from Dan and Hannah nearby, from other voices she recognized, and many she did not, soothed her until she became the breath of the spoken prayer, offered on high. "Come to him," Ida sang. "Come down and kneel."

It was dancing to raise her tired legs. It was dancing to kneel before Melissa, to take the goblet containing the wine, to drink it and feel it—*did* she feel it?—transform to Christ's blood in her mouth as she swallowed. The warmth that came touched her heart and radiated to the rest of her body.

"Sweet surrender, sweet submission," sang Melissa.

Back at her place, she knelt and listened to Melissa, singing, until, towards the end of the prayers, when the final Hymn to Christ began, it was not Melissa's high voice that she heard, but the voice of Christ himself.

Afterward, she rose and touched Dan and Hannah. Hannah had tears in her eyes and even Dan was silent. The congregation began to mill towards the door.

"Ida?" It was Brusneck, Adenour's assistant.

Ida looked at him in confusion, staring at his hand on her arm. Words seemed foreign objects at that moment. Dan and Hannah stood next to her.

Brusneck released his hand and apologized. "Imam Adenour would like a word with you."

Ida looked at Dan and Hannah and back to Brusneck. It seemed the outside world had come in with them. She waved Dan and Hannah on and turned back to Brusneck. "Sure." Ida followed him into the back of the Mosque.

Brusneck led her to the back of the building, past the meeting rooms, Melissa's quarters, and into the Mosque Garden. Melissa waited for her there, watering the plants. She was dressed in jeans and a loose shirt. She'd taken down her hair.

"Melissa?" said Ida quietly.

Melissa turned to her and the two women embraced. "Ida," she said warmly. "How are you?"

Ida shook her head in confusion. "Fine. You sent Brusneck to get me. Surely, it's not because you want to see how I *am*."

"I always want to know how you are. But that is not the reason I sent for you."

They sat together on the bench. Ida and Melissa had grown up together back in Salisbury. Ida had been merely devout. Melissa had been devout and *called*. Ida could tell she was tense.

"What's wrong?" Ida asked.

"I need to know about foves."

"Why?" Ida exploded in frustration. "What is going on?"

Melissa nodded. "Bear with me. Speak to me of foves."

Ida shrugged. "You've seen the news, haven't you?"

"I need to hear it from *you*."

This made Ida uncomfortable. She shrugged again, irritated. The joy she'd felt at prayer was gone now, evaporated under this interrogation. Ida felt the lack.

"Foves are animals modified into a new species that can breed true," Ida said. "They are not sterile, like most modified animals."

"Aren't all artificial animals foves?"

"No." Ida shook her head. "Most artificial animals are grown from rootstock. Monsanto's slugs, for example, are grown from modified eggs. They cannot reproduce themselves. It's *hard* to make a new species. You have to make sure the germ cells will produce an embryo that will self-assemble into the target animal. It's hard in the natural world, too. If you take a frog population and modify them to chirp at twice their normal frequency, you've behaviorally isolated them from the parent population. But they're not physiologically isolated. They *could* interbreed but for the new behavior. That's usually referred to as a sibling species. A fove is different."

Ida gathered her thoughts. "It's currently impossible to create complex living organisms completely from scratch. Instead, we modify an already complete organism to fit our needs. Until recently, a *reproducing* animal was too difficult—again, Monsanto's slugs are a good example. Monsanto has to modify each egg. A *fove* would be an animal altered from the rootstock with new needs and drives and a new niche that can interbreed with itself but can't interbreed back to the parent stock with any success."

Melissa nodded. "Are the Amazon pangolins foves? The whole animal was modified there."

Ida shook her head. "Not all. Only pieces of the animals were modified. In fact, the pangolins were intended *not* to be foves—they were supposed to be sterile and die on cue, all while competing unsuccessfully with the native stock. You know how *that* turned out. That's the pangolin problem. It has nothing to do with foves." Melissa looked blank. Ida needed a better example. "Say you want a fox to tap-dance, okay?"

Melissa looked confused. "What do you mean?"

"I mean you want a fox that's able to tap-dance like a human. You have to modify the spine to bring it erect, and the hips to handle upright posture. You have to change the myotonic reflexes so that the muscle tremor is modifiable—that changes how spinal processing works." Ida grew excited. It had been a long time since she'd even thought about design. "Then, you maybe want the fox to *understand* tap dancing, to *comprehend* the heritage and technique of the past so it could reinterpret it for the present—like any artist. That's all manipulation. But if our tap-dancing fox breeds, it just produces little foxes. The fox's embryo is directly modified to develop tap dancing—normal modification. *Foving* the fox embryo modifies it to develop tap dancing plus genes in the sperm and eggs that can create embryos that can also develop tap dancing. Foving is *much* harder than straight manipulation."

"How is it done?"

"Manipulation is done psychically—that's the main business of the Hopi Development Corporation."

"Why psychically?"

"That's the kind of thing Cori Phenomena is best at: fine operations where not much energy is involved. 'Rains of stones' are pretty rare." Ida smiled. "High energy phenomena don't happen. The occult craze is hype: like radium drinks or electrotherapy."

Melissa bit her lip and looked around the garden. "Foves breed true?"

"That's what makes a fove a fove." Ida watched the tension in Melissa, the crook of her shoulders, the set of her mouth. Maybe she was one of those people who were afraid the livestock would get out of control. "Reproduction is what makes foves the goal. Right now, new complex organisms are all one of a kind. This is why they're simple—slugs. Wasps. Spiders. Foving would be a breakthrough. Breeding is a much better way to recoup your investment."

"Who's doing it?"

"Nobody," said Ida, simply. "We can't do it. But for the first time, we can see it from here."

Melissa nodded absently. That wasn't what was bothering her. "Is a fove an animal?"

"Of course, it's an animal."

"Your fox, who understands tap dancing—*loves* tap dancing like any artist. Is *she* an animal?"

"Sure," said Ida uncomfortably. "She's still a fox."

"If she's not an animal, she's a slave," said Melissa, more to herself than Ida. "Mohammed had specific instructions about slaves and their treatment. If they're animals, there are specific instructions there, too. If they are not animals and not slaves—they can't be human, can they, Ida?"

Ida shook her head mutely. What was Melissa

talking about?

"Have we created demons, Ida?" Melissa spread her hands. "Not animals. Not human, but with human volition."

"Come on, Melissa," said Ida softly. "You're scaring me. The most complex animals we've built were modified for specific, expensive, and dangerous jobs. Nobody's foving. Nobody's building volitional animals. Nobody would dare build *volitional* foves." Ida shuddered at the thought. "What would be the point?"

Melissa looked stricken. "Jesus said 'For I have come to set a man at variance against his father, and the daughter against her mother.'" She shook herself and peered closely at Ida. "I had a dream last night. You were in it. I was in it with you. There were animals dressed as men, dancing beneath a full moon. A wolf laughed, clutched my hands, and forced on me a gift, then cried out, 'Go use it!'"

"It was just a dream, Melissa."

"I've been thinking about it ever since. I thought it might have something to do with foves."

Manipulated animals weren't something Melissa would ever like, thought Ida to herself. Melissa had never been easy with animals that didn't stay in their place. "What did the wolf give you?"

Melissa didn't answer.

Ida took one of her closed hands. "It was just a dream. It doesn't mean anything."

"Then, how do you explain this?" Melissa opened her hand.

There, glowing above her hand and imbued with a soft brightness like foxfire or the combustion of cobwebs, burned a tiny bush that was not consumed.

Chapter 1.3

‹ 1: Lethias, 3/15 ›

From the moment he was brought to the mainland, Lethias felt himself to be part of a great and inchoate machine. A giant wheel rolling towards Boston. Before, when he had come to the labs to spend time with Parkin, or for esoteric lab tests and experiments, things had been social, somehow. He had been centered in the process of things, a supporting beam in a great house. Now, however, he felt outside, the rim of the spinning wheel, directed from within the mechanism but not part of it.

He was prodded and vaccinated. Biopsies were taken from vaguely defined regions inside his belly—subsections of the liver, kidney, and spleen. He was embarrassed to find that he was, against all his self-conceptions, able to arouse himself enough to give a gentle but professional aide a sperm sample. The aide came in on him before he was quite done and it took Lethias several moments of staring at his own penis to recover.

Outside, the aide took the sample and examined him. "I'm surprised at the size," he commented.

Lethias was aghast. "Beg pardon? I didn't produce enough?"

"The penis size." The aide looked straight at him. "I'm surprised they modified it to be larger. The unmodified gorilla penis is tiny. Yours is as big as an average human's."

Lethias wanted to strike him and he wasn't able to think past that for a moment. He closed his eyes and turned from the aide. It made him feel small, threatened, and angry to be stared at. He had learned to endure it from LeRoy or Monty or even the doctors who came regularly to the island. But to be stared at by a stranger was appalling. Lethias struggled with himself, managed by an act of will to turn rage aside. The effort depressed him. "I was told it was an artifact of how they implemented the upright posture," Lethias muttered wretchedly. "I really don't know."

The aide touched him gently on the shoulder. "Cheer up," he said kindly. "We're almost done. I've been to Boston—you'll have a good time."

Lethias nodded. They put him up in a LifeWorks apartment to wait for the train to Boston. That night he dreamed Kong towered over the island and stared down at Lethias silently, his expression unreadable. Try as he might, Lethias could not get Kong to speak. Lethias woke frightened in a cold, strange room. He pulled the pillows tight to his belly and tried to pretend their gathered softness was Catherine nestled spoonlike against him. He tried to imagine he could smell her.

Lethias was glad to see Sims when he knocked on his door.

"Just heard you were down here," Sims said. "Monty says you're coming to visit."

Lethias was pathetically grateful to see a face he knew. "Yes. Soon, I hope. I hate it here."

Sims nodded. "I understand. I bet Monty's got something devious up his sleeve. Don't let him twist you around, okay?"

"Twist me around what?" asked Lethias, genuinely confused.

Sims shrugged and fell into a distracted silence.

This was not an unusual behavior for Sims, but right now it made Lethias, lonely as he was, terribly nervous. The ape looked around the room. He pulled

Sims to him. "Get me out of here," Lethias said softly. "Send me home."

Sims looked mildly surprised. "You can go home anytime you like. I don't suppose LeRoy will send you to Boston against your will. It might be a bit difficult to get hold of him right now—he's on his way to Washington. Still, Amanda ought to be able to take care of everything. Shall I call her?"

Looking at Sims, capturing for a moment the distance between Sims and the rest of the world, Lethias knew that he could do this: walk out right now and be on the next ferry back to the island. All of the obscure, romantic images he had of what he would do when he reached Boston, how Marcus would interpret what happened to him there, seemed naive.

Lethias would still have to explain to Marcus, to Runs-From-Water. And to Catherine. Lethias realized her good opinion had become important to him.

"I'll stay, I guess," Lethias said softly, thinking of her.

"Good. It'll be nice to have a visitor—though I understand you aren't going to be living with us. Monty got you your own place but it's not far away." Sims nodded. "When you get a chance, come over and I'll show you my eggs."

"Your eggs?" Lethias had a sudden fear he'd missed some obscene idiom by accident.

"Well, not just my *eggs*, mind you," Sims said, waving his hand. "The eggs are just part of it. They measure the fine structure constant of the Cori base state. I have a small collection of natural objects that have been influenced by Cori Phenomena. I use them in my work."

"Is that what you're doing here? Working with eggs?"

"The eggs are in Boston. And it's not just eggs,

remember," he said testily. "No, I'm here making money. Widnergog is still having problems. He dug himself deep into a bad hole and it's taken the last two years to lift him out. It's just money work—I got all the good stuff out of him years ago. My collection— eggs and all—is the basis of my research. When I'm not back on the island."

Lethias had no idea who or what Widnergog was. "Into Cori Phenomena."

"Into Cori's model of the phenomena. Part of it, anyway."

"I'm lost." Lethias looked around the room. He felt disoriented. Talking to Sims always made him feel that the floor of the world was a little tilted—due, no doubt, to the fact that Sims seemed to delight in lifting it up to see what was underneath. Right now, it made him dizzy.

"Cori tried to bring psychic events into the realm of physics and failed. That's the long and the short of it. His models violated momentum rules, conservation rules—lots of things. So, he constructed a model that included," Sims held up three fingers and counted them off. "Conventional Newtonian and relativistic mechanics, quantum mechanics, and what he thought of as psychic phenomena. He did it by stepping outside the system and modeling it on finite automata. He said, in effect, that the universe behaves as if it were a rule-based simulation of a system based on both quantum mechanics and relativity. The rules of normal physics were a *subset* of the simulation capabilities. However, the automata could be invoked in ways that violate that subset without violating the underlying simulation structure. In effect, he said, that everything is an illusion that we agree to accept."

"Nothing is real?"

"Not a damned thing," said Sims cheerily.

He does this on purpose, thought Lethias. He must. It makes him happy to tear down the world. When Lethias was a child, Quinote had told him Coyote stories, always tearing down and remaking the world in new and ridiculous ways. Lethias wondered if Sims was like that.

Using mythology and religion, humans had remade animals into humans since pre-historic times. What would apes remake? What *could* they do? Turn humans into gorillas? Humans use everything, even their mythology, to define themselves. *What do we have?* Lethias thought bleakly. Once he had committed himself to leave the island, the scope of humanity had become something terrible. Something palpable and huge, hanging over him. Over and over again the same thought came back into his mind: we know *nothing!*

‹ 2: Tamar, 3/17 ›

Tamar had traced public records and freenet speculation to a *flying* violation for Carmine Ranquiz. The certified report stopped when the boy reached the Cambridge Police Department—there was, in fact, no actual record he was ever taken to the CPD. Was he taken to a hospital? Was he spirited away to Italy? The CPD wouldn't say.

As far as the Cambridge Police Department was concerned, he had disappeared underground like a mole. None of the freenet reports she followed panned out. One took her to meet a *muralista* who worked for the Islamic Baptist Union. The Sufi-Baptist had known nothing. A report from Allston had implicated a tea house in Brookline. Another dead end. She'd changed strategy, then, and tried to reach first Quinote and then Parkin at LifeWorks. Parkin didn't return her phone calls. Quinote's proxy did but it was too sophisticated a piece of software to give anything away. Tamar never saw Quinote himself.

A freenet picture surfaced of a shadowy figure taken into an ambulance. Maybe Carmine had been hurt?

Tamar began to follow Carmine's complex trail through the health system. But medical data was even more protected than the Cambridge Police Department. The City of Cambridge required public disclosures of arrests, court cases, and sentences. Nothing like that was required of hospitals and physicians.

Finally, she grew desperate enough to try Wide Ida's office: the Division of Biological Affairs. Ida's office proxy listened carefully enough—it was much better than the usual government software—but in the end, it told her sweetly that even if there were an injured biodesigned human in Cambridge, wasn't he entitled to his privacy according to the 37th Amendment? And besides, since she wasn't either registered or certified (bonding didn't officially count with the government, though nobody but a fool would ignore a bonded reporter), she had no business even asking. Isn't that right?

Tamar fumed for several minutes staring at the now blank display. There was no respect for the press anymore.

When you were bonded, they at least had to talk to you. She lived to put that little golden owl next to her name when she broadcast.

Tamar gave up and started working on other topics: the introduction to the US market of pangolin soap ("Scrubs you twice as clean!"), pangolin body armor ("20% stronger than neo-Kevlar!"), and pangolin window cleaner ("The scales have fallen from my eyes!"). A week or so after she had tried to reach Ida, she received an e-mail packet containing a set of key combinations and an address. The packet was anonymous but the trailers suggested it came from the government and the timing suggested Ida's office.

Thank you, Ida! Tamar thought and wondered what kind of payback would eventually be required.

The address was Mount Auburn Hospital and the keycode combinations got her into Carmine Ranquiz's room. Carmine had been hospitalized for three weeks. He was watching *Mister Coyotee* on the screen opposite the bed with interest but without comprehension. The boy was on Acrostamine, a preferred drug for patients with severe broken bones. Acrostamine was especially effective and reducing propriospinal pain and prevented acute distress from turning into a chronic condition like fibromyalgia. Technically, it was not really a pain reliever, since it did not affect pain perception. Instead, it removed pain *significance* so that a patient didn't react to it. Acrostamine patients were awake and fully capable and therefore better able to participate in their own therapy—though they were a bit odd. Pain was still there but not registering properly. Since the pain reaction was blocked, they acted out in different ways. A side effect was the inhibition of the transformation of short-term memory into long-term memory; they never remembered anything that happened during therapy. This gave the drug the nickname of "the Doctor's friend."

Tamar considered Acrostamine a friend also, since Carmine was quite talkative about his father, Doctor Montague Quinote, LeRoy Parkin, and LifeWorks, Brazil, the role of magic in everyday life, UFO sightings, and the perception of God in a teacup. She took copious notes and was so encouraged by Carmine's cooperation that she kissed him (he wouldn't remember it anyway) as she left. None of it was admissible in a court of law, of course.

Acrostamine would constitute *under duress.* But Tamar wasn't interested in *trying* Carmine's story. She was interested in reporting it.

Tamar finished the story with satisfaction, reread it, and sent it to Fred. She left her apartment in South Boston and walked down the long curving harbor greenway. Even though the bright March day was breezy and cold, people strolled along the water, admiring the prairie grass and the cathedral American elms—modified, Tamar knew, to thrive on salt water. Did they reproduce? Were they foves? Tamar didn't know.

As she watched the harbor, Tamar thought of this walkway leading north from Fort Independence, through the piers, and along the shore of the harbor as far north as Marblehead and as far south as Cape Cod. One long path on the east coast of Massachusetts, filled with people joining each other and parting. Watching the same boats as they progressed along the coast. It was a thought that made her feel small and insignificant and one of a crowd, a spray of water against the sea.

Tamar heard something and looked up. In the channel, a boat bit through the water and roared distantly past her. A small, pale man was steering in the front. In the back, a huge black man seemed to be laughing. He waved to her and before she thought, she waved back. Then, the boat turned east and she couldn't see them for the spray.

The March wind seemed to bite through her jacket and she caught the underground into Brookline where the BioNews production studio was located. Fred was waiting for her.

"Did you read it?" Tamar asked, suddenly excited. He would like it—how couldn't he? It had everything: a child remade before he was born, a crime family, a tie-in to one of the most famous bioengineering firms in the country.

Fred nodded. He looked at the ceiling and out the window. He picked up a pen and fiddled with it in his hands.

Slowly, the import of these little actions began to add up in Tamar's mind. "You're not going to let me run it."

"Not yet. There's no proof."

"No proof? I have a *witness*. And look at the timing. This is Pulitzer material. Think about it: the most famous, most moral, most ecologically correct bioengineering firm in the country is caught with its pants down. It's like catching the American Hospital Association trafficking in illegal cigarettes." She held out her hands. "The big newsnets would kill for this story."

"No, they wouldn't." Fred leaned his elbows on the table. "You've got a collection of rumors and innuendo here based on the ravings of a kid high on Acrostamine, for Christ's sake!"

"A kid modified to fly."

Fred waved the comment away. "Drug ravings. You're not bonded. You're not certified. You're not even *registered*. Besides, this could hurt both LifeWorks and the biotech business."

"Come on, Fred. We're BioNews. This is what we're supposed to be doing."

"No, it's not." Fred stared at the tip of his pen. "We are a trade journal. We track companies. We find new developments. We print how a company is doing—not how they're involved with international crime. Our readership doesn't care about that. What do you think would happen to us if we broke the story that hurt our industry? Look around you, Tam. Isobanna's Oregon Initiative is in play."

"It won't win."

"You don't know that. If we broke the story now,

on *this* evidence, LifeWorks would have no choice but to sue us. Who would *possibly* talk to us if we were the target of a suit from Parkin? And *if we won?* Who would talk to us if we were the instrument of a company's downfall? We'd be on the shit list of every biotech company in the country either way. If I pass that story, BioNews folds in a month—three months, tops."

"Fred—"

Fred shrugged. "I could run a story about a new cosmetic surgery product in the wings. Or a new line of Monsanto slugs mining the closed landfills in Concord. Or new bacteriophages to use against emerging leprosy strains. But you have real news here."

"Yes!"

Fred looked up at her and his face was sympathetic and that made Tamar even angrier. "News—real news—is a buzzsaw, Tam," he said. "It's politics and disaster and crime and it chews you up and spits you out if you're not protected. Sometimes, even that's not enough. It's not why I founded BioNews."

Tamar stared at him. "They got to you, didn't they?"

Fred shook his head tiredly. "Don't be naive."

"Don't lie to me!"

"I'm not. They didn't have to." Fred stood up and leaned towards her across the desk. "BioNews is a network trade magazine. We are not a news service. We exist because we are either convenient to the industry when they want to advertise or leak product announcements or because we aren't enough trouble to worry about. Between these two extremes, we do our job."

"This is our job!"

"*No!* This is a buzz saw. Our job is not and never

has been real news."

"Then I'll take it to some real news services!"

Fred closed his eyes. "Do it and you're fired."

The words stung her into silence. She started to speak: take your fucking job and... thought better of it. Jobs in the newsnets were not easy to find. She'd never get bonded if she were fired from her first job.

"Tam," Fred said softly. "Jesus, you're young. You're good at this—this story you found proves it. But don't go to the mat on this one. This is not the hill for you to die on. It's just not important enough."

If I were bonded, he'd have to listen to me. That goal seemed farther away than ever. "Okay."

"Tam—"

"*Okay!* Okay, for Christ's sake." She exhaled slowly. "You made your point. What next, then? Do we just drop it?"

Fred was quiet for a long time. "We'll wait and see. Keep following them. This is an election year, after all. We'll see what happens." He nodded towards her. "Maybe we can use it as background for another story."

"Right," she said, holding her words back. She knew this was merely a gesture. "Right. Whatever you say." *Someday,* she thought. I'll be bonded. Then, they'll have to listen to me. They won't have any choice.

‹ 3: LeRoy, 3/18 ›

A tall, cadaverously thin white man boarded the business class of the Boston-Savannah subsonic train. Though the car was crowded, he selected his seat carefully and took his time placing his luggage. Then, he stood over the seat and eyed it critically, choosing a moving pattern for the seat covers that matched other similar patterns around him, but also complimented his suit. The seat was near the window and he watched the passing countryside silently, occasionally watching the advertisements that paced across the public display area at the top of the window. His face was pale and his eyes were a deep, formless black.

About an hour after the Boston-Savannah left Charleston, an active area of the window flashed a message: "Call for Richard DiMotto."

The man nodded, took a device from his jacket pocket, and placed the receiver in his ear.

"Hi, Boss," came Amanda's voice.

"I thought I said never to call me here," responded LeRoy.

"You picked a good mask. I saw it on the pickup."

He brought up his image in the window. A young man, pale as paper, stared back. The name *Richard DiMotto, Apotech Machining* was displayed beneath him. Only Amanda's voice was real and that was scrambled. LeRoy turned his head to the left and the right.

"Do you like it?" LeRoy asked.

"Except for the little fold behind the ear, it's good work. Sheffield down in props, right?"

"Yes." LeRoy smoothed down the skin. "Better?"

"Much. Still, you don't look good white."

LeRoy ignored her. "As long as I pass muster."

"Why disguise at all? You're going to testify in public as LeRoy Parkin."

"Practice. So, when I leave the senate chambers, I'll have it down. I'll drop the mask in the limo at Union Station and put it back on when I leave Senator Luther. Bring me up to date."

"Lethias is fine, though depressed. Sims is talking with him. I found a good courier to take him from the Boston train station to the house in Cambridge. You got three different invitations for spending Solstice—

one from Monty, one from the island, and a public function for Monica Shuman. I said no to all of them. Do you want to change that?"

"No." LeRoy liked spending Solstice by himself. "Is the courier good enough for a longer term contract? We'll likely need someone to protect Lethias."

"I'll check on him and let you know." She continued. "After the hearing, Senator Luther will be waiting for you at Cheezy's—there'll be a cab waiting for you at the steps. The Senator's aide, Roman Bronsky, will accompany you. From there, a masked transport to a protected room in the Watergate. You'll call me in the morning?"

"As soon as I get up. Probably not until then."

"Good luck, Boss."

The man in the window appeared to finish his presentation. He bowed and the image disappeared. There were other people in the business class car, but LeRoy had no desire for conversation. Beyond the window, the marshland of South Carolina reappeared. The Die-Back had been over and the Restoration achieved for twenty years but people still clung to each other in cities, leaving the natural world to the robots and the wildlife.

For a long time, LeRoy watched the soaring hawks and ospreys migrating north in the brief glimpses of the landscape afforded by the train. He tried to distinguish the surviving natural birds from the renewal stock. He couldn't. They looked the same. On occasion, he saw fields of corn or soybeans tended by robots. Rarely, he saw mysterious, bare, robot industrial complexes without smokestacks, effluent, or windows.

For a time, he dozed. It was a private fear that this newfound ease of sleep (new since he was seventy) signified a growing senility. It was such a fear that had prompted him to ask Amanda to help him.

Proxies were common and computer personalities, even very complex ones, were no novelty. However, Amanda had been designed to not only be his aide but a test of his flexibility. She was all of that. He thought of the teapot. Disguised trips such as these were a godsend since Amanda was constrained from playing tricks on him.

There were two methods of maintaining anonymity in this world: generate enough noise that the single note of truth could not be recognized, or don't generate any noise at all. Of the two, he preferred the latter.

LeRoy awoke when the train stopped at Union Station, disembarked, and took the limo downtown. In the automated privacy of the limo, privacy insured by law and the limo company and further insured by devices LeRoy had in his briefcase, he removed the mask and gloves and replaced them carefully in their case. The limo stopped in front of the capitol dome. He checked the time: there was at least two hours before he had to testify. Time enough to talk to Luther's aide, Bronsky, and go over the testimony. It was a relief to pursue the Life Banks Bill, a relief to do something unconnected with the island, the apes, and Lethias.

After he and Bronsky left the Senate committee chambers, LeRoy felt uncomfortably sweaty. Annoyed, he stopped in front of the restroom. "Look, Roman, you go on," he said. "I'll be a minute."

The men's room on this floor was stark: the paint on the walls was peeling, the mirrors dingy silver, and the stalls were the archaic water flush type. Even the light was provided by a naked pair of incandescent bulbs hanging high from the ceiling. LeRoy stood there, lost for a moment, thinking perhaps he shouldn't be in here. He realized with warm embarrassment that the room had been remodeled to look like this, as if, here, in the Senate, the world was the same as it had been in the—twentieth century? Early twenty-first? LeRoy looked at the toilet, an ancient tank, the condensation beading on the sides like pebbled glass. Depression? World War II? He had no idea.

He washed his face and looked at himself in the mirror: portrait of a thin-nosed black man surrounded by a white paint frame. At that moment, he hated himself for being here, isolated in this world from that which he knew in his bones to be important, to discuss the stuff of life in the same manner as one would talk about regulation of commodities futures and international trade. I should never have taken over a business; I am not cut out for this.

Malcolm was waiting for him in the limo.

"Thought you'd meet me at Cheezy's," said LeRoy as he sat down.

Malcolm Luther was a beautiful man, in the same way that an animal is beautiful. He had wide cheekbones and black skin with a depth of color suggesting midnight. His hands and shoulders were large and now, in middle age, he had taken to shaving his hair at a slant so that he looked regal. His voice was low and controlled.

"This seemed more expedient." Malcolm held his hands out, palms up. "I don't want to be seen with you after the hearings."

"Why, Malcolm!" LeRoy leaned back in the seat and watched him. "We've been friends for a long time. You hurt my feelings."

"I hope not," Malcolm said in that beautiful voice. LeRoy always wanted to just nod and close his eyes to keep him speaking. Once, at a party in the early days of the Restoration, Malcolm had leaped to stand precariously on the back of a sofa and delivered the mad priest's soliloquy from Weiss' *Marat/Sade*:

So stand up
Defend yourselves from their whips
Stand up stand in front of them
and let them see how many of you there are

LeRoy had sat on the floor that night and just stared at him, washed along in the river of words. Malcolm had been forty. LeRoy had already passed a hundred. *This*, he had thought, *this is our future.*

Now, Malcolm looked worried.

"What's wrong?" LeRoy held his hands in his lap.

"According to my sources, there is a growing dissatisfaction with the emerging fove technology. A lot of religious feeling on the right—there's even talk about forming yet another political party." Malcolm snorted and looked uncomfortable.

"Do they understand what a fove is?"

"Does that matter? With the Brazil situation—"

"We have Brazil under control—"

"LeRoy," said Malcolm heavily. "Brazil is a disaster. To me, for backing it. To you, for letting the pangolins get out of control."

"No one could foresee—"

"*Disaster.* The discussion of non-existent foves is only the visible part of the problem." Malcolm leaned forward earnestly. "We live at the political interface between necessity and distrust. We *have* to have biotech. We *have* to have robot industry. Without both, the Restoration is impossible. But because of everything that happened during the Die-Back, no one trusts either. So, we ignore them. As long as nothing disturbs the illusion, we can blithely go along." He gestured towards LeRoy. "Then, Brazil happens. That's terrible but it's a long ways away. Now, people are talking about foves."

"The pangolins are not foves," said LeRoy.

Malcolm leaned back. "You told me they were

designed never to breed. Did you lie to me?"

LeRoy shook his head. "We didn't *make* the pangolins to be a separate species—to be foves. But we thought we'd isolated them from breeding with the native population. They bred anyway and the *result* is a new species but it's not one we created."

"Wonderful." Malcolm snorted. "'Native.' Old World species alive and well in the New World."

"Can't blame Lifeworks for that. That was a Texas solution to the fire ant problem. Might have worked, too, without the Die-Back."

"Hindsight is always 20-20." Malcolm waved him away. "My point is everybody's worried that foves— whether or not they exist—could turn into one of those big polarizing non-issues, like abortion a hundred years ago. Or guns. Or vaccination. A point of contention that represents a lot of other things and gets traction." He shrugged. "You're one of my largest donors. You wanted to talk to me. I wanted to talk to you. But discreetly."

"Do you need another contribution to your reelection campaign?"

"Always." Malcolm sighed. "Reelection is dicey. But especially this year."

LeRoy shook his head. "I've been backing you for a long time. I helped put you in—I was the one to talk to old Senator Grand to pick you for his successor. Because you'd done a good job for Charleston."

"I know that. But people don't like you, LeRoy. Not just because of Brazil." Malcolm leaned forward, his elbows on his knees. "Plumbers can't make money like they used to because of the new recycling forever toilets. That's a LifeWorks product. They don't thank you for that. Cities are still struggling with water and sewer because of the rising water and the losses of the Die-Back—cities like our dear Charleston. New regulations—some of which benefit LifeWorks—don't make things easier. They would dearly love to blame some convenient industry. They do. Yours. Like the few remaining rural poor who are both too stubborn to come into town where the jobs are and unable to make the new wave of cottage industries work for them. You're a convenient face. When a machine takes your job, you blame the manager. When an animal takes your job, you get pissed."

"No animal is taking anybody's job. That's not how biotech is used."

"Facts make no difference. To them, it's one step from slugs laying mortar along brickwork to a mason out of work."

"We still have too few people. There's work enough for everyone—you can see it in the government statistics."

"Again, you're talking like facts matter." Malcolm leaned back and stared outside. The limo was driving near Dupont Circle. "Look," he said. "South Carolina—our state—has three big constituencies I have to satisfy: we have the Appalachian Corridor to the west, the farm vote, and the cities. The Corridor is pro-bio, networked from north Georgia up into Maine. They vote very carefully on issues. They trade votes between state boundaries. People who don't work with them have a nasty way of ending up out of office. *They* like me."

"The Corridor buys a lot of our products."

"They like *you*. But there aren't many of them. They're a big minority, but a minority nonetheless. Then, there's the farm vote. The big robot farms are politically invisible but there are a lot of small farms. They aren't monolithic. There are the middle farms, the swamp farms, and the coastal fisheries. *They* don't have problems with robots like most folks. But they see your biodesign as upcoming competition and they're not happy about it. And they have to live next door to the failing rural poor I mentioned before. All of them vote. That leaves the cities. They shift with the fashion. One election they like me. The next they think I'm the devil himself."

Malcolm lifted his hands and dropped them. "I have to keep everybody happy. The fisheries lobby would have been happier if I hadn't voted for the Near Shoals Preservation Act. But if I had sided with them and voted against it, I would have lost the Appalachian Corridor—heavy conservation vote. The fisheries lobby lived with it because I voted for the increase in western state subsidies—their biggest market. But *that* pissed off the middle farmers. The swamp farmers are still upset about the farming exclusion amendment in the Wetlands Preservation Act of two years ago. But the amendment was the only way I could make the middle farmers happy. The cities are the tax base. They want cheap food and services and low taxes. But subsidies for the Corridor and fisheries have to be paid for by an increase in taxes. And that means either corporate, income, or total use taxes. Which pisses off the cities."

"I know about taxes," LeRoy said dryly.

"I know you do, friend," said Malcolm. "You aren't the lightning but you *are* the lightning rod. If the Brazil project weren't so public... if you were a faceless company like Johnson and Johnson, or Eli Lilly..."

"Don't remind me." LeRoy brushed his pants with his hands. "Why are you talking to me at all?"

"I need your money." Malcolm spread his hands in a great orator's gesture. "What do you need?"

"The Life Bank bill for one."

"That one's hard—"

"And an amendment to the renewal of the Biosystems Regulatory Act for another."

Malcolm looked thoughtful. "What do you have in

mind?"

"Life form protection."

‹ 4: Wash, 3/19 ›

A small courier job, Ralph had said. South Station to Cambridge. Enough scratch to pay off the Cambridge cops. Easy money.

Who's the client?

Some guy who wants to get to Cambridge without being observed.

Convenient, Wash had thought. Anonymous, but most of Wash's contracts were anonymous. Ralph checked him out and while he couldn't identify the client, he could make sure there was no halo of police, government, or mob connections.

And Wash needed the money.

Wash caught the trolley to Park Street. There, he took the underground to South Station and got out to walk down past Fort Point Channel salmon farms towards the Iron Bridge Dock. He entered a small grocerette. The clerk eyed him morosely as Wash purchased a case of Coca-Cola.

"You got a thirst on, eh?" said the clerk.

"Yeah," said Wash. "Just can't get enough of the stuff."

"I have cold soda. That stuff's warm."

"This is what I want."

"Don't drink it all at once. Warm soda's bad for you," said the clerk.

"I can handle it," said Wash shortly and left holding the eight-pack.

The day had fully started and people were walking purposefully on unknown errands along Atlantic Avenue when he reached the marina. Wash could feel the mercantile bustle that began a couple of months before the summer Solstice. Christmas in the summer, he thought. Instead of buying presents, people bought things to spend on the night itself—fireworks, streamers, drugs, sexual protection. Solstice and Christmas: the two nights of the year Wash refused work.

Wash drank the first one as he inspected the boats from the railing, then slowly ate the bottle. The clerk was right. Warm soda was the worst.

He glanced at the half-eaten bottle. Maybe Jake was right and Coke did taste better in plastic—Wash thought he could taste the oatmeal from which the bottle was made. When he was done, he had decided on a particular boat.

The office was set up from the marina in a flimsy shack. There was a fat, balding man inside, asleep in his chair. The name on his desk said, "Drew Fielding."

"Excuse me?" said Wash in a loud voice. "Mister Fielding?"

Fielding awoke with a start and lost his balance, leaning nearly to the floor as he saved himself from falling. This left him in an awkward crouch. He was still for several seconds, looking shocked. Then, his face relaxed and he stood up smoothly, leaned over the desk towards Wash, and stuck out his hand. "Drew Fielding, here. What can I do for you?"

"I want to buy a boat." It was good to have an expense account to go along with the contract.

Wash made sure not to purchase the boat too easily, but after an hour he had the boat he needed for a reasonable price. It was an obsolete model, a Chriscraft Neptune, made at the height of the Second Boston Harbor Cleanup, just as the Die-Back began. The Neptune speedboats had a good, if limited, brain and a metabolic motor that had been originally designed to be fueled by the organic muck in the water. The more the boat was run, the cleaner became the harbor. Eventually, this caught up with the Neptunes and they could no longer find the fuel they needed. Boats are rarely junked, and the unhappy Neptunes went from being speed boats to being slow and reliable harbor fishing boats. Not one of them liked the change.

Wash threaded the little boat slowly out of the marina and into the broader harbor. "Hey, fella. Pretty day, isn't it?"

"Yeah, Boss," the boat responded. "If you say so."

"I always heard you guys were fast. Smart, too."

"Smart as a dog—smartest boat you'll ever see." A bit of static burst from the boat's speaker. "Faster than any of these old tubs. Hell, you don't know."

"Could you have made it out past the harbor and back at high speed?"

"No sweat."

"Want to show me?"

"Can't, Boss. Harbor's got no taste to it anymore."

Wash hefted the soda bottles. "Got a fuel tank?"

"Sure, but it's dry—"

"I can give you one more chance for speed. But it's going to be the last time. This will blow the engine."

The boat didn't say anything for a long minute. "I always wanted to go out with a bang. Set it up, Boss. You gonna' see some speed."

Wash filled the fuel tank with the Coke and then cut up the bottles and dropped them in as well. He topped off the tank with a half-liter of brown powder. "Okay, fella," he said finally. "Let's go up the channel where I can pick up a friend. Then, we'll go for a ride."

‹ 5: LeRoy, 3/19 ›

The 37th Amendment mandated the protection of personal information. A mélange of court cases, legislation, appeals, and relegislation made legal implementation spotty. Nobody was happy with the result but nobody wanted to open that can of worms again. News drones were limited to a prescribed distance but were allowed telephoto lenses. Telephoto lenses were allowed but not parabolic microphones. Publishing LeRoy's birthday was illegal but a casual image of the Watergate where he happened to be walking up the steps was not. Imagery of the crowd on the street was perfectly publishable as long as none of the faces were identified. Someone taking that picture and then associating names with faces was perfectly legal, but not publishable.

The Watergate had a secure entrance for the limo. With the life mask, LeRoy felt more or less safe as the limo checked him in. It was a point of pride for the Watergate to provide this feature: completely private and anonymous places to stay in a not-so-private world.

LeRoy walked through the private tunnel to the elevator wondering if it would be enough.

The room was spartan in the bland, unremarkable sense of hotel rooms across the world. The bed was broad and had several features that were carefully detailed in a short pamphlet on the end table, proving that the Watergate had a large customer base that used its privacy suites for other than business purposes. The picture window was well simulated—the suite was underground. Windows were too obvious a security breach. The walls were a bland rose, though he could change that if he so chose. All of this was described in the bedside pamphlet.

Still holding his briefcase, he walked over to the desk. On it were two medium-sized bowls. One had a sign of a sperm and an ovum on it. The other had the same sign overlaid with a red circle and slash. For a moment, he was confused. Then, he chuckled: fertility symbols and anti-fertility symbols. He rummaged in them for a moment to see if there were any actual drugs or devices but none were obvious.

Amanda could tell him when he finally called her. If he wanted to ask.

LeRoy set his briefcase on the bed and opened it. Inside, next to papers and electronics, was a black box with a bright red button on the top.

"Shit," LeRoy muttered. "What's she got for me this time?" Gingerly, he pressed the button.

Silently, the box opened and inside was a bundle of fur. It opened one eye at him.

"Gah!" LeRoy stepped back.

It unfolded itself, jaw hinged into place, tail unrolling. A fox—mostly fox, at least. She stood up, her head coming up to his chest, female, complete with human breasts and figure, and anatomically complete. She was wearing fishnet hose and her red fur was extremely silky. LeRoy had an almost irresistible urge to pet her. He restrained himself.

"Hey there," she said in a soft, sexy voice. "M'names Molly."

"You're supposed to check the room, right?" LeRoy sat down next to her. "Did Amanda have anything else she wanted you to do?"

She yawned again and scratched herself, looked at him. "She did have some ideas—"

"Just check the room."

Molly reached down inside the box and turned on some music—a jazz band, from the sound of it, LeRoy decided.

She jumped down on the floor and tapped her foot until she caught the beat, then began a tap dance across the carpet, along the edge of the wall, on the desk—

"What are you doing?" asked LeRoy.

"Securing the room," she said over her shoulder without missing a beat.

The music faded a bit and she began singing:
It ain't the meat, it's the motion,

that makes this lady want to dance.

"Do you have to sing, too?" called LeRoy.

"Do I tell you how to do your job?" she said on the downbeat, and continued, beginning now to dance up the walls.

The song ended in a rousing chorus with the fox dancing around the ceiling fixture. She dropped to the floor, breathing heavily. "Got a towel?"

LeRoy got her one from the bathroom.

"How about a cigarette?" she said softly.

"I don't smoke."

"How about twenty minutes of your time?" Her voice dropped several notes and became sultry.

"I don't think so," sighed LeRoy. "Back in the box."

"I'm reusable," she said as she curled up inside his briefcase. "Activate me again some time." She seemed to fall asleep and folded up into the box. The box resealed itself, its button red and prominent.

"I don't know," LeRoy said to himself. "Maybe it's time to change Amanda's programming."

He pulled out the papers he needed and began to work as he waited.

An hour or so later, the bell chimed that a passed person was entering. A young black woman entered the room. She looked across to him. "Damn it, LeRoy. Take off that damned mask."

"Sorry. I forgot." He took off the mask and she removed hers.

"Hey there," said Monica Shuman, President of the United States.

‹ 6: Marcus, 3/19 ›

Marcus hauled himself over the edge of the parapet and held himself against the edge. Below him, new and shiny spring leaves were limned silver by the moon. The effect gave a thin and insubstantial look to the world as if everything Marcus could see was a mere reflection. He wondered if perhaps younger apes, with their new generation of eyes and brain, saw it differently.

Marcus sat on the damp roof and stared at the sky. He grunted, content for the moment that he was alone. Scratched his shoulder. Stopped himself. If he scratched it too much it would bleed.

Few of the apes had his predilection for wandering alone at night. Most sought each other's company and nestled together, gathering warmth and solace from the close smell of another warm body. But since Jefferson had gotten old and his children had grown, Marcus had come to enjoy a certain amount of solitude.

In the distance, he heard the dry wash of the Atlantic. If he strained, he could hear now and then a faint hoot or mutter from the apes below him. Here, however, there was no one. The sounds he heard, the odors he smelled, the world he watched, seemed his alone. Complexity fell away and he could imagine the spider workings of the world better than it really was. He hooted faintly to himself.

And heard an answering call from below.

Cursing, he stood and turned to the edge. Without thinking, he identified the sound of breathy muttering as two apes, one larger than the other. After a moment, the creaks of the climbing bars told him it was a chimp and an orang. Then, he smelled Maxwell and Lao-Tzu as they made their way toward him. Neither shared Marcus' love of nighttime scenery so this could be no coincidence. Marcus drew himself as erect as he could. Being third generation, he could stand fully erect—more than Lao-Tzu could, anyway. At least, he had that on the orang. Not being fourth or better meant that standing erect hurt—which Maxwell, being fifth, could not have known.

Maxwell peeked over the edge. He bobbed his head once. "Hello, Marcus."

Lao-Tzu followed Maxwell onto the roof. "We had hoped to find you here." He coughed a moment.

"I'm here, all right," said Marcus shortly. "What do you need this late at night?"

"Sister Hanna has been saying that Catherine is pregnant." Maxwell scratched at himself.

"Lethias hasn't been gone long enough to know for sure." Marcus snorted. "Hanna's crazy. She always has been—even for a chimp." The last was said to irritate Maxwell: Marcus had more than enough irritation to share.

Marcus wasn't disappointed. The hair on Maxwell's head and shoulders rose and the chimp grew tense. Still, he did nothing. Maxwell was hot-headed and impatient, but he wasn't stupid enough to attack a gorilla that outweighed him by a hundred forty kilos. Marcus lost his irritation and felt depressed. Always, they were arguing.

"Sorry, Max," said Marcus suddenly, surprising both Maxwell and himself. "That was uncalled for. Look, what are you getting at?"

Maxwell relaxed visibly and even brightened up some. "It's all right. Sister Hanna is a little odd. Comes from good stock, though."

Yeah, thought Marcus sourly. A *little* odd. But funny. You had to give her that. Nothing made him laugh like watching Sister Hanna.

"It is not just Sister Hanna," spoke up Lao-Tzu. "The Empress Dowager, one of my wives, has also mentioned this alleged pregnancy. We did not even know that Lethias had joined with Catherine."

"Where is Catherine?" Maxwell looked thoughtful.

"Down in Women's Country," answered Marcus. Women's Country was near the middle of the island. It was a glade in the bamboo forest where ape—and even baboon—females and their young children congregated from all the different species. Females went there to give birth. Next to Women's Country and the Soft Gate, was the graveyard.

Male apes were not exactly excluded from Women's Country. Neither were they welcomed. It was common for newly mated females to spend some time there. *Doing God knows what*, Marcus thought.

"So's Jefferson. Hell, Max. Maybe women can tell quicker than the tests." Marcus shook his head. "It's not a big thing."

"I have also overheard the Empress Dowager speaking of a baboon named Comes-At-Noon. Do you know him?"

Marcus went cold. "Yeah, I know Comes-At-Noon. It's Lethias. Runs-From-Water named him."

The announcement created silence and Marcus could hear the Atlantic again.

"I've never heard of that happening," said Lao-Tzu slowly.

"Tell me about it. I don't know if it has *ever* happened before. Lethias and I didn't want anything to get out—there was enough nonsense going on with him leaving. Runs-From-Water agreed after I made it clear to him what I wanted." And Marcus didn't want it getting out that Runs-From-Water had known about Lethias before Lethias had appeared. They had enough problems without adding in coincidence and superstition.

"Then, who told who?" Maxwell's voice lost all expression. Marcus wondered what *that* meant.

"Who do you think? Some baboon female saw what was going on and told some ape female down in Women's Country." The reasoning made Marcus uneasy. Marcus would have expected it to come up in the male community first. After all, the baboons, though separate from the other apes, were by no means strangers. Baboon society followed a promiscuous grouping with a leading male descended from a leading female. When the apes fraternized with the baboons, it was usually along gender lines: males mixed with males, females with females. It was the male, Runs-From-Water, that had named Lethias. When Marcus hadn't heard anything about it for a while, he'd assumed the secret had held. Had Runs-From-Water mentioned it to a female and the female took it to Women's Country? Or had the information made it there by some other means?

"Two females think—say they in fact *know*—Catherine is pregnant," said Lao-Tzu slowly. "And other females speak of an event they should not know at all. This seems to me to be cause for some concern."

"Come *on*," said Marcus. "Maybe females can smell pregnancy sooner than anybody thought. I'll ask Jefferson. Besides, Lethias and I were sitting on an open beach—*anybody* could have seen us. Maybe some female orang from the bluffs." He was blustering and he knew it.

"As a community, we are coming to an important decision," said Lao-Tzu reproachfully. "No event should be considered unimportant within the larger pattern of things."

"You should have told us, Marcus," said Maxwell dryly. "The baboons think it's important even if nobody else does. Otherwise, they wouldn't have named him."

"Listen, goddamnit," Marcus rumbled angrily. "We sat on our asses for three *years!* I wasn't going to let anything derail the *one* decision we've made in all that time. If I'd said squat, you guys would have yammered over it for *another* three years before you'd have done something. I couldn't take that chance."

"What's so urgent, Marcus?" asked Lao-Tzu, quiet

now, with the same voice he'd used when he analyzed the dream.

Marcus had come to hate that voice: it told him that Lao-Tzu the orang and friend had become, for the moment, Lao-Tzu the mystic. Marcus would have felt better if he had an answer to the question.

"I don't know, Lao. I don't know. I just *feel* it." Marcus looked at Maxwell, expecting a sneer.

"Maybe it'll come to you in a dream," said Maxwell softly.

Marcus searched his face for any sign of sarcasm but Maxwell seemed sincere. "Maybe. I'll talk to Jefferson, anyway."

Maxwell nodded. "I'm going back to the compound. I don't think there's much more to discuss tonight."

"I concur." Lao-Tzu got to his feet. "We will leave you then, Marcus. We have interrupted your meditation enough for one night."

"No, I'll come with you," Marcus said miserably. The night had become alien to him. He wanted to smell others around him once again.

Above him, the moon seemed cold.

‹ 7: Jefferson, 3/19 ›

Most of the bamboo shoots in the grove were too tall for Jefferson to reach easily. If she were younger, she could have bent the thick boles down by climbing them, plucking the sweet spring bits from very top. But her back and legs hurt this morning from the night's damp and her eyesight wasn't too good anymore. Her chest hurt, too, as if she had a deep heartburn. She contented herself by searching the back edge of the grove where it abutted the honey locust trees, thinking their thick thorns might have discouraged other apes from looking for spring shoots on that side.

Jefferson was successful and found a tasty collection. It seemed to ease the heartburn. She was, she thought, chuckling, like the great toad who had fallen into the cream and by the virtue of his faith, churned the cream to butter until he was saved. At least, that was how Lao-Tzu told the tale. Jefferson didn't like the taste of cream or butter and therefore paid little mind to the story.

Sitting in the warm sun, comfortably satiated on the sweetest of foods, she dozed, dreaming of Marcus. When she awoke, she remembered the dream and thought fondly of him. Thinking of Marcus slid easily into thinking about sex with Marcus since the weather was warm—*oily weather*, the apes called it. Warm enough not to think about the cold. Warm enough to feel that life was lubricated, the sharp edges smoothed, the crooked made straight. It was no accident that most of the women came into season near this time, nor that most of the children were born near the turn of the year. Jefferson had reached the age where coming into season, and therefore sex, was no longer urgent. Still, she could remember the languor of it. Gorillas and orangs took their time. It was only the chimps that came and went like a handclap.

Although, maybe she should take a lesson from the chimps. They had sex out of season all the time. Gorillas not so much. But maybe Marcus would be inclined.

Jefferson chuckled again. Marcus had been such a lusty boy. So different from her previous, second-generation, husband, Little Jack. When Marcus had asked for her, he had been small, his back had only a hint of silver, his shoulders still narrow. Her children by Little Jack were freshly dead—she'd never been able to keep her sickly babies alive. Maybe a young one, she had thought. And there had been something vital about him, so much more alive than Little Jack. To be clear, she had not exactly been Little Jack's favorite, either. She liked Marcus' voice, soft and inviting, and different from her own scratchy whisper. And she liked the grace of his sign.

"Jefferson?"

Jefferson recognized Catherine's voice on the other side of the honey locust. She sighed and eased up on her legs and knuckles—another thing she had liked about Marcus was the effort he put into standing up. Of course, he was third generation. Jefferson was second. For her, standing was harder.

She sidled around the locust trees and waved to Catherine.

Catherine came to her out of breath. There was sweat on her face, highlighting the white patch and the three thin, red lines. "Sister Hanna and Jezebel sent me to get you. They want you to see her."

Jefferson saw no need to speak and signed instead. ==Who?==

"The figure in Jezebel's painting. The Deadly Woman."

Jefferson nodded. The Deadly Woman had been generating ripples in Jezebel's dreams—and therefore her paintings—for a year now. Some were convinced that it was the Deadly Woman that had given Marcus the dream to send Lethias to the outside world. Jefferson knew better.

==Take me to her.==

Jezebel was staring intently over a small painting in the dust, her orang hair was so deeply orange it was nearly crimson. Jefferson sat just behind her, in the sun, and waited for her to speak.

Jezebel was young to live in Women's Country. She had moved from her orang quarters when she was barely pubescent and had never left. That had been ten years ago. She was beautiful. With that hair and lustrous skin, combined with the delicacy of her fingers and the richness of her fragrance, she would have been pursued anywhere on the island except here. Jefferson knew that was one reason she had come. Jezebel had no interest in men.

Jezebel pulled back from the sand painting and stared at it for some minutes. She added a few grains of red here and there, then a thread of yellow beneath the image.

"There," she said and looked up at Jefferson. "See for yourself."

Jefferson looked over Jezebel's shoulder. The dark face of the Deadly Woman, a shadow descending from her right eye, down across her cheek and down her neck. She had moved towards the white ape. They were dancing towards each other.

==Is she death?== signed Jefferson.

Jezebel shook her head. "Nothing so simple. It could be a woman, or a host of women, or an attitude. I think it's a single woman, though that's nothing more than a feeling. She's not good for us, anyway. I'm certain of that."

Jefferson studied the painting thoughtfully. ==What is this?== Jefferson pointed to a winged shape flying about her head.

"A spirit, maybe? An idea? A helper? An annoyance? I don't know. It's vague. Maybe it's just a bird." Jezebel looked troubled.

Jefferson touched her arm in comfort. ==The woman will be difficult to find. We will look out for the bird.==

‹ 8: Lethias, 3/19 ›

The train had moved fast enough that Lethias thought he could see the seasons reverse before his eyes. March was already early summer in South

Carolina. By the time the train had passed through Washington, the trees were green. New York was covered with a late spring rain.

The train arced beneath the earth near Quincy and the windows became obsidian plates. Lethias didn't like the effect: it made him feel buried alive. He didn't want time to reflect; he'd had enough of that over the last six hours since he had boarded the Boston-Savannah in Charleston and the previous few weeks since he'd first spoken with Marcus. It was nice to have a private car but all of his preparation urged him towards humanity. Postponing it yet again made him nervous. He'd had a bad hour when the train traversed Pennsylvania, when his manmind had gone offline and his solitary apemind had become frightened and lost without understanding the context of the train. He'd spent part of the time staring out the window and whimpering, another slamming his fist against the glass. Afterward, he was glad the glass had not broken. *More control*, he told himself. You cannot give in to emotions.

He called Catherine—using Amanda as a secure link—but she was gone to Women's Country. Instead, he talked to Jefferson, the two of them signing silently to one another about innocuous things: the difference in the weather, the change in the light as he moved North. But when he tried to talk to her about his new marriage, and his leaving the island, she resolutely turned the conversation away. Frustrated, he finally said goodbye, then stared hurt and fuming out the window.

"When you get to South Station," said Amanda. "You're going to be met by a hired courier."

"All right," Lethias said hesitantly.

"He'll take you up to Cambridge where Montague will meet you."

"Why isn't Montague meeting me himself?"

Amanda shrugged. "Monty has some ideas on how you're going to fit into Cambridge life and they don't include any connections with LifeWorks. Catch you later."

‹ 9: Monty, 3/19 ›

Monty did not dream as he had when he was younger. Or, rather, he dreamed as he expected people like LeRoy dreamed: confused, vaguely Freudian, psychosexual meanderings that reflected more the dreamer's chaotic mental state than any spiritual advancement. The apes held true dreams in high esteem. They were valuable experiences that instructed and guided. Monty felt the same but he seldom dreamed that way anymore.

It had been this way since he was a child. All of the natives prized dreaming. There had been great dreamers among the Hopis, the Navajos, and the Mojave. Even the Paiute had had their share of men and women who could dream something strong, with conviction and power, where the truth of things stood straight out and cast a long shadow. Not that everyone had this talent; far from it. But dreaming was like seeing. Where most people could detect the gentle falling of photons on the retina; fewer could extract truth and facts from the image. Seeing clearly was a learned skill. Dreaming was the same. Monty had always stood aside when real dreamers had spoken.

All but once.

Monty had been born in New Oraibi. He had danced the dances as best he could with withered arm and withered leg. He fasted the fasts and ate the corn but he saw nothing beyond the seeds and hunger. Many of the faces he saw were white or Mexican—it had gotten to the point where any tribal event was descended upon by groupies, false prophets, and outright thieves.

When he was twenty, full of youthful angst (angst was in demand on television that year) and feeling, perhaps, the precognitive whisper of the Die-Back on the wind of the evening news, he went out to Hotevilla, the village founded by Yukiuma, and slept in the back of his pickup truck in the open ground near the Community Center. He slept, hoping that like Jacob, he might dream of a ladder piercing heaven. Nothing happened. He limped north past the bluffs until he couldn't see anything but bluffs and scrub. He did not eat food or drink water. It was the middle of January and he was deeply cold at night, looking up at the Pleiades and asking help from one sister to the other. Still nothing.

On the third day, he was angry and hallucinating on the edge of some nameless mesa, shouting at the spirits, at the bats, at the snakes: "Give me a dream or let me go!" That night, when he slept, he was given the only dream he had ever had; the one that would keep him going for the rest of his life.

In his dream, he was sleeping in the pueblo with his grandmother next to him—which felt strange, since she had died drunken in a car wreck long before he was born. She woke him up and said, "Come outside. The sun is shining and it is warm." Monty was cold and followed her outside.

There, he found he was standing on a cliff with his grandmother standing next to him on his right. The whole world was arrayed out before him. He could see as far west as the Colorado River, blue and violent, not half stagnant and polluted as he knew it was, and farther west to the glittering Pacific Ocean. The pueblos were numerous and filled with a strong, proud people. They had become a force to be reckoned with, a nation to be respected.

"That man," she said, pointing to his right, "is important to you."

Monty saw a tall man, thin as a rail, his skin the shiny blue-black color of a beetle. He seemed to be roughly Monty's age. The man appeared in a foul mood. He was dressed in wool and seemed hot in the sun, though he didn't have sense enough to take off his jacket.

"All this," the man said, "will I give to you if you will come and serve me."

Monty looked at his grandmother. The marks of the car wreck that had killed her were still fresh on her face. "What should I do?"

"Do what you will," she said softly. "But if you go with him, you will lose your soul."

His own soul did not seem much worth when weighed against what he saw. Down in the valley, there was a gathering of the people and he saw it was the Night of the Washing of the Hair. He could see children being initiated into the clans. There were no white tourists around them and the dance had a deep and solemn rhythm.

His soul seemed a small price to pay.

"I will," Monty said finally.

"Come East to me," said the black man.

Monty woke up. The sun had just risen and the land was black shadow under the glass bowl of the sky. Every broken part of him ached. He drove back to his lonely trailer and ate. No one celebrated his return with song. After breakfast, he began looking for Eastern colleges to attend.

This night, years later, Monty awoke feeling the fragments of a dream, a true dream, pass through him. It was gone before he could make sense of it and he was bitterly disappointed. While all of his true dreams invariably reflected that first dream, they were all precious.

The only wisp left of it was flavored with gorilla. Female gorilla at that. With all that was happening, it made him uneasy. He decided he would call in a favor. He made a call to Sims.

‹ 10: Sims, 3/20 ›

What makes this game interesting, Sims wrote in his journal, is not the determination of clues. Instead, it is the means by which a clue is defined. In any detective story, the implication is that clues are left by clubfooted villains. In my investigations, the nature of what makes a clue must first be ascertained. Of course, that is, itself, a variable. Nothing can be considered constant. Coincidence is king.

He leaned back in his chair and stared out into the Richmond evening. Sims wondered who he was writing to—he'd kept a journal all of his life, writing it by hand into expensive paperbound books. For a moment, he felt lonely, thinking about being away from home.

Sims lived in two places: his lab on the island and Cambridge with Monty.

He loved the island, with the smell of apes mingling with the smell of the Atlantic. He'd come there along with Monty before the Die-Back and reluctantly left for opportunities on the mainland he could only find in person.

But Sims enjoyed Cambridge. The fresh smell of the canals down Massachusetts Avenue. The half-rotten smell of the Charles in flood. Walking along the river with Monty—slowly to make up for Monty's limp. Noticing the relative coolness that fell beneath the trees in summer only because of that forced slowness—like fall, he thought. The coolness is like autumn. He felt homesick but he was not sure for which home.

This trip had been worthless. Widnergog had been an incompetent twit. He'd completely misread the data, even with the help of Sims and Jim Secondson. The whole mole rat network had been ill-conceived—it could never work. The one bright spot had come two years ago when Sims had reproduced the same network in Boston. System capacity was measured in Hawkings—one Hawking was the ability to fully simulate one human brain in real-time. The mole rat brain network could not exceed a Hawking rating of .01 but as a laboratory mechanism for Cori testing, it had worked well in a limited fashion. As a control system, it was terrible. The intrusion of mole rat brain Cori Phenomena into normal operations that worked so well in Sims' lab was impossible to control in the field.

Sims had found nothing to fix Widnergog's problems—not one blasted thing. Sims had felt so confident in Boston when LeRoy had called him in on it. Filter out the Cori Phenomena and leave the MRBs to be a control system. That was what he'd intended.

The universe had not cooperated.

Sims cracked his knuckles in frustration, then chided himself. How do you catch a bird? By patience and observation. He'd been stalking the underpinnings of the Cori Model for over seventy years. He remembered the Zen koan from his days at college: *First, there is a mountain/ then there is no mountain/ then there is a mountain.* How do you track the physical world when it operates according to *that?*

You're getting old, Carroll. Admit failure and get back home. Boston? Sure. It would be nice to see Monty.

The idea of return warmed his heart.

Sims laughed. He got up and went to the open window and stared out. The air sang with insect discussion. It had rained earlier and Sims could smell the wet concrete, dusty as the urea smell of snakes. The air seemed actinic and alive. "Give me a sign, damn it!" he called out to the sky, laughing. "An egg. A sighting, An unusual stone. Show me some magic!"

Quiet fell outside the hotel window and he stopped laughing, feeling a sudden sense of dread. A pigeon came in, landed, and tumbled across the carpet. It rolled itself upright and stared at him with a pigeon's dead gaze as it walked around the room, pecking at the carpet here and there.

Sims stood absolutely still as he watched it strutting across the carpet, cooing maniacally to itself. It stopped by the corner of the desk, squatted, and made a small grunting sound. It stood up straight and preened itself, flew out the window, leaving behind a brown and white mottled egg.

Sims picked up the egg and stared at it. It was mottled and discolored, but there was a face staring at him: a woman with a shadow descending from her right eye, down across her cheek and down her neck. The picture was clear as an etching.

His hands were shaking as he wrapped it carefully in toilet paper and put it in his luggage.

The room phone rang and he almost dropped the egg. He didn't answer until the egg was safely stowed away.

"Yeah?" said Sims, standing in the window and watching the night sky.

"Oh, Romeo, sweet Romeo—isn't that your line, standing on the balcony?" Monty chuckled.

Sims turned to him. "I should be in Boston tomorrow."

"No hurry. If you like, you could do me a favor."

Sims cocked an eyebrow at him. "The last time I did you a favor it cost me in installments."

Monty waved his hand. "That was in another country—"

"Brazil, I believe."

"—and besides, the wench is dead." Monty's face sobered. "Marcus called me to ask about Catherine, Lethias' wife."

"Is she all right?" Not that Sims knew this Catherine at all. But he liked Lethias.

Monty looked a bit confused. "Not exactly. It seems that she has sequestered herself in Women's Country. Marcus is worried about her."

"That doesn't sound like Marcus. Come on, Monty. You're making this up."

"Not exactly," said Monty crossly. "The truth of the matter is Marcus called me to ask if there were any differences between the human component of the male and female apes. I told him no, of course. And that's true as far as I understand it—that is, we never saw any. Of course, we weren't looking for them. And there could be postpartum developments. Then, he told me a couple of odd things that occurred on the island and it got me to wondering. I think the island should be checked—something's not right."

"Cori Phenomena?"

"I don't know. I want you to check. Perhaps nothing is happening—"

"Of course there is, Monty," Sims smiled. He looked at the wrapped egg nestled in his underwear. "The apes are saturated with the stuff. That's the way we designed them."

‹ 11: LeRoy, 3/19 ›

Monica murmured against his chest. "This is the best part."

LeRoy looked at her. "I beg your pardon?"

"You're too old to be insecure." She snuggled closer.

"Ah." The simulated early evening light from the

window limned her face without shadows. He kissed her.

"Perhaps I was mistaken." She giggled and kissed his nose.

"How long have you got?"

"What time is it?" A glow over the end table showed a clock. "I can't see a damned thing without my glasses," she said crossly and pulled herself towards it. He felt her breasts pull over his chest, reached out and cradled her behind.

"Maybe an hour," she said, snuggling again next to him.

"I need to talk to you."

She sighed. "I know you're not married—I checked. Don't try to weasel out of this."

He laughed shortly. "I talked to Malcolm today—"

"Oh, God," she said wearily. "Business. I thought we agreed, no business."

"I know, but—"

"We've kept to that—discretion, privacy, and no business. You agreed."

"Monica—"

"So, let's consider this a minor lapse and forget it, shall we?" She kissed his nipple. "We still have an hour."

He was motionless and silent.

Monica looked at him for a moment. She sat up and pulled her hair out of her eyes. Her face had high, thin cheekbones and her lips were thin to match. Her breasts had a maturity to them he found erotic.

"You're beautiful," he said.

She shook her head and pulled on her shirt. "Right. What do you want, LeRoy?" Her voice was stern suddenly, like the sound of bending iron.

"The biotech regulation renewal comes to a vote tomorrow—Malcolm told me."

"If this is about that damned Life Bank. Christ,

LeRoy—"

He shook his head. "That's important but this is something different. It's an amendment to the higher animals law, protecting them from frivolous slaughter."

Monica looked at him full in the face. "Talk to me, LeRoy. What's this about? You don't go out on a limb for some piss-ant amendment on a two-bit bill."

"I'm worried about it."

"You don't know from worrying. What's going on?"

"I got it on paper." He reached down and rummaged in his briefcase.

"Paper? For Christ's sake—"

"Can't network to it here." He brought out a sheet of paper and handed it to her. "It—"

"I can read."

"I thought you couldn't without your glasses?"

She smiled briefly at him. "That's only for clocks across my lover. I can read legislation in the dark. Half the time I have to."

After a moment, she put it down. "What do you want me to do with this?"

"Not veto it."

"This thing protects enhanced animals—would that require you to get a permit to destroy a lab animal?"

"Not quite." He leaned next to her. "It's modified somewhat in the second paragraph. Only neurologically enhanced animals."

"Like Beck's Law?" She looked at him.

"But more broad." LeRoy pointed down the page. "Here, where the neurological definition is."

She didn't say anything but continued staring at him. He gestured to the paper, suddenly helplessly embarrassed.

"Whose lab is doing this kind of work? Yours?"

"No," LeRoy lied. "And nobody else I know of."

LeRoy put his hands behind his head. "But it's going to happen and it's going to happen soon if it hasn't already. This is more to protect anybody that can exist rather than does exist."

Monica was quiet again. "Who would it be protecting?"

"Somebody like the Abravomitch super-geniuses."

"They were human."

"That was questioned."

Monica waved that away. "Besides, they're dead."

LeRoy shrugged. "So what? Like I said, somebody's doing this or will be. The genie is only in the bottle because it's been legislated there. Bodywork's been going on for years. Brainwork—"

"—hasn't been a problem since Chen and the China War in the late 2040's just before the Die-Back." Monica put down the bill. "Don't remind me. "

"Sorry."

"What does Malcolm say?" Monica stood up and moved around the room.

"He likes it." LeRoy watched her body peeking out from under her shirt as she stood in front of the fertility bowls. The stiffness of her, the distance, made him think he didn't know her. He realized, suddenly, that people around her in the White House must see her like this: distant, guarded, inscrutable. "He thinks the biotech lobby would like it because it protects them from suits on behalf of the enhanced animals. And the ASPCA would like it because it prevents any uncontrolled slaughter. The regulatory agency would like it because it modifies the hearing procedure for the certification of new animals. So, it's got sponsorship."

"And the opponents?" Monica picked up one fertility token, turned it over in her hand, dropped it back in the bowl.

LeRoy didn't like her this way. *This is my fault*, he

thought. But still, the way she stood, half-clothed, looking at fertility objects, she seemed to look like a shaman or a chief of a lost tribe. He had the feeling everything she said, every movement, was choreographed in some strange way, using obscure methods in the service of dark purposes. *Crazy thinking.* LeRoy shook his head. "Only the same people that would oppose the renewal anyway. For them, the whole bill is objectionable. It should pass with or without the amendment. The bill needs renewal."

"Right." Monica took off her shirt and shook herself, held her hair up and rubbed her neck. Idly, she rummaged in the fertility bowl and brought out two rings, apparently of bone. Each had a talisman hanging from it. She pinched them and individual brown knobs blossomed from them like small, fleshy flowers. She pressed one on each breast so the rings hung over her nipples and the talismans dangled below. She twisted the knobs until drops drop of blood rose from the skin of her breasts like small, red pearls.

LeRoy felt fear rising in him like desire.

"Tell you what," Monica said distractedly. "I'll call Malcolm and have him leave the renewal bill until towards the end of the summer session. It'll have more chance of passing out of committee in the pre-recess rush. Then, schedule it for a vote just after the election—if I can. If there's a lot of *sturm und drang* about this amendment, I might just tell him to let it go."

"After the election?"

"Win or lose I'm a lame duck and I can do what I want." She sat down next to him and touched her fingertips to the blood on her breasts and drew them in a red line down his sides until he shuddered. Touched the blood again and drew signs on his chest.

He looked at the bloody marks. "Monica—"

"Do you know about these things?" She touched the rings and set them swinging.

"Not exactly." LeRoy felt nervous. He didn't know what to do. There was something in her eyes that looked dangerous.

"The talisman's for fertility—you could guess that. But the rings turn blue if you're pregnant after sex. Tells in a couple of hours. LifeWorks makes them. Science making magic." She set them swinging again. "Made from modified leeches."

"Monica, I'm sorry I brought up—"

"Hush." She touched his lips and smiled. "I've been thinking about having a baby."

"You're sixty—"

"And you're over a hundred-thirty." She smiled at him. "The perqs of national security and Die-Back luck." She rubbed her hair. "So what? The joys of modern medicine. I'd be the first president to give birth in the White House." She laughed. "Your baby, LeRoy. How about it?"

"I had a vasectomy," he said, suddenly ashamed, unmanned in some obscure way.

"I know." She laughed again. "I know lots about you, LeRoy. We've been doing this too long for me not to know about you. You were an AIDS baby, ultimately treated by RL5. Treated into permanent remission but not cured. Healthy and voluntarily sterile so you couldn't give it to a child. You told me. Remember? And Cindy agreed to that. She died fifty years ago still agreeing to it." Monica kissed one of his nipples, bit it gently. "But *I* didn't agree to it."

"I'm still sterile." The light caught her teeth and she looked feral.

"Magic, LeRoy." She bit him again, lower this time, harder. He gasped. "Let's make some magic."

Some hours later, beneath the sheets he was

awoken by lips. He smiled.

"Monica," he said sleepily. "I thought you had to go."

He suddenly felt sharp teeth. He cried out, reached down, and felt fur. He pulled her off him by the scruff of her neck. Molly watched him levelly, smiled at him, and licked her lips. "Time for your wake-up call."

He put her down. "Already?"

"We have some time…"

He shook his head. "Never mind."

Just before Molly folded into the box, she looked up at him, a sad, earnest concern on her face. "Did everything go okay?"

LeRoy looked at her and felt a sudden kindliness. "I hope so. I truly hope so." He reached down and scratched her head. She rubbed her head against his hand. LeRoy patted her until she lay down. "Go to sleep," he said.

‹ 12: Carmine, 3/19 ›

Carmine felt very comfortable swimming. This struck him as odd—with his wings, the water had never been an inviting place. But now, in the warm water, he felt at home. Curious, that. Curious, also, how he had learned to breathe underwater. He didn't remember ever quite managing that before.

The water was the color of *cafe con leche*, a pale brown coffee that Carmine had associated with the word "sordid" since he was thirteen. That was when he learned the circumstances under which his father liked to drink it. Carmine had refused to admit to himself that a bordello was not a place entirely safe for one of Carmine's light bone structure—sex done well, according to Papa Carlos, was supposed to be violent. Carmine told himself it was merely that the place offended him. "Sordid", he thought to himself. He was above such things.

"I made you a bird—I bought that for you," Papa Carlos had said. "I'm proud of that. A bird is free. But you should be a man, too."

Carmine had flown over Rio de Janeiro for hours afterward, letting the wind heal the bruises. His father had never pressed him about it again, seeming to feel he had done his duty to his son and was now content to watch him fly.

Do this if you can, Papa, Carmine called down to him. *Then, tell me how I should be a man.*

Papa Carlos had watched from the bordello roof, smiling, sipping the coffee and milk with his right hand, the other resting on the inside thigh of his mistress. When Carmine had banked around the building, Papa Carlos had raised the cup in salute.

Swimming now, Carmine grinned. There had been this germ of truth in what Papa Carlos had been trying to teach him: for those who could not fly, women were one reason for living. Women and power had together been enough for Papa Carlos. *Not quite,* he amended to himself. Women, power, and Carmine.

The water seemed lighter and he could see streaks of light breaking through it. He swam for the surface but it seemed a long way away. The water was thick, holding him back and he found he couldn't breathe after all.

He remembered her name, then: Bicita, with pendulous breasts and dark, glistening skin. His own smell of excitement compounded of hormones and fear of her thighs around him, thighs that could crush him in meat and sweat. The air was thick and he was so afraid he could not breathe. "*Meu querido. Meu coração,*" she murmured and her hands pulled at him, pulled at the folded flesh of his wings. Carmine felt squeezed, bent by her strength, and the fear and the excitement carried him away and he cried out—

—the police, the fall—he remembered hitting the pavement—

"Steady, boy."

Carmine felt Quinote's hand on his shoulder. He grabbed it and tried to sit up—he felt his wings hold him down and for a moment he panicked and whatever held him tore.

Quinote's other hand took his other shoulder. "Steady," he repeated. "It's only gauze. Come on, Carmine. It's time to wake up."

Carmine shut his eyes tight, fear struck down into the bone, cracked and splintered bones from the fall. Then, as the pain didn't come with the memory, he gradually relaxed, still afraid He looked up at Quinote, at his sweaty, greasy sympathy. Carmine wouldn't give Quinote the satisfaction of seeing his fear. Instead, he grinned crookedly. "Hello, Doctor. I was just carrying my coin collection when I tripped—"

"Quiet, Carmine," said Quinote softly but with a hint of impatience. "Just wait a moment." His face eased. "We've been working on you for a little over a week. This is the first time you've been awake and sober."

Carmine shrugged off his hands and chuckled hollowly. "Am I fixed?"

"Fixed?" Quinote came around the bed, his good hand checking the braces and bandages, the other held close to his chest. "Torn ligaments. A sprained sheet of interior binding muscles. A couple of broken bones—one of which is unknown to anybody else in your class of vertebrates. Not to mention all of the resultant soft tissue damage. I've pulled most of the pieces together and fast-tracked the healing where I could. But *fixed?* I don't think so." Quinote snorted.

"You can't get out of it this time, Carmine. You're going to be doing a lot of physical therapy in the next few weeks."

"Don't be so stuffy. I'll do it in my off hours."

"You'll do it here for a bit."

Carmine looked at him in sudden fear. "I'm not *damaged*, am I?"

"No." Quinote rubbed the bridge of his nose. "No. No permanent damage. The processors did their job. The *damage*, as you put it, is repaired. The *healing* will take some time."

"Then don't worry about it. What's your problem?"

"I hate to see my work wasted." Quinote inspected the cast on Carmine's leg. "The cast is going to stay for a few days—the hard calcium has already been laid down but the cell matrices haven't settled yet. That's not a problem in and of itself but it'll be weak for a while." Quinote snorted. "Maybe it'll slow you down. The wings didn't require as much work. Still, they'll need special exercises that I'll probably have to design from scratch. Let's look at them. You remember, don't you? *Os—*"

"I hate you sometimes. You act like I'm stupid."

"You hate me *all* the time, Carmine. I'm the bad guy in your personal story," said Quinote tiredly. "You're not very easy to like either. Come on. *Os—*"

"*Os spinus interior*," snapped Carmine. "I know the drill."

That night, he dreamed of a woman's eyes, deep, dark, that moved him so that he wept as if she were something divine. He wanted to reach out to her. Carmine awoke in darkness. A woman stood at the foot of his bed as still and perfect as if she were carved out of his dream. The same woman from the roof. Her eyes glowed with reflected moonlight. He found the curve of her face, the arc of her neck, heartbreaking. He sat up.

"Who are you?" he breathed.

"Good evening, Carmine," she said in a deep and sultry voice, captivating him utterly. "I'm Joanne Biri. I've wanted to meet you since I first knew you existed."

‹ 13: Lethias, 3/19 ›

Lethias followed the courier through the long dark corridor dubiously.

"This is the way out?" he asked.

"That's right," said the courier cheerily. "Through the long dark into the light. Isn't that the way it always is?"

"If you say so." Lethias shifted his duffel bag from one shoulder to the other. "You *are* the courier Amanda sent for me, right?"

"That's me. The last scion of cultural integrity in an otherwise completely corporate family." He shrugged expansively. "It's a living."

"You have some kind of family business?"

"Drug production. It's more of a family tradition. I decided it was not for me. They disagreed. I left." The courier leaned against a large fire door. "Mister Lethias—"

"Just Lethias."

"—welcome to Boston!" With a dramatic flourish, he opened the door.

Outside, were a set of stairs leading down to a small dock. Both sides of the dock were bracketed by tall, straight hulls of transport ships looming over them and leaving them in shadow. There was a long narrow strip of blue sky that stretched out towards open water. Lethias felt as if he were in an alley. It was low tide and the stench of ocean rot was strong.

"Some welcome," Lethias muttered.

The courier dropped lithely into a boat tied to the

dock and motioned Lethias to follow, then he busied himself with the controls in the cockpit.

Lethias lowered himself carefully to the edge of the craft. This boat was much smaller and not as stable as the ferry to the island. It tilted alarmingly as he eased his weight into it and startled him. He had a quick vision of a pair of shoes placed carefully next to the railing and suppressed it with a shudder. Involuntarily, he grabbed the railing and cracked it off. He scrambled back onto the deck ladder. He stared at the railing in his hands foolishly.

"Come on, fellow," said the courier encouragingly. "You've come too far to back out now."

"Easy for you to say," Lethias said softly. This time he grasped the edge of the boat and held it to the dock as he climbed in. There were seatbelts on the back seats and he strapped himself in firmly.

"Don't be so afraid of the water," the courier said over his shoulder. "The worst you can get is a dunking."

"I can't swim."

"So, do the dead man's float, eh?"

Right. Lethias decided he definitely did not like this man. "What's the plan?"

"We're going out at high speed," he said. "Play in the harbor a bit and then come back, go up the Charles to Harvard Square where you walk to your new home."

"Why?"

"You're obviously modified. The trick to anonymity is not to hide it but flaunt it. This will show you're someone wealthy enough to show off. The high-speed boat reinforces that. People might think you're eccentric instead—" He glanced at Lethias. "—instead of whatever you are. Don't tell me. I haven't been hired to know."

He released the mooring and slowly backed out of

the slip. After a moment, the boat faced the harbor. He paused. "Besides, Boston is best introduced from the water." He spoke at the boat. "Ready?"

"Yeah," the boat answered.

"Let's dance."

The boat surged forward and Lethias cried out, grabbing the seat arms. They broke off in his hands. Damn! Why can't they build things strong enough? He held onto the cleats.

The boat ran forward between the two ships and shot out into the sunlight. Lethias looked around and above him, glittering and green, covered over with trees and ivy, was the city of Boston. The boat breached the city's shadow and out again, around the pier, and north. The April sun beat down on him and he laughed nervously. He was here. The courier yelled into the spray and laughed as well.

Thrilled, Lethias clapped his hands. They passed an old stone fort. He waved at it.

Yes, he thought in the spray and the sunlight and the cloudless sky and remembered Catherine, his new wife, Marcus and Maxwell, and the vague and formless mission before him. *Yes*—he was filled with the thought of things to do, things that could be done, and a great feeling that something new and complete was awaiting him. *Yes!*

Chapter 1.4

Carmine was released from the hospital—and out from Quinote's care—a little less than a month after the accident. He half expected the Cambridge Police to be waiting for him but he exited alone. No doubt there they had too many people to bludgeon. He had to wait his turn.

A tiny one-seated automated cab was waiting for him. No doubt called by Quinote.

"Home, sir?"

"Yes," said Carmine shortly.

Carmine owned—rather Papa Carlos owned—a three-decker in North Cambridge. All the way there, as the little cab navigated the occupied streets, Carmine kept thinking about Joanne Biri.

Since his first time mediated by Papa, Carmine had no shortage of sexual company. Carmine might think he looked like a bat, but he was still capable of flight. That alone made him attractive. In addition, he was fairly good-looking in a miniature sort of way. It didn't hurt he had a brittle self-confidence grounded in his unquestionable uniqueness.

Maybe it was the way Papa Carlos had introduced him to sex by way of a transaction. Or maybe it was his intrinsic physical vulnerability. Regardless, Carmine kept himself at a distance. He partook of physical relationships when they came his way and when he could control them enough to protect himself.

Carmine was tiny. He had bat wings. He knew

what he looked like every time he looked in the mirror. He saw women compensate for it when they looked at him. *At least, he can fly!*

He didn't see it in Joanne's eyes.

Her *voice* sent shivers through him. Deep. Dark. Registers and frequencies unknown to the mind of man.

Carmine unlocked his front door and walked up the two flights to the third floor. Keynes, his apartment software, had a list of communications ready for him on the wall's active surface when he entered the kitchen. A follow-up medical note from Quinote: detailed instructions regarding the binding of his wings which were *not* to be unbound until physical therapy, dates for physical therapy, the required list of those outside the hospital to be informed of his medical issues. This included the Directory of the Economics Department and his advisor, Henry Farrell. Carmine noted Papa Carlos had not been informed. There was a request for confirmation that the notification list conformed to his listed requirements.

Carmine initialed the confirmation.

There was a note from Farrell describing changes in the timing of his online courses because of the hospital stay along with a request for them to meet. Papa Carlos had sent a message asking how he was— suggesting Papa might have learned through other means. Carmine marked it for later. There were bills and requests for charitable contributions but none were marked urgent.

Carmine walked down the apartment and outside to the balcony.

April had turned hot. His cast itched. He ached to stretch his wings and cursed physical therapy, root and branch.

He took off his shirt and sat on the couch.

No woman had occupied his mind like this, ever. Usually, he discarded them from consideration minutes after he left them and occupied himself with more suitable pursuits.

Joanne had merely sat by the bed and they had talked for two and a half hours. Nothing consequential. He remembered her laughter, her attention when he shyly spoke of his interest in the economics of moral choices. Listened carefully as she described an esoteric branch of mathematics called "State Theory" that sounded more like wishful thinking than rigorous equations.

Joanne came twice more before he was discharged. He looked for her each morning when he awoke, during the day as he worked out, had tests, and submitted himself to the indignity of electrotherapy. When she did appear, it was as sudden and unexpected as a cool breeze in the desert. When she left, it was like losing necessary water. He carefully avoided asking Joanne what had brought her here. He didn't want to know. That didn't stop his mind from giving him unpleasant possible reasons.

That part of him would not be denied for long. "Why did you come?" he asked her the day before he was discharged. "Why are you *here?*"

Joanne looked away.

Carmine felt his heart stop. This was nothing more than some fetish. Some perverted attraction.

"I'm older than you," she said. "Not much but a few years. I read about you when I was a teenager. You couldn't have been more than ten."

Oh, my God! Pedophilia.

She gave him a slight smile. "I have my own problems. My own obstacles to overcome. But you have a longer distance to travel than I do and you do it with style. I admired that."

Carmine didn't quite know what to make of her.

"So, I kept on and solved my problems. Now, I'm working for Doctor Carroll Sims."

"Sims?" He stared at her. "Quinote's housemate? Or lover. Or soul mate—no one seems to know."

"Yes. Once I heard about you and Doctor Quinote, I planned to introduce myself eventually. Doctor Sims told me that Doctor Quinote said you could use some visitors."

Carmine closed his eyes a moment. "Let me clarify this. You heard about me when you were a teenager and I was a child. Did it... excite you?"

"Excite me?" Joanne stared at Carmine for a moment. Then, she burst out laughing. "You thought I was—as a child? Oh, that's—" She dissolved into laughter again. She sobered. "Did that happen often to you as a child?"

"No," Carmine said shortly.

"What kind of home life did you have that would make you think of that?"

"Never mind!"

"Did you need visitors?"

"What?" Carmine shook his head in confusion.

"Was Doctor Quinote right? *Did* you need visitors?"

Joanne was looking right at him. He had the sudden sense she could *see* him. See who he was. See who he had been—any embarrassments, regrets, and failures he'd experienced were just little blips in the arc of his life as far as she was concerned. There was no judgment. No sense of superiority. She was just looking at him.

Joanne reached over and took his hand. "Carmine Ranquiz, your life has had an impact on mine that I value. That was the sole reason I wanted to meet you." She smiled.

"I'm glad you came," Carmine said. "I did need visitors."

Now, Carmine was home, sitting on his couch on the balcony, alone.

"Keynes?"

"Yes?"

"Call Joanne Biri."

A moment later: "She's not available. Do you want to leave a message?"

"Ask her to call me back. I'd like her to come over and have dinner. Or something." Carmine waved in the air. "Scratch that. Say that I want to see her." *What did he want?* He realized he wanted to be with her. Every day.

Carmine was appalled.

‹ 2: Ida, 4/7 ›

Ida boarded the trolley in a fury. She sat down on the bench and stared stonily down the street as the trolley cruised past the brick buildings on Beacon Street. The benches were wooden—the building of furniture, even the benches in a trolley, being one of the few socially acceptable reasons for cutting down trees.

Certainly not the writing of letters. *Letters.* Delivered by *mail.*

The trolley closed its doors and rattled down the street. It was sharp-angled and small, with a trellis of vines enfolding the door, both enshrining and lighting the advertisements inside. Since the creation of the Boston trolley system over two hundred years ago, the shape of the cars had cycled from the original ornate Victorian to streamlined, art-deco forms that suggested winged Mercuries, to narrow boxy shapes that resembled nothing so much as a gasoline-powered city bus, to obese, inflated cylinders, and now, back to a neo-conservationist design that seemed oddly Victorian.

She uncrumpled the letter from her pocket and reread it. It made her furious all over again. How *dare* this Sunshine character criticize her for evicting the Pedersens! Jake had broken the *law!* She was the Director of Biological Affairs for Eastern Massachusetts—was she supposed to overlook such a violation when it happened in her very own *department?* Where she *lived?* After a moment, she grudgingly admitted to herself that Pedersen had been tried, convicted, fined, and *then* she had fired him. Okay, maybe her assistant had suggested it, but the responsibility was ultimately hers. Should that have been enough? Did Ida need to evict him, too? But still: she was more than a public official. She also had a responsibility to uphold the public trust, didn't she? Sourly, she shook her head. It was also intelligent PR: it didn't look good for a public official to be a convicted felon. She *had* to move before the press did.

Even so, to get a letter such as this on *paper*. It was insulting. Sunshine must have had to find a supplier—paper was rare. The letter felt thick. Could the paper be handmade? Maybe he had commissioned it. Could he have made it himself? That would explain the time it had taken to reach her. Sunshine would have probably composed the letter on his home unit, and then written it on the paper. Was he a calligrapher? Ida had thought it a lost art. Had he taken the month to transcribe the letter? The letter was written in a shaky hand, but it had been so long since she had seen something written on paper, she couldn't be sure. Years long. She wondered if he had learned calligraphy just for this letter. If so, she was impressed.

She'd never met this Washington Sunshine. Ida resolved to correct this at the first opportunity.

Ida replaced the letter in her pocket. She'd recycle

it later—do something creative with it. Something
nasty. The momentary satisfaction she got by
contemplating "something creative" paled. The letter
wasn't important. It was just the lightning rod. The
storm came from somewhere else.

She felt thickly depressed. This alternating anger
and depression had become the bracketing ends of
the swing of her mind's pendulum in the few weeks
since she'd spoken with Melissa. Right now, Ida
wished she'd never seen a damned burning bush on
Melissa's hand or anywhere else.

Melissa had decided to pursue the Oregon
Initiative.

"Melissa!" Ida had cried when she was told. "What
difference does it make? It won't pass. It won't even
make a ripple—state referendums never make any
difference nationally. This one's barely got any
support. "

Melissa sat at her desk and stared back at Ida.
"God doesn't put us here just to pray to Him. The
world is a place where the steel of our faith is
tempered into instruments of His Will."

"What has that got to do with the Oregon
Initiative."

"I'm convinced this referendum is part of that
Will," she stood and restlessly paced in front of the
window. "What is the most fundamental thing Allah
requires of us?"

"Submission," Ida said promptly.

"Exactly. How can it possibly be submission to His
will to usurp His divine act of creation? How can we
be so arrogant?"

Ida said slowly: "Humans have been modifying
animals for twenty thousand years."

"Not brains. We've not elevated the animal into
our own image."

"No one is doing that. It's a fiction of the

Initiative." Ida shook her head. "Besides, doesn't it say in Genesis that God put us in charge of the animals and the land? Doesn't that give us the *right* to manipulate them?" Ida reached over to Melissa's desk and started to page through Genesis in search of the passage.

Melissa recited it. "'And God blessed them, and God said unto them, Be fruitful, and multiply, and replenish the earth, and subdue it: and have dominion over the fish of the sea, and over the fowl of the air, and over every living thing that moveth upon the earth.' Genesis 1:28. I read that passage and the relevant commentary last night." Melissa smiled. "The key phrase is 'dominion over the earth'. That's a stewardship. We are caretakers of the Earth for God, but the Earth belongs to God."

Ida frowned. "What about the parable of the three servants in Matthew? The first two servants invested the money given to them and were rewarded but the third buried the coin to keep it safe. He was rebuked. That would suggest that mere stewardship isn't enough. Perhaps your miracle suggests you should *oppose* something like the Oregon Initiative—which would suggest passive stewardship—not *support* it."

Melissa nodded slowly. "I hadn't thought of that particular passage, but it isn't unique. Consider *halal*—no amount of prayer and blessing will change a forbidden animal into an animal allowed to be eaten. There are limits to what we can or should do. In addition, it is not enough that we raise good meat according to proper husbandry and according to the laws: the meat must be *blessed* by God. The implication is there are limits to the power of our stewardship that can only be sanctioned by God's grace." She didn't speak for a moment. Then, she smiled. "You remind me of Zacharias and his angel: he never understood anything until it was spelled out for him. Finally, even the angel got frustrated."

Ida felt vaguely irritated, as if she were being belittled. "An uncertainty that Muhammad never shared in the Recitation," she said carefully. "Like you, he, also, witnessed a miracle."

Melissa's face darkened and she looked away. "The miracle came to me, not you. God does not make frivolous choices. Perhaps, like Muhammad, I just need to have the courage of my convictions."

Ida shrugged and the silence filled the room.

"I want you to come work for me on this initiative," Melissa said at last.

"I can't do that." Ida spread her hands. "I'm in the Civil Service—it's against the law."

"What about submission?"

"Didn't Jesus say give to Caesar that which is Caesar's and to God that which is God's?"

Melissa nodded shortly. "Jesus also said give everything away, take up your cross, and follow me."

"You're not Jesus."

Melissa stared at Ida and her eyes burned. "I'm not asking you to follow *me*. I'm asking you to follow *Him*. Remember who was given the miracle." She paused. "Many are called. Few are chosen."

Ida bowed her head. *Didn't He also say let Thy will not Mine be done?* "Show me the miracle. Please."

Melissa held out her hand. It was empty. Then, in the next moment, the flame appeared as if it had never left. "It comes now when I need it." The flame disappeared. "And goes when I do not." She looked at Ida. "Then, I heard the voice of God saying, 'Whom shall I send?'"

"Here I am," whispered Ida. "Send me."

That had been weeks ago. Since then, she had helped Melissa procure a political consultant: Orfeo Johannsen, a man who had been recommended to Ida as one of the best in his particular business but who she also found personally repugnant. Orfeo had introduced Ida to the world of virtual PR, re-directed news, inadvertent net transfers, and sideband interest generation—the techniques the political world used to get and hold the interest of an apathetic, technologically over-stimulated public. "It's all signal-to-noise, Ida," Orfeo kept saying. "We can either boost the signal or reduce the noise."

It was against the *law* to work for the government *and* Melissa. Ida could go to *jail*. Each time she thought that way, she heard Melissa's voice: *Saint Paul was in jail for years. Can you do less?*

Once he had been convinced of Gabriel's authenticity, had Muhammad wondered at the Recitation? Had he questioned the power and truth of the words he spoke? Or had he closed his eyes and let his mouth sing the praises of the Lord? Isaiah said, "Here am I; send me." As a member of the Islamic-Baptist Union, she was used to looking for confirmation from two sources; and here she had it. The message was clear: maintain faith in no one but God. Both the Commandments and the Qur'an demanded it.

As she looked out of the speeding trolley, she could recognize the metallic blue of the escaped Toyota advertisement flowers. The sight of them depressed her. Another escape. Another blot on the natural world. It depressed her that the Oregon Initiative was not about these pollutions, only about new creations possessing will and volition. Creations that existed only in the broken minds of those who had conceived the Initiative. She thought of the trees in Government Center, pulling the gratings out of the ground, a jibe at the political powers that put them there. The manipulation of life was necessary—they did have stewardship of the earth, as Melissa had said. Yet, the good steward was judicious and didn't use trees as political favors or flowers for advertisement.

On the other hand, what if someone did create volitional animals that could never be any better than their creators? Ida knew it was only a matter of time and technique. They had intelligent robots. Intelligent animals weren't that far away. Intelligence, compassion, and consciousness marked the human experience. A dog had compassion and consciousness. An elevated dog would be intelligent, compassionate, and conscious—in effect, a person. A *foved* elevated dog would be independent of human beings entirely. The world had a desperate need for more human beings since the Die-Back. What was the need for a non-human people? Why weren't people enough?

The trolley entered the station and she stopped her ruminations as she swung heavily to the sidewalk. Orfeo was waiting for her and they walked together down to the small production studio he had rented. He talked continuously but she only paid him half a mind. She would resign from the Department tomorrow. There can be no more important thing to do than God's work. From the lofty point she had reached, even Orfeo seemed more reasonable.

"Orfeo," she said suddenly as they turned onto Park Drive. "All our effort has been aimed at just getting the Initiative to win in Oregon. "

"Right. And I have a lot of new ideas—"

"What would be necessary to get it on the *national* referendum? And what would it take to get it to pass?"

Orfeo's mouth opened and nothing came out. Clearly, the idea had never occurred to him. His expression was so comical she began to chuckle. The chuckle grew. The two of them stood there, beneath a clear blue sky and ancient trees, the water of the Fenway beneath them, a man sputtering under the weight of a new idea and a woman bending forward, her hands on her knees, laughing.

‹ 3: Carmine, 4/15 ›

After what felt like months of physical therapy, Carmine could stretch out his wings. He couldn't fly yet—unless, as Quinote said, *you want to rip those pretty wings to pieces*—but stretching them was pure joy.

Joanne had visited a few times. They had walked together in the nearby park, spent time in the apartment, sat on the balcony couch and talked. Carmine felt an unusual desire to *not fuck it up*. He had let her take the lead and she had not moved past holding his hand. She *had* suggested he go out on his own. Carmine didn't know what she wanted. Carmine didn't know what *he* wanted.

With his wings folded and wearing clothes, Carmine looked like a hunchbacked child. Sometimes, he had exploited this and wandered about Cambridge slack-faced and drooling, a mutant relic of the chemical excesses of the twentieth century come to haunt the post-Die-Back world. Other times, he ignored it. Tonight, with the painful twinges of his last flight deep in his fragile bones and the light, the almost invisible brace on his leg dragging at him, and palpable Joanne-derived confusion washing through him like an inky river, he pulled a cape around his shoulders and wandered Cambridge in the dark, disguised.

The unpredictable New England weather had gifted the April evening to be clear and crisp. This would not remain much longer. As a result, the night had a holiday air about it. As cool as it was, the streets were crowded and bustling and filled with cooking smells. Solstice was only a few weeks away and the town had the same feeling it had in the first week of December. Solstice and Christmas were the two holidays around which the year moved, pegged in place by First Night and the 4th of July. As Carmine stalked along the river, melodramatically dressed in black and silver, street musicians and dancers were already playing to small crowds. Mystics, fortune tellers, and courtesans operated out of small booths beneath the bridges and sycamores. The river air smelled of jasmine and incense.

The cool air oppressed him. It felt heavy, earthbound. He stopped and bought a charm from an overweight woman dressed in a blue tartan.

"The ancient Scots had the proper sense of magic, sir," she said eagerly as he examined the trinket, a small pearl encaged in filigree. "They'd give the aborigines a run for their money."

He smiled and didn't answer, bought the charm when she told him it had both the power of contraception and glowed in the dark.

Carmine worked his way through the crowds, past two opposing booths with evangelists more interested in attacking each other than attracting converts, a patent medicine show for a pangolin extract that would cure sterility, baldness, and the common cold, and came to rest on the bridge over the Charles River. He leaned over the edge of the bridge and looked down on the moon's reflection in the river and wished he was finished with Quinote's damned physical therapy and could just fly away.

Who was Joanne Biri and why should she have this power over him? When he thought of her, he remembered her voice and eyes. Her eyes had held him and when she had spoken, the rolling cadence of her voice seemed to shudder and ring inside him like the sound of bells.

Look for a woman to listen, Joanne had said. It's time to talk about yourself with someone other than me.

"What the Hell does that mean?" he said morosely to the night. It had seemed full of significance and portent at the time. What woman? Joanne had seemed to think he would know her. Carmine closed his eyes and still saw Joanne. She had reached him in a way no one else had, just by her eyes and voice.

"Hey, sailor," came a low woman's voice.

For a moment he thought it might be her but as he turned, Carmine realized the voice was wrong. Instead, he saw a rather attractive dark woman and her taller companion and a dog. Carmine wondered if he found her attractive now because Joanne was small and dark. Both women were dressed against the brisk spring air. The smaller woman wore a thick sweater with a maroon glow strip along the shoulder and arms. The color of the strip set off similar highlights in her eyes and Carmine judged the effect pleasing. The taller woman wore a sharp-lined jacket that dimly pulsed the color of raw meat. It was a kind of clothing he recognized as parasitic and of which he vaguely disapproved. Carmine noticed the dog and watched him narrowly.

"Do I know you?" asked Carmine politely.

The smaller woman laughed. "Not exactly."

"I'm sure I would remember," Carmine said gallantly.

"It doesn't matter. I'm Tamar Longren." Tamar gestured to her companion. "This is my friend Carrie."

"And this is Brutus." Carrie patted the dog and looked up at Carmine. "He's not very tame and a bit touchy." She smiled coldly at him. "Pleased to meet you."

"Of course." *What a twit.*

"We were going over to Idleman's to see if there was any good music," said Tamar.

Carmine grinned. "Good idea. They have the best

stout in Cambridge. I think there's a good jaxx band there—Los Olvidados, I think."

Carrie shook her head. "Not jaxx—I hate that stuff. It's like manic-depressive klezmer music."

Carmine shrugged. There was no accounting for tastes.

Tamar looked speculatively at her. "I'd kind of like to go, Carrie."

"Oh, Tamar—"

"Tell you what," said Tamar. "You go on home and I'll call you later."

Carrie stiffened. Alert to her every movement, Brutus came to his feet and growled faintly. "If that's the way you feel..."

Tamar smiled. "Don't be like that. I'll see you later."

Carrie nodded shortly. "Come on Brutus." She left them on the bridge and walked away towards Brighton.

Carmine watched her go. "That was a bit cruel, don't you think? Clearly, you two are attached in some way."

"You don't really care, do you?"

"No. But I didn't like her."

Tamar chuckled. "Sometimes I don't either. Idleman's?"

"Stout!" Carmine offered her his arm and they walked up the cobblestone streets towards Harvard Square.

"What are you studying?" she asked after a moment.

"What makes you so certain I'm a student?"

She laughed.

He liked the sound of it. "I'm studying economics."

"I'm surprised. I thought you would be studying aeronautical engineering."

"Ah. No doubt you recognized me as the bird boy

of Cambridge." His small notoriety irritated him. He didn't want it. He just wanted to fly. *And take Joanne to bed at the first opportunity*, he amended. He looked at Tamar.

"Let's just say you've been pointed out to me."

"It's lucky we met. One should always meet their heroes if possible."

She flashed a wide smile at him that was far too innocent.

"This is too much of a coincidence," he said after a few minutes. "Regretfully, it makes me suspicious. Were you looking for me?"

"Yes."

Perhaps this woman would serve as Joanne suggested: to speak about himself. "How did you find me?"

Tamar pointed to a man on the street corner near them, then a woman in the window of a restaurant, and an open window of one of the Harvard dorms. "Pretend that any of them had a small camera and a net hookup. Each a hobbyist doing low-level unbonded reporting on the newsnet."

Carmine felt nettled. He shook his head. This wasn't what he expected at all. "Nobody knows me tonight. I've seen nobody I know."

"That's true. But consider a young man walking along the river in Cambridge with a hunchback— especially if he is as handsome as you are—many people might think it worth mentioning as a kind of local color. If someone were looking for a person of that description, she might have a watchdog on the net…"

"That's a lot of digging."

"It's an expensive program. I like to get my money's worth."

Tamar's hand was warm against his. Why was Joanne paying attention to him? He had no idea. Why had she sent him out on his own? They should be together. Carmine had done everything correctly, hadn't he? He'd given her space. He hadn't pressed. But nothing had come of it. Maybe Joanne didn't care for him at all. Maybe he was being used. Who was she anyway? What the hell did he owe her? He looked over at Tamar. "I hope I'm worth it."

"We'll see." Tamar smiled and Carmine thought it made her face light up.

They walked past the subway stop and were suddenly enveloped in a chattering group of musicians rising suddenly from the underground like Lazarus. A street magician on Brattle Street pulled a rose out of Tamar's jacket and presented it to her.

"To a lovely couple," he said.

Tamar looked embarrassed. "We're not—" began Carmine.

The magician grinned, gestured, and she took the rose. Carmine felt vaguely guilty but couldn't figure out exactly why.

The club was crowded and smoky and the dancing sweaty. The band did play something which to the unkind might indeed sound like manic-depressive klezmer. They left before midnight and wandered the streets looking at the solstice displays in the shop windows.

Tamar fingered the pearl charm hanging from his neck. She smiled. "I didn't know you believed in charms."

Carmine snorted uncomfortably. "I don't."

"Really?"

"Given my circumstances, perhaps it's appropriate that I have more than a passing interest in the truth of such matters. I am one of their results."

Tamar laughed. "I love the way you talk."

He leaned towards her and smelled her scent, a mixture of cloves and cinnamon, in the cool air. "I was told it has great contraceptive powers."

Tamar's face was close to his. Her eyes were dark and reminded him of Joanne's. "Let's test it," she said and kissed him.

Later, she tried to undress him but he gently held her hand away. "It's better if I do it myself."

He undressed himself. She was not Joanne, but she reminded him of her. As he watched the rise and fall of her breasts, he thought wryly to himself: Joanne who? He thought again: what did he owe a dark woman who had appeared at the foot of his hospital bed? Nothing? Everything? He had no idea.

Carmine shook his head. Back to the moment. He considered taking off the harness and decided against it. His wings were still fragile. The harness would give him some protection.

Tamar pulled him hard against her and he caught his breath at the impact.

"Gently," he breathed. "Let's go a little slower."

Tamar kissed him so strongly he felt like he couldn't breathe and almost panicked.

"Easy." Carmine tried to pull away but she was too strong. "Wait a minute."

She looked at him. "Something the matter?"

"You're going to hurt me—I just got out of the hospital, remember?"

"Right." She gently kissed his neck, shoulders, across his chest and down.

Carmine caught his breath and sighed. "That's better."

Some indefinite time later, she straddled him and eased down, pulling him inside. The weight of her hurt his thighs. He said, "This might not be—"

Tamar didn't seem to hear him. Her breath whistled through her teeth and she reached down and dug her fingers into his thighs and pulled him deep into her. It hurt. He tried to lift her off.

She caught her rhythm and started moving faster, pounding him. A sudden vision of the policeman grabbing him, breaking his leg, filled him and he cried out, pushed her to one side, and scrambled to the other side of the bed.

"God damn it!" she shouted. "What's the matter now?"

Carmine looked at her, dark skin flushed, chocolate nipples erect, almond eyes wide. *Damn.* "I hate to say this. You're too rough for me."

"What?"

"I don't like saying it any more than you like hearing it. But I'm a thin-boned bird man and you are going to break me."

She sat back, looking confused. "I'm too rough?"

"Let's say, too enthusiastic."

"First time I ever heard *that* as a criticism."

"Consider this a special case."

"Hm." Tamar stood and rummaged in her closet and found a robe for herself, tossed him one.

It fell to the ground on him. "Is this Carrie's?" Carmine asked.

Tamar nodded. "Want some hot chocolate? I'm going to have to think about this. It's never happened before."

Carmine followed her into the small kitchen. He sat and watched her take bars of solid chocolate, melt them, and mix in the water. She whisked the mixture into foam and then added hot milk.

"I've never seen anybody make cocoa that way," he said.

"I learned it from my grandfather," she said as she brought two mugs to the table. "Too rough. I'll be damned."

He spread out his hands and saw they were shaking. He clasped them together in front of him. "Don't take it personally. I'm what you might say an exception."

"True." She looked at his wings bound in the harness. "Are they uncomfortable?"

He shrugged. "I'll spread them out later."

"You could spread them out here."

"There's no room. They're fragile."

She cocked her head to one side. "You're fragile all over. You think about it all the time?"

"Not in the air."

"But you don't fly all the time. On the ground, you always have to worry about it. It must wear on you. Do you ever resent what was done to you?"

Her sympathy seemed so professional Carmine laughed. "What are you, a reporter?"

"Well, yes."

He stared at her. "I'll be damned. Is *that* why you were looking for me?"

She looked into her chocolate. "Partly."

"Is it why you took me to bed? To report on the experience?"

"Only the bonded reporters get to do that and be taken seriously. 'I slept with an elephant, and ladies, the size doesn't matter myth isn't true!' *That* would make a small hit on the net. For anyone else, it would be pornography."

"Are you writing pornography?"

Tamar shook her head. "Hardly. I looked for you because I'm following up on a story I wrote a while back. I never published it and it's a sort of hobby of mine. On the bodyworks in Brazil. I didn't know I'd like you."

"You're doing this for love, not money, eh?"

She laughed. "Look, I wouldn't sleep with someone just for a story."

"What do you want to know?"

"You must have hated your father for doing this to you. Doesn't it haunt you? Always watching what you're doing so you don't inadvertently hurt yourself? Like an arthritic old man."

"Flying is worth it." Carmine paused. "And I don't hate my father."

She brushed that aside. "I believe you. But doesn't the rest bother you?"

"Are you sincere?"

"Yes." Then, she grinned and he liked the look of it. "This time, at least."

Carmine leaned towards her across the table. "Just once. Just *once*. I'd like to hit somebody without worrying about breaking my arm. Hit some rude son-of-a-bitch. Just hit him. And not break."

"An angry young man."

Stung, Carmine settled back in his chair. "You asked. Tell me, Ms. Longren," he said bitterly. "What's your secret fantasy? Besides to be preternaturally nosy."

"I want to be listened to," she said simply.

Carmine considered that. "You have more ambition than I do. I'd be happy with a comparatively simple physical blow. Besides, Papa and I have buried any axes between us." *Talk about yourself*, he remembered. How had Joanne known? Maybe he *did* owe her.

Carmine sipped his cocoa. "Papa gave me a gift. To do this, he made me a cripple and a freak. Is my father insane to make over his only son into something more pterodactyl than man?"

"I would say so."

"So would I, some years ago. But he could not know what that gift would mean. He took a chance— a crazy, insane chance—that the gift of flight would make up for it. My father is a gambler."

Tamar watched him levelly. "And?"

Carmine shrugged. "After several years with some very good therapists, I decided he had won his gamble. It is worth it."

"I find that hard to believe."

"So would say anyone who has not done what I have done. You cannot know, can you?"

Tamar watched him silently for so long he began to be uncomfortable. She smiled. "Right. So, you think I shouldn't follow up on Papa Carlos."

"I can't say what you should do. Only that I have nothing to say on that subject. Quinote, on the other hand, is another matter."

She raised her eyebrows. "Who?"

"The good doctor Montague Quinote, MD, Ph.D., sage and sachem." Carmine gave her a wan grin. "He's a ghastly man. He made me what I am today."

Tamar looked at him coolly. "Made you?"

"Oh, Papa bought the service." Carmine stared into his cocoa. "But it's not a good thing to hate your father. This was explained to me. And flying... well, flying is worth almost anything. It's as good as sex. Better, sometimes."

"Excuse me?"

Carmine held up his hand in apology. "No offense meant."

Tamar chuckled. "None taken. We can talk more later. You have presented me with a challenge. Would you like another dance?"

"If I can stand the strain."

Tamar came around the counter and pulled him to her slowly. "This time," she murmured. "You lead."

‹ 5: Wash, 4/15 ›

Wash rarely watched the certified news. This was bigotry on his part. He had his own sources and standard news reporting never measured up; he always felt a thirst for more information when he turned off the net.

However, Rocco suggested it as soon as he

returned from the courier run.

Wash dropped the soiled clothes to be washed.

"Mister Sunshine," said Rocco as Wash stepped into the shower. "Something on the certified net."

"What have you got?"

"I don't know."

Wash frowned through the mask of soap bubbles. He rinsed and stared upwards. Rocco had no particular center of consciousness but Wash was in the habit of addressing himself to the ceiling. "Tell me more."

"Remember you asked me to check out the condors flying over the Boston area?"

"Yes. You said there was nothing to it." He toweled himself. "None of the condors had been sighted below Tewksbury. I believe you referred to it as an 'act of overeager imagination'. Or some such."

"Forgive me."

Wash grinned. "Forget it. What are friends for?"

"I was premature in my judgment."

"What do you mean?"

The surface of the mirror grew opaque. Then a color display showing the skyline of Boston appeared—it looked like someone taking stock footage of the city. Across the field of vision, came a flying figure. Slowly, gracefully, it turned towards the camera and sported a large erection. It laughed silently and banked away.

"Freeze it," said Wash. Obediently, the boy froze in mid-air. He was beautiful, his long bat-like wings catching the early afternoon golden sunlight. He was as natural in the air as Ariel, a primeval Pan of the air. Wash remembered the ambulance leaving when he fought the police. Allowing himself to be bundled off by the police—meekly since he was in enough trouble. Paying off the fines and under-the-counter bribes—he'd taken the courier job for that.

"He has no tail," commented Wash, not quite breathing as he watched.

Two threads were highlighted in the display. They extended like ribbons below the boy and terminated in flat tufts of feathers. "I believe that these act as a tail. Some species of lyrebirds have similar designs."

"He's beautiful. Who is he?"

"I don't know, sir. I only gave it a superficial scan. He's not blocked on the net, exactly, but the net service doesn't list him easily. I don't have his name, yet. Though to be fair, he could be spoken of quite often in hearsay and still not appear on the net."

The design work was flawless to his perfect fingernails, no longer or shorter than his needs. There was a furred appearance to his chest and legs—there would be something like down on his body; flying was high energy activity but it was also an energy sink as the wind bore away any shred of heat. Wash loved the compromise in the chest, shoulders, and back: ropy muscles in all places, but not so great as to require the breastbone of a bird. He could see the burgeoning shape of muscles less constrained in the shadows behind the boy's head. And the bony hook at the wing joint was genius: the boy was able to add force where it was necessary, making up for the lack of a bird's breast muscles. Wash did not doubt that the bones of the wing were collapsible—perhaps erectile tissue or a solid/gel matrix.

"When did I divert on my trip to Cambridge the other day?"

"3:05 March 11."

The time signature on the video was 3:07, March 11.

"I was chasing a man who was a bird," Wash said softly. He sighed. "That was over a month ago. Why are you showing it to me now?"

"A flying man doesn't intersect any of your alert

parameters. Subsequent freenet discussions likened this event to the new condors. Enough of those and the condor alert was triggered."

"Find him," Wash said to Rocco, looking upwards. "Use any means necessary."

‹ 6: Ida, 5/4 ›

As in horse racing, to Win was not the same as Place or Show.

In Place and Show, it was enough for Orfeo to seed the clouds of the newsnets with artificial events to gain the rain of publicity. Winning required action.

Brusneck—the most zealous of the zealots in Melissa's church—Orfeo, Ida, and Melissa sat around the table to hear the Orfeo speak.

"I'll say this right up front," Orfeo said nervously, playing with the tassels on his shirt. "We don't have a snowball's chance in hell. Okay? That's just so we understand each other."

"Why bother if we're not going to win," growled Brusneck. Sitting next to her, Ida was reminded how achingly large he was. There were not many people that made Ida feel small. Brusneck was one.

Melissa gave Brusneck a hard glance. "When God sent Mohammed into Mecca, did Mohammed ask conditions?"

"Begging your pardon, Melissa," said Brusneck slowly. "Mohammed had *miracles*."

"So do we," replied Melissa, and Ida held her breath. So far Melissa had not revealed the light in her palm. "We have the miracle of God."

Ida sighed in relief.

"Okay. We've gotten past that." Orfeo held out a calendar. "The final date for a referendum to get on the national ballot is by the end of August. To even be eligible for the vote, we have to get the Initiative on the national ballot. To *win*, we have to do something to capture national attention."

"How do we do that?" asked Melissa calmly.

"We don't, exactly." Orfeo grinned at them. "You have to understand how the national referendum works."

"Everybody knows that," said Ida. "Get enough petition submissions to get it on the local ballot as a national entrant in the national submission queue. Win the local ballot that puts the entrant in the national queue. Then, vote for the candidates in the national submission queue. Win there and it's on the national ballot."

Orfeo shook his head. "That's just the way the 34th Amendment is worded. See? You only *think* you understand it. It goes: petition to get on the local national candidate list. Win to transfer the article from the local list to the national submission queue. Win *there* to put the article on the national ballot. If it wins *there*, it's passed up to Congress to implement within two years. That's the sequence: petition, vote, vote, vote. Petitioning is just turning a crank. The problem is the elections."

Orfeo took a deep breath. "Three elections. Two of them—the local to national queue and national queue to ballot—don't take majorities. Fifteen percent of the actual vote is enough. We're lucky the article is starting in Oregon. Preliminary referendum ballots typically have low turnouts so we're only talking about a yes vote of maybe four thousand votes. The national candidate election is more difficult but still only fifteen percent of the vote—no more than a few hundred thousand. The national election requires an actual majority."

"It sounds absurdly complicated," said Melissa.

"Oh, it is." Orfeo chuckled. "It's *supposed* to be. Nobody in government trusts the mob. It's not an accident there've only been two articles in the last fifteen years to even make it to the national ballot. Only one of them won and *that* was the start of the *absentia* amendment. The only reason Congress ever passed National Referendum was to head off a Constitutional Convention."

"Why?" asked Ida.

Orfeo stared at her. "Are you serious? The 1787 Constitutional Convention was just intended to tinker with the Articles of Confederation and look how *that* turned out."

Orfeo sipped at his water. "Back to the subject at hand. Lots of locals will vote for a national entrant before they'll vote for a local article—if the local article wins, they're stuck with it. Not so a national entry. So, we should be able to get the referendum past the petition and first vote steps if we spend enough money. That puts the article on the national submission queue. Remember, though, even if they get on the national submission queue, most articles die there."

Orfeo paused and looked at them to make sure they were following. "Now, it starts to get difficult. The article has to be voted off the submission queue and onto the national ballot. Only six national articles have made it onto the national ballot in the last fifteen years. None of them passed. Everybody knows this and that makes voting an article onto the submission queue an easy vote of conscience. It's like voting for a Red Republican in a Green Democrat district: the vote is meaningless symbolism. Same thing if you think the article is likely going to die. Voting the article out of the submission queue onto the national ballot is a different animal. Fifteen percent of the vote in Oregon is one thing. Fifteen percent of the vote of the United States—well, that's as much as six hundred thousand people across fifty-six significantly different states, each with different agendas."

"Not all of those states are populated," Brusneck said.

Orfeo snorted. "You worked for Senator Kennedy. You should know better. Remember the *absentia* referendum? Only referendum to *pass* in the last twenty years? Generated a constitutional amendment? It's why those depopulated states have representation. You can argue voting twice—once for your locale and once for the locale of your heritage— is stupid and unconstitutional. Except that by virtue of the 41st Amendment, it *is* constitutional and merely stupid. Regardless. That only means you have to convince the *absentia* voters twice. It would be nice if they were always of like minds but a substantial number of them vote their local vote and *absentia* vote differently so they're always a headache."

Orfeo spread his hands. "My point is the process is intentionally nearly impossible. Articles rarely get on the national ballot on their own. Local people are happy to vote an article onto the national submission queue. The very same people are often reluctant to vote that very same article onto the national queue."

Silence filled the room.

Melissa finally asked, "It's been done, so it's not impossible. How does it happen?"

Orfeo grinned. "You put a face on the article by embodying the article in a human being."

He leaned back in his chair. "The Oregon Initiative already has enough support to be a local article— that's what put it on the state fall ballot. We have all of its petition data so we know who to contact. We go to the Oregon Green Democrats again. This time to get their support to get the same article put on the Oregon ballot to be transferred to the national submission queue. Since they already voted for it as a local article, we shouldn't have much trouble getting enough petitions for a national entry—like I said, that vote is cheap. We only need fifteen percent. Locals love to see their state showing up nationally. There must be thirty local articles like this one across the country already and I bet half of them get put on the national submission queue."

"At which point we need a national presence," said Ida.

Orfeo nodded. "Exactly. Referendums come up every two years but this is a presidential election. National issues need to be captured by a national presence and *this* year, that presence can best be embodied in a presidential candidate. National candidates automatically bring national attention to an issue and, thereby, their chosen referendum article. Once a candidate takes on an issue, it's bandied about and interest groups get charged up by it. Enough, maybe, to push the article onto the national ballot."

Ida thought for a moment. "Joe works for Senator Kennedy. Maybe—"

Orfeo shook his head. "No. Kennedy isn't going to help. National issues need a national presence to carry them. Articles in the national submission queue are national issues. No senator or representative is going to bat for a referendum article—the only votes that count for them are the ones that keep them in office. National support doesn't do diddly unless they're running for higher office."

"Then who do we get?" Ida was beginning to have a nasty feeling about this.

"Nobody. There's *nobody* who would be fool enough to take a stand on an issue like this. A congressional or senatorial candidate may agree with the idea but the risk is too high." Orfeo pointed at the calendar. Circled in big red letters were the words, 'National Filing Date.' He grinned. "No, we don't *find* a candidate. We *build* one. Our one and only Reverend Melissa Adenour, candidate for President of the United States."

Melissa stared at him. "You're kidding."

"Not at all." Orfeo spread his hands. "You have absolute freedom with your platform. You run on this one issue—you can even say why you're doing so. After all, it is your citizen's duty to bring attention to a national tragedy, blah, blah, blah."

"I can't be president," Melissa said softly.

"You won't be. *You* are going to *lose*. Therefore, your only *possible* motive is the betterment of your fellow humans. That will help pull the article first onto the national submission queue—not that we need it but every little bit helps. Those who would vote for you in the primaries—and there will be quite a few—will also vote for the article. If we're very, very lucky, it will be voted off the submission queue and onto the national ballot."

"Where it will fail," said Ida.

Orfeo shrugged. "Unless the party candidate pulls the article along into the national election. And the party candidate isn't going to Melissa."

Ida shook her head. "What about all of those techniques we're using to get the initiative on the ballot? Do we just stop them to run Melissa's campaign?"

Orfeo shook his head. "Not at all. We continue that. It helps our cause. In addition, we link Melissa and the article in the eyes of the media. It'll maximize exposure for her and she pulls the initiative along." He turned to the calendar. "We file today for presidential candidacy. She starts her campaign *immediately*. As soon as we have the votes to put the initiative on the national submission queue, she starts campaigning for it. With any luck, we can even get Melissa on as one of the lesser speakers at one of the conventions. July or August. Any preference on party affiliation?"

"Green Republican, of course," said Melissa firmly.

Orfeo shrugged. "July, then. It would be a little easier with the Red Republicans, but what difference does it make? Any luck at all, this show will be on the road by Solstice." Orfeo stopped and tapped his teeth with his stylus. "It'd be nice to have a bonded reporter on our side. Usually, they avoid connection with anything religious. Bad for ratings. Any ideas?"

Ida watched them. No one said anything. She remembered the kid that had called her about some favor—wanted to be bonded but didn't know how. Tommy or something. She'd never spoken to her—the proxy had handled it. She would check. Maybe there was something there. "Could we elevate somebody?" Ida said suddenly as the idea occurred to her.

Orfeo snorted. "Not likely. It takes a *lot* to get the Guild to move. It'd be nice to have one of our own, but we'll have to make do with the ones that are already there." He thought a moment. "Chang-Tsu might be interested. There's always Arban Mondal. He's fond of lost causes. I'll sniff around." He looked at them. "This will take money. A *lot* of money. And a good deal of luck. Do you have what it takes?"

Melissa glanced down at her closed hand. "With God, Orfeo," she said sweetly, "all things are possible."

‹ 7: Carrie, 5/10 ›

Carrie walked along the waterfront waiting for Brutus to finish. "Damn it," she muttered to herself. "A hundred years of biotech and we still have dogs that have to shit outside. Couldn't you use the toilet? No, that would be too easy. That's too damned intelligent."

"Carrie Tomo? Previously, executive vice president of Boston Bank Systems? Previously, Restoration Financial Advisors? Currently, assistant editor, BioNews? I'm sure there's a curious story there. Good evening, Miss Tomo."

She whirled around to face a short, dark man—Persian, or something. He was leaning negligently against the railing over the water. He was consulting a handheld—that caught Carrie's attention. Handhelds were incredibly expensive.

"Current worth six million, two hundred forty-three dollars and sixty-four cents." He consulted the handheld again. "Correction. Forty-four dollars and thirty-nine cents. Interest, you know." The man straightened and stood, his hands easy in his jacket. He moved as if he was much lighter than he appeared.

"Brutus," she said quietly.

The dog turned immediately and stared fixedly at the man, muscles tense and ready to spring.

"Nice dog," the man said quietly. "Expensive, too—Mug-Not is a subsidiary of Ford. Did you know that? A joint venture between Mitsubishi and the—"

"Get away," Carrie said. "Brutus can kill you where you stand."

"Yes, well..." The man squatted until he was even with the dog. Brutus growled. The man pulled out a vial and crushed it. The air was suddenly filled with the smell of jasmine. "Hot. Flower. Cat. Mustard," he said loudly.

Brutus stiffened and stopped growling. She was suddenly scared. "Get him, Brutus." Brutus was motionless. "Go on! Kill him!" Brutus stared fixedly at the man, unresponsive.

The man stood and walked towards her. She backed away from him. He leaned over Brutus and felt down the spine. He pushed something and Brutus collapsed. "Brutus can't help you now. Don't run," he said.

"I have an identifier—" She stood and faced him. "They're recording. A team is heading here right now."

"Then there's no harm in listening, is there?" He grinned crookedly. "This is a ransomware attack." He held up the handheld. "You're being ransomed. You're going to give me the verbal keys to account..." He looked again at the handheld. "Bay State account 516993." He pressed a button on the handheld. The unit spoke:

"A withdrawal of one hundred thousand dollars in the form of biocoin is to be withdrawn and transferred. Enter the verbal keys, please."

The man gestured to her.

Carrie shook her head.

The man brought out a hypodermic. "London flenser," he mouthed.

That was enough.

"Plywood 989 Moonset Hardware," Carrie said.

"Keys accepted. Transfer complete."

He pushed a button and put the hand unit in his pocket. "Easy. Since this is recorded, it's clear you were under duress and you'll be reimbursed by insurance. Don't forget to change the keys. Someone could have overheard."

He looked around. "No team. Maybe they're busy." He gestured with the handheld. "Or maybe I jammed them. But they should get the signal later." He nodded to her. "You'd best go home. Brutus isn't feeling well."

Brutus was lying dead on his side, slumped in a pool of urine.

She started to stumble away when he called after her. "Don't worry about being safe on the way home. I'll be watching over you."

With that, she ran, panicked, released, choking,

sobbing until she came to rest holding herself against a building, crying that she couldn't run anymore. Carrie looked behind her. She saw no one. She was missing a shoe. She walked the last two blocks to her building, continuously looking over her shoulder.

Carrie had regained some of her confidence by the time she reached her apartment. As she unlocked the door, she felt a light, sharp poke against her back. She shrieked and spun around. It was a paper airplane. She unfolded it to be a note: "Remember to change those keys."

In her hands, the paper darkened and seemed to bubble away like dry ice. A moment later, her hands were empty.

‹ 8: Tamar, 5/23 ›

Solstice was less than a month away. The excitement bubbled through Boston. People met for drinks. Small gatherings. Large parties—all in practice and preparation for Solstice.

Tamar was no exception.

She had taken the afternoon off to cook dinner for her friends. Tamar liked to cook. Liked the sense of taking constituent materials that were inedible or repugnant—egg whites, raw meat, sesame oil—and turning it into food. Tamar regarded cooking as deep and mysterious magic.

Her apartment felt small when there were more than three people in it. This Sunday morning there were twice that many. The crowd made her feel comfortable and anxious at the same time. Others might have the gift of hospitality and know unerringly which meal went best with which occasion or what mix of people would come together as smooth as pudding. For Tamar, any such attempt was blended with the fear of failure. She was finishing the dinner as she listened to her guests in the living room. They were no longer discussing the latest *Mister Coyotee* episode.

"Come on, now. The tree does what it was supposed to do: it holds up Trinity Church. It holds up the Hancock and Prudential towers. As an example, it doesn't count."

That would be Fred, she thought as she turned the roast. Always bringing up his favorite topic: biotech failures. He had brought a friend, Mickey. Tamar had found herself liking Mickey as soon as he spoke; he had a soft, creamy voice as comfortable as buttered bread. Fred had embarrassed him twice over wine and his black face deepened in color. Tamar liked how he blushed easily:

"Come now, Fred," she heard Carmine say. "You're just baiting him again."

"I'm not!"

"He's right," came Mickey's soft voice. "The tree does exactly what it is supposed to do: it supports those structures. It's just that nobody expected the Hancock Tower to be supported ten centimeters off the ground."

"That's an exaggeration," said Fred. "It's just a slight crack in the bottom floor. The lower branches brace the tower just fine."

"That's why the plywood's on the base?" asked Carmine.

"The Plywood Tower!" chortled Fred. "Okay. Okay. I'll accept that one."

She ran over who was supposed to be here: Fred and Mickey, Carmine, Mike and his new girlfriend, Jean Willamena, and Carrie. Carrie said she would be late—something about Brutus.

"Okay, I've got one," Fred chuckled. "Remember about six years ago the spray you could put on snow shovels and the snow would slide off."

"I remember that," Mickey replied.

"Worked like a charm, too, didn't it? Well, it turns out the stuff was a rapidly binding polymer that bound to the flat surface of the shovel. You were supposed to wait five minutes for the stuff to set. No one ever did and they shoveled the snow without letting the stuff cure. Lots of people here in New England pile snow next to their houses. The uncured polymer bound to the snow instead of the shovel and raised its melting point by about thirty degrees. That June, all over Boston, house after house: mountains of snow. People standing out in front, staring at these snow boulders, scratching their heads. Some of them lasted until July."

Mickey laughed. "Okay. That counts."

There was the sound of the door opening in the front room and a sudden hush.

"Good God," said Fred quietly.

Tamar checked the roast and walked out to the front room.

Carrie stood in the doorway holding a leash. There was a satisfied smile on her face.

At the end of the leash was an animal made more of sharp points than anything else. It had hulking shoulders and a gray, leathery hide. Its head was big and held a jaw filled with what looked like shark's teeth. The spine was prominent and knobbed with muscle. The animal held its tail still—which relieved Tamar. The tail ended in a spiked ball the size of two fists. With yellow eyes, it watched the room closely.

"Good God," repeated Fred, looking at the thing. "What is *that?*"

"I had to turn Brutus in. He was ineffective. This is Horatio—Brutus' replacement." She scratched the animal's head between the ears. Horatio didn't notice; he was too busy watching everyone in the room.

"Jesus, Carrie," laughed Tamar suddenly. "I swear you worshipped that dog. Why did you replace him?"

Carrie's face looked stricken for a brief moment, then the manic smile returned. Tamar wondered what nerve she had struck.

"Dinner's ready," Tamar said to cover up the sudden silence. "Carrie, you know where everything is. You set the table. Carmine, help me get the stuff in the oven. Fred, start uncorking the wine you brought."

"Such domination." Fred looked at Tamar and grinned. "Does this mean we'll get into the whips and chains later?"

"In your dreams, buddy."

Carmine followed Tamar into the kitchen and quietly helped her carry vegetables, casseroles, and the meat to the table. Carmine said little and Tamar wondered if he felt a little odd that both he and Carrie were here. Get used to it, she thought. The proximity of Carmine—more a friend or an acquaintance than a lover, but a physical intimate—and Carrie together gave her a warm feeling. She wondered if Carmine wanted to stay after the party. As she carried the meat to the table, she decided that if she wanted anyone to stay, it was Carrie. Tamar realized she wanted the feel of a woman's skin tonight, not a man's.

"We need to talk," said Carmine as he was arranging the salad.

"Not here," she said quietly. "Call me tomorrow and we'll talk."

Carmine nodded, subdued.

Despite herself, Tamar felt concerned. "You okay?"

Carmine nodded. "Nothing that can't wait."

As they sat around the table, Tamar smiled at them. "Ladies and Gentlemen, I give you steak."

"Steak?" said Mickey dubiously. "Where did you get it?"

"New company." Tamar served him. "Manatee-by-Mail—it's steak from the things that keep the canals clean. There are some in the Mass Ave Canal this week."

"I've seen them." Jean began slicing her steak. "In the coastal cities down south, the city water treatment canals get choked with water hyacinth and these manatee teams come in and eat them. There must be a few thousand of them working up and down the coast."

"That ought to count," commented Mickey.

"Water hyacinth?" asked Fred. "Tell me what it is. I forget."

"It's that bulbous green stuff," said Jean. "They use it to process sewage and gray water. Cleans the city air, too." She grinned at them. "Washington doesn't have a big sewage control plant out in the ocean like you do."

"Is that where you're from, Jean?" Carrie delicately cut away pieces of the steak. "I couldn't place the name Willamena."

"Arlington, Virginia," Jean said shortly. "It's a deceitful name in a way."

"Virginia?" asked Fred.

"No. Willamena."

"What do you mean?" Tamar let the taste of the meat linger in her mouth. "The steak seems more like veal, doesn't it? More delicate."

"Like veal," Carmine repeated as he stared at his plate.

Tamar realized Carmine hadn't eaten anything.

"Willamena is the feminine form of William, but it should be Wilkes." Jean sipped her wine.

"Wilkes?"

Jean looked straight at Tamar. "I am a direct descendant of the Southern patriot, John Wilkes Booth."

"Booth didn't have any descendants," said Mickey. It had the air of a long and repetitive fight.

"He traveled the country and sired several illegitimate children," said Jean. "He met my many-great grandmother in Saint Louis."

"Right," said Mickey.

"Booth?" Tamar felt stupid for a moment. "The assassin?" She glanced at Mickey and he looked bored and a little irritated, as if this were a long-standing and tiresome subject for him.

"The patriot," said Jean, proudly.

"I don't understand."

Jean drew herself up and Tamar for a moment could see her, eyes bright, sending young men off to war. "A patriot is a man who puts the welfare of his country before his own, who will give his life for a single act. John Wilkes Booth was such a man."

"But Jean," protested Fred, smiling. "Booth made it Hell for the South. And look what he started. You could say all the racial issues we had until the Die-Back stem from that assassination."

"Let's not forget all the slavery," said Mickey.

Fred nodded. "But Booth's act prevented the country from confronting it after the war."

"That's debatable," said Mickey.

"No one is responsible for what History makes of them." Jean smiled. "If he had done it earlier, and the South had won, he would have been a hero."

Carmine looked at her. "Hear, hear." He stood. "Let us honor our patriots who gave their lives for their ideals."

"And consort with them no more," said Fred, raising his glass.

They drank the wine together. Carmine sat back down and turned his attention back to his plate.

"When was the last presidential assassination?" asked Mickey, mildly.

"There was Chen—" started Carrie.

Fred waved that aside. "Chen was shot waiting for trial. Besides, he was Secretary of Defense. Not the same thing at all. There've been attempts. Let's see..."

Carmine looked up. "Kennedy. He was the last one since the Die-Back."

"Kennedy was killed long before the Die-Back," pointed out Fred. "How about Weisner?"

"Weisner died from one of the early Die-Back plagues. The last *killed* president was Kennedy." Mickey looked around them. "Over a century and a half."

"And hasn't it been a peaceful one?" said Jean sarcastically.

There was a moment of silence.

"Hey, I got one," began Mickey. "Aphrodisiacs— ten, twelve years ago there was an over-the-counter cream that a woman would use to help prolong the man's erection—some muskol derivative. Worked, too. But, unfortunately, it resembled the pheromone used by queen bees to draw the hive during swarming. Well, the safety tests were done in December. No bees. FDA passes it. Then, that summer, weird reports start coming in from Mississippi—"

"Swarms in the swamps!" Fred laughed. "Report at eleven!"

After dinner, the party began to break up. Mike and Jean announced they had somewhere they needed to be—Tamar wondered if Jean's announced ancestry had something to do with it. Fred and Mickey left with them. Tamar asked Carrie to stay and help clean up and Carmine stayed as well. Tamar thought this might be a little awkward but accepted it for the moment.

As she dropped the scraps down the sink into the disposal—and tried not to listen to its eager, slurping noises—she dwelt on the feeling of standing next to Carrie, feeling the heat from her.

"What happened to Brutus?"

"Brutus was killed. He was ineffective." Carrie gave Tamar a brittle smile.

"Jesus." Tamar stood, hands on the edge of the sink. What would it take to kill Brutus? She shuddered. At least Horatio made sense now. "What happened?"

"A ransom attack. Somebody figured out my net worth and decided they wanted a piece of it." Carrie held her arms. "A backdoor in Brutus' programming. It was so easy. A scent in the air, a couple of words, and a switch. That's all it took." She looked at Tamar. "Like stopping a gun by putting your finger in the barrel."

"I'm sorry."

"Mug-Not said it should not have been fatal. Something about a flaw in Brutus' design." Carrie shrugged. "Brutus failed me. That's okay. I'm alive. And Horatio will make sure I stay that way. He will protect me."

"How did you get Horatio?" Tamar stared at her, the glitter in Carrie's eyes, the strange, small smile on her lips. Tamar felt vaguely horrified as if she had been told a distant cousin had been murdered.

"That," said Carrie, pointing in the air. "Now, that is an interesting story." She poured herself another glass of wine. "I wanted to be safe. All my life, I've wanted to be safe. So, I brought home Brutus' body. There are funeral homes for pets—did you know that?"

Tamar nodded, unwilling to stop the flow.

"They picked up Brutus and left a brochure." She tapped her fingers on the table. "They had a lot of options. I had him skinned and the body cremated. While I was waiting, I ordered a replacement from

Mug-Not. They were happy to help. This time, I didn't spare any money. Get me the best, I said. They were very apologetic about what had happened. Inside information leaks or something."

There was a sound from the living room and Carrie left the kitchen and returned a moment later followed by Horatio. "He gets lonely when I've left him too long. Don't you, boy?" Horatio didn't respond. He just watched Carrie, then Tamar, then Carrie again. "By this time, I'd received everything back from the funeral people. I took the skin and mounted it to the wall of my apartment. The ashes came in an urn with this little stand, so big." She measured with her hands. "So, I put the urn on the stand and placed it in front of Brutus's skin. And I sat there, in front of it, for hours."

She looked at Tamar. "Brutus wanted to protect me. I knew that. It was just too much for him." Carrie sipped her wine. "It finally dawned on me that just thinking about him wasn't enough. So, I tried praying to him—not anything weird, you understand," Carrie said hastily. "I'm still a good Catholic. But *kind* of praying to him. For days. Then, I got a call from Mug-Not."

"About Horatio?"

"Yeah." Carrie leaned over Horatio. "That's you, honey. Something had happened in the vat. Something odd. They apologized for the delay. I said I wanted to see it. They didn't want to let me. But I said I'd call the Division for Biological Affairs—I lied and told them I knew Wide Ida personally. Even then, I had to have Daddy twist their arms." She sat on the floor next to the animal. "And you were there, weren't you? Like you knew me." Carrie looked up at Tamar. "He knew who I was. He knew what I wanted. I took him home, right there. They couldn't stop me."

"Carrie," said Tamar, backing away from them.

"You're telling me he's an accident?"

"Of course not," Carrie crooned to the dog. "He's not an accident. He's the answer to my prayers. Aren't you, Horatio?"

"Right." Tamar wiped off the table vigorously with a rag. There was no way she was sleeping in the same apartment as Horatio. "All done, Carrie. I think I'll go to bed." She suddenly realized that she hadn't seen Carmine for some minutes. "Did you see Carmine?"

Carrie shook her head. "He wasn't in the front room with Horatio. Maybe Horatio scared him off." She leaned over Horatio. "Maybe Horatio ate him. Did you, Huggums? Did you eat the nice little man?"

"Whatever." Tamar threw the dishcloth on the edge of the sink. "Time to go to bed. I'll see you tomorrow, Carrie."

Carrie continued to talk to Horatio. "Tamar doesn't want Carrie to stay, does she, Huggums? That's okay, though; we have each other." Carrie stood up. "See you tomorrow."

Horatio moved ahead of her to the front door and waited.

"'Till tomorrow," said Carrie lightly and let herself out the door.

Tamar checked the rest of the apartment to see if Carmine was still there. She half expected to find him in the bedroom. But no Carmine. Talking with Carrie made her feel itchy inside. Tamar was glad Carmine had left; he'd probably been spooked by Horatio—Tamar sure was.

Tamar took a long, hot shower, lying in the damp, warm pool at the bottom of the tub. Every time Carrie's voice or face intruded into her mind, she pushed it away until there was only the steamy, jungle warmth of the water pouring over her body.

Tamar woke when the automatic cutoff cut back the water and a draft blew over her. For a long moment, she was dreaming: Carrie was standing over her, holding Horatio's leash, her eyes red and glowing, saying: "You didn't really want me to go, did you?"

Tamar sat up sharply and looked out of the shower. The bathroom door was open. Holding a towel to her, she walked outside and through the apartment. There was no one here. Just a dream, she thought.

Tamar pressed a button on the phone as she sat on the bed and started brushing her hair. "Any calls?"

"A message from Carmine Ranquiz and Ida Sung, Director of Biological Affairs for the Boston District."

"Carmine first."

It took seconds to read the text. Carmine broke up with her. He was committed to someone else. He was sorry.

Tamar's first reaction was anger. How *dare* he tell her he didn't want to see her again like that? How *dare* he do so by message? Then, she realized that was pride talking. Tamar didn't have all that much interest in Carmine as a sex partner. After all, he was too fragile and she had gotten from him what she wanted.

Still: it stung.

Fine. Put it behind you.

"Ida, please."

"She asked that you call back personally. I have the numbers."

Ida? Maybe it was payback time. Damn, again. It'd be irritating to have to return a favor for something that had done her absolutely no good. "Why did she call?"

"She didn't say."

"Set up a call with her for tomorrow. Sometime in the morning." She lay down and the lights dimmed. At that moment, she thought of Carrie and then

Carmine and felt her tears come. She and Carrie hadn't had much, but at least Tamar hadn't felt quite so lonely. Now, Carrie scared her and Carmine was gone.

Tamar rolled over on her side, wishing there was someone to hold, someone to keep her safe as a *giant lizard-wolf chased her. Its face was Carmine's and its claws were tipped in stone.*

"Tamar?"

Tamar awoke instantly, staring around the room.

The wolf seized her by one leg and brought her crashing (slowly, slowly) to the ground, pinned her, and licked her slowly in the small of her back. She looked back at its face: Carmine? Carrie? She couldn't tell.

"Tamar?"

She looked for the voice, remembering the piercing of the wolf's teeth into her leg, the warm sensation of its tongue on her back.

"Tamar? Are you awake?"

It was her room, there. It was the proxy—*her* proxy—speaking to her.

"Yes!" She shook her head, the dream finally receding. *Christ, I hate Mondays.* "Yes. I'm awake. What do you want?"

"Ida Sung's proxy has returned your call from last night and inquired if you would like to speak with Ms. Sung this morning."

Tamar stood up. "Sure. I'll talk to her." It's never a good idea to be rude to the public sector. There could be consequences. "Tell her she can call me in an hour: I need a shower and a cup of coffee."

An hour later, she was sitting at the table in the kitchen. The kitchen unit chimed and the window next to the table became suddenly opaque.

Ida Sung's hair was very short and black and covered her head like a helmet. Her face was pale and devoid of expression. Tamar thought the eyes of a fish possessed more warmth.

"Good morning, Director," she started warmly. "It's a pleasure—"

"Your memo suggested you had a lead you were following concerning Carmine Ranquiz. There was some talk of being bonded." Ida looked at her speculatively.

"Yes. Thanks for the information."

Ida didn't respond for a moment. "Tell me about it."

Tamar choked down her irritation. "It is my hope to be bonded, one day. That's what I said—"

"It's bloody unlikely. You admit that, at least."

"Are you *trying* to antagonize me?"

Ida laughed shortly. "Maybe. Many are called, few are chosen."

"I beg your pardon."

"A quote I heard recently." Ida watched her a moment. "Not just everybody who tries for it gets bonded. You have to be dangerously good or lucky."

"So, I understand," Tamar said dryly.

"It helps to have a sponsor." Ida inclined her head towards Tamar. "Sometimes the Guild can be persuaded."

"I'd heard that," she said finally. "But I've never heard anyone admit it."

Ida ignored her. "If you're dangerous, convince me. If you're dangerous to the right people, it's possible I could do something for you."

"You're fishing for something. What?"

Ida laughed again. "You're not thinking—not surprising. When you're bonded, you can be only accountable for reporting things that you have *personally experienced*. To be dangerous enough to be bonded—or to have me sponsor you—you have to know something you can say you've *personally experienced* that is special or dangerous." She leaned towards Tamar through the display. "I am the Director in Boston. You are a reporter for BioNews. Think carefully. Now tell me, Tamar Longren, do you have anything you've *personally experienced* that is dangerous enough so that I can sponsor you to be bonded."

Tamar stared back. "What does your sponsorship do for me? Can you guarantee it?"

"Now, that's a good question." Ida leaned back. "I'm not sure. It's possible. Let's say I can help if you have the right information for me. The wrong information would do nothing for either of us."

"What would the right information be?"

Ida waved her hand. "I have no idea. But I know its shape. I'm looking for something detrimental to biotechnology."

"Detrimental?"

"That's right."

"Considering your position—"

"—and yours, remember."

"—and mine, that's surprising." Not so surprising, Tamar thought to herself. Preserving the status quo is not dangerous. Changing it is.

"Isn't it?" Ida held the palms of her hands together and considered Tamar. "So, tell me: do you have anything for me?"

"Not yet. I know that—"

"Send me everything you do have. I'll see what I can do." Ida's face disappeared.

Tamar stared where Ida's face had been. She realized she knew nothing about this woman.

Tamar opened some search windows. Born in Salisbury, New Hampshire. Came to Boston to study at Boston University when it reopened. Joined the Division for Biological Affairs of the Department of the Interior right out of school down in Washington.

Transferred to Boston a year later. Director of the North East Division four years later. Member of the Islamic-Baptist Union.

Tamar remembered the *muralista*. She didn't know much about the Sufi-Baptists.

Down the rabbit hole again.

Islamic-Baptist Union founded by Hanif Robertson to join Calvinist and Islamic philosophy into a single religion. Robertson declared his church in the middle of the Die-Back. A *pastiche* religion—not the only such to come out of the Die-Back. There was nothing like having every neighbor, relative, and friend die in front of you to make you think you need to do *something* about it. Roundly disliked by both Christians and Moslems. *Hated* by Christian and Moslem zealots.

Current head: Jacob Adenour. Two children. Farouk and Melissa. Farouk's whereabouts unknown. Daughter, Melissa Adenour, running the Boston chapter. There was a story *there*. Jacob grooms his son to follow him and Farouk disappears. No one left but Melissa so he sends her to start a Boston church for him. Or, maybe, she always wanted to follow Papa but Papa didn't want her because she was a girl. So, she moves down to Boston to start a church on her own.

Tamar gazed out the window for a long time. She realized slowly that if she found something sufficiently powerful, sufficiently *useful*, Ida had as much as promised her a bonding. If Ida could be trusted. If she had the power she hinted at. Tamar wondered what the price would be. Not the IBU story—that wouldn't interest Ida. It would be personally repugnant and insufficiently useful. The whole Parkin/Quinote/Carmine story might work.

Tamar had the feeling she was in a dark forest full of wolves and all she could see around her were their eyes.

‹ 9: Ida, 5/23 ›

When Ida received Tamar's packet, she went over it carefully. Innuendo, inadmissible evidence, suspect interviews. Enough to start rumors but not enough to influence the Guild to bond her. Ida sent back her thanks but no thanks.

Bluff. Conceit. Lie. Cheat. Steal. Ida rested her head on the table. The cool surface felt good against her face. She was so very bad at this.

Did Ida find out what Tamar might have before she committed to anything? *No!* That would have been *smart.* That would have been *intelligent.* No. Instead, she had made a dubious bluff to get what information Tamar did have. So what? Tamar could have state secrets for all Ida cared! The question was whether or not Tamar would be *useful* to her.

But it wasn't much of a commitment, thought Ida. She had only said she'd see what she could do.

Did Allah care about the size of a promise or the fact of it? Ida knew the answer.

What's happening to me? she thought.

Ida knelt on her prayer rug and gave herself over to He who never forsook her and always listened.

‹ 10: Wash, 5/25 ›

Rocco failed to find any records of a flying boy. They gave up. But a month and some change later, Rocco served up the Cambridge Police Department records on Carmine Ranquiz.

"I thought you couldn't find anything."

"I couldn't. But after we terminated the search, I kept a background thread running in case anything new turned up. The thread found a hook into the Cambridge Police Department. The hook had barely any security at all."

"Odd. You would expect better from a police department."

"Yes, sir."

Suspicious, even. "Any trojans in the data?"

"No, sir."

"Collecting this data might have put a target on our backs."

"I considered that. I camouflaged the theft. Hopefully, it was sufficient."

The deed was done. Wash had instructed Rocco to use any means necessary and that phrase was coded to a specific risk assessment profile. If someone came after him now, it was Wash's own fault.

Carmine Ranquiz lived in an apartment in North Cambridge. He was born in Brazil and was nineteen years old. He was studying economics at Harvard. Wash raised his eyebrows as he read: the son of Papa Carlos Ranquiz. Wash had never met that man, though he had heard of him. According to his reputation, Carlos Ranquiz was a man both ruthless and kind—the sort of personal contradiction that encouraged fanatic loyalty in an organization. He had retired somewhere in the Mediterranean when the corruption scandals erupted in Brazil. Wash wondered if Carmine had inherited any of the old man's tricks. "I'm planning to take the day off. What's happening?"

"A Mister Mitterand has asked for an estimate for a commission against the King of France."

Wash chuckled. "No, thanks.

"Doctor Quinote would like to commission you as a bodyguard for the Mister Abramovitch you brought into Boston."

Wash shook his head, then sipped his coffee. "No. I don't want to take any local jobs."

"His proxy was very insistent."

"Answer's still no."

"Hal and Jake Pedersen sent you a message."

It was just a quick note saying they were fine. Andy loved it there. Jake was sober. Hal was adjusting.

They had enclosed a picture from Washington—a town Wash didn't know existed until the Pedersen's moved there. As depopulated as western Massachusetts was after the Die-Back, at least it was deep in the Appalachian Corridor. Jake, Hal, and Andy would be safe there. The Corridor took care of their own.

The picture was interactive. He moved around in the image. Jake's family farm was barely a kilometer from the Appalachian Trail. Wash could see corn drying on the stalk. Several small robots were walking in and through the corn, poking in the soil and checking with one another, doing whatever it was agribots did.

Andy was riding a horse. He waved at the camera, then took off out of sight.

Then, Jack and Hal showed up in the picture and waved. They looked good out in the country. They looked happy.

Wash secured the apartment and left to work on his new hobby, Carmine Ranquiz.

He took the Ring line from Brookline to Harvard. After he got out at the Law School station, he crossed Soldiers Field Road and started across the footbridge. Halfway across, over the middle of the Charles River, he stopped and stood, watching the sculls on the water, listening to the early morning sounds.

The bridge here was upstream from where the Mass Ave Canal drained into the Charles. But even without the infusion of available nutrients, life on the river was lush. Wild rice lined the banks. Ducks and geese were on the water. He could see a carp the size of a desk swimming contentedly below him. Here, as the river had risen, buildings had been demolished and replaced by trees. The reclamation of the land by the river had been gentle. Buildings on unpopulated parts of the river had been left to decay in place.

The birds wheeled overhead and he said their names as if the words brought them to life: double-crested cormorant, *Phalocrocorax auritus*, common loon, *Gavia immer*, herring gull, *Larus accidentalis*. He said the words as he saw the birds, and it was as if his words had taken flight.

Wash crossed the bridge and walked between the ancient brick buildings of Harvard, through the Commons, and up Massachusetts Avenue along the Canal. Only the breakfast restaurants were open and he could faintly smell the burnt charcoal of buttered grills, the aromatic fat of eggs, and frying bacon. Some things, he thought, did not change.

This made him think about the road he was on, the changes it had seen, and its age since before the country was born. Once a dirt track, then a concrete road, and after that a sprawling street, choked with traffic, smelling of dirt and automobile exhaust. Now, half that size as a road again and divided by the long Canal of slowly moving water, flowing to the river, flowing to the sea.

Wash leaned on the fence looking down into the Canal. It smelled faintly of marsh—or sewage? He wondered. The water treatment began in the higher hills of Arlington but the Canal didn't emerge until the Cambridge border. Since Arlington was largely depopulated, there were pumping stations placed discreetly all through Cambridge that took water to be treated and pushed it uphill to the treatment tunnel.

The water was supposed to go through final filtration before it reached the Canal. He supposed some smell was inevitable. Regardless, it did not smell precisely of marsh or sewage, but of an amalgam of human intervention with natural processes. He could detect people in the smells of the Canal as easily as if they had left their sweat or their old shoes. An olfactory signature written on the plants, turtles, frogs, and even in the movement of the water. It was not unpleasant; just distinctive.

Two pond turtles sunning themselves on a branch watched him warily. When he straightened and started to walk on, they fell into the water with a loud slap that made Wash laugh. Frogs imitated this behavior as he walked along the Canal, leaping into the water with a great *squawk* as his shadow passed over them, heralding his passing by a meter. By the time he reached Rindge Ave to make the turn towards Carmine's building on Jackson, he was smiling.

Before he left the Canal, he leaned quickly down over the fence and caught a frog in mid-air as it leaped away from him. As he held it, it looked back at him with cold, stupid, frog eyes, its arms waving helplessly in the air, its legs caught. Even with all its activity, the eyes were still absent, unengaged with the situation.

He remembered Jake Pedersen, then. Jake liked walking around the city with Wash, early in the morning. It had been an occasional thing they had done over the years. Wash had a sudden desire to see Hal and Jake, to sit and drink coffee with them, to partake of their companionship along with Hal's bagels and tea. He tossed the frog into the Canal and turned up Rindge Ave.

Carmine's apartment was on the top floor of a flat-roofed three-decker apartment building. Wash pressed the button marked with his address and waited.

"Who is it?" came the answer immediately.

It had to be Carmine's proxy. "Washington Sunshine. I'd like to speak to him about something important. It's about his accident."

"Just a moment."

Wash relaxed. He'd guessed that the proxy would ask Carmine what to do next, but he wasn't sure.

"Christ," came a different voice. "It's seven in the fucking morning."

Wash listened to the voice, made grainy by the speaker. He heard the Old World pronunciation of the English words and the leftover sibilance of Carmine's original Portuguese. *Belonging to a man as a bird—or a bird as a man?—roughened by the wind and holding within it the clarinet call of a loon.*

He'd have to remember that and write it down.

"I'm Washington Sunshine—"

"I *know* who you are. Keynes told me."

Wash blinked. "I beg your pardon."

"That's my proxy's name."

"Of course. I was there at the scene of your accident. I'd like to talk to you."

"What for?"

"I thought you might need a witness—"

"I'm not suing. What the hell do I care?"

Wash leaned towards the speaker. "Perhaps you might need some help with the police—"

"Right. Sue the Cambridge cops for brutality above and beyond the normal brutality of duty. Not interested."

"But—"

"Look, it's fun to be rude to people who woke you up out of a sound sleep but it's wearing a bit thin. I'll be getting—"

"Wait!" Wash stood still for a moment. "I'm Washington Sunshine of the Summit Ave Block. I thought you were a condor, so I followed you. Please let me in."

There was no immediate response.

"Summit Ave Block?" said Carmine. "The bird research people? You manage that refuge up in New Hampshire, right?"

"We're part of that, yes."

"Why do you want to talk to me?"

"I've loved birds all my life."

"I'm not a bird."

"You're closer to them than I'll ever be."

It seemed to take forever for Carmine to respond. Wash felt depressed and sad. He'd take a cab home—he didn't want to walk home, now. Maybe he'd call Jake. Or get Rocco to read the Audubon biography to him.

He heard footsteps through the door, the scrabbling of locks.

The door opened and a boy stepped from behind it, barely a meter and a half tall and seemingly humpbacked under his clothes. A narrow, eager face with wide, blue eyes that ferociously glinted like owls or eagles.

"Come on in," Carmine said.

Wash followed the owl-child into the house. He felt at ease, comfortable, wherever Carmine might go.

"Tell me the truth, now," said Carmine delightedly as he led Wash up the stairs. "Did you *really* mistake me for a condor?"

‹ 11: Carmine, 5/26 ›

Joanne did not come to Carmine in a dream but on the phone, like a normal person, shortly after he returned from Tamar's apartment.

On the wall screen, the sender showed as unknown but he knew it was her before her face appeared.

Joanne was smiling, her dark eyes aglow.

"Good morning, Carmine."

"Good morning." He stared at her. "It has been six weeks since you spoke to me."

"I've been busy," she said.

"That's an excuse."

Joanne watched him. "Yes," she said. "I like you, Carmine. It's not clear that's something good for me. I'm conflicted about it. I have obligations. I have been busy. You have interfered with that."

Carmine gave her a mock bow. "With the best of intentions."

"Yes," she said. Silence fell between them. "I could use your help."

"The real reason you called."

"Yes," she said. "As I said, I'm conflicted. Will you help me?"

"Of course," said Carmine. "Here I am. Send me."

"I've been told someone might contact you."

"By whom?"

"I can't say. This man thinks of you as a bird."

"Really." Carmine snorted. "Please. I get that enough already."

Joanne laughed. Carmine loved her laugh.

"That is correct," Joanne said.

"I am to be an object of bird lust to yet *another*." Carmine shook his head. "I think I will be burdened with friendship."

"You must be patient," Joanne teased. "All things come to he who waits."

"*All* things?"

"Come now. Don't you have a new lover? You can afford to be patient."

"I am breaking it off with her," Carmine said simply. "I would have done it tonight but there was no opportunity."

Joanne stared at him. "Why would you do that?"

"I have concluded there is no one for me but you."

Carmine shook his head. "I knew that afterward."

"Oh, Carmine," Joanne said gently. "I will be no good for you."

"There it is. Accept me or reject me. I am yours."

"Don't make promises you won't want to keep."

Carmine didn't say anything for a moment. The declaration stood on its own or it didn't. There was nothing more to say about it. "Who is this person I am to befriend?"

Joanne pursed her lips. "I'm not sure. He is on his way but I don't know his identity. You will know him, I think, when he finds you."

"I will make him my long-lost brother," Carmine said.

Joanne watched him for a long time. "Oh, Carmine. I'm going to break your heart."

"I know," he said. "It's yours to break."

Joanne nodded and disconnected.

Carmine let out a breath. "That went about as well as could be expected," he said aloud to the room.

With that, he showered and went to bed, expecting to spend the next ten or twelve hours asleep.

Instead, he was awakened in the morning's early light by Keynes insisting someone was at the door. Carmine almost sent the man packing but he remembered what Joanne asked of him.

He listened with half an ear until the man revealed he'd thought Carmine was a bird.

Ah.

Carmine was young enough to be excited when someone admired him, whether or not that admiration was merited.

"Tell me the truth, now," Carmine said. "Did you *really* mistake me for a condor?"

Chapter 1.5

Lethias walked up the steps to the door wearing a great overcoat. *Quinote must have had this made especially for me*, he thought. Hot as it was at the end of May in Cambridge, the coat kept him cool. The cab waited as Lethias tried the door. The knob turned easily. He stepped into the foyer and looked back to wave the courier on, but the cab was already gone. Inside, there were lights on. He walked to the dining room.

A familiar, withered, old man standing before the window turned to him. "Hey there," said Montague Quinote.

"Hi." Lethias tossed the keys on the mantelpiece and the coat on the floor.

"You should hang that up," said Monty. "If you fold the radiant surfaces too many times, they become ineffective."

Lethias picked up the coat and hung it on the hook in the foyer. "I was wondering when I would see you."

"Life is complicated just now."

"So, I guessed. I told Sims I thought I would stay with you. He corrected me."

"How do you know this isn't my house?" Monty cocked his head and stared at him.

Monty reminded Lethias of a grand and ancient bird. "I guessed your house had furniture." He gestured around the room.

"It could be I liked space more than comfort, but

you are correct." Monty limped around the room "I wanted you here where you could partake in humanity. That said, I planned to meet you when you came in, but somebody's watching me so I left you to your own devices. Like a summer cold, the Brazil business is coming back to haunt me a bit. Nothing catching, I'm sure, but prophylaxis was in order."

As an on-screen image, only Monty's face could be seen: dark with coal black hair, a hawk nose, and a pair of black, unfathomable eyes. In person, as soon as he turned away, the limp became apparent, the withered left hand, the curved and broken back. His habitual hat and cane enhanced the effect. It was so unsettling in this most cosmetic of cosmetic ages, that those who did not know him only remembered a jumble of features: the eyes, the hands, the nose.

Monty gestured to the room. "How do you like the house?"

The house was three stories with a peaked roof. It was smaller than either neighbor and the back balcony was hidden by chestnut trees. Beyond the trees was the greenspace where crops were grown.

"It's huge. I feel lost in it," said Lethias. "I haven't met anybody."

"Likely you won't," said Monty. "They don't like me."

"Why not?"

Monty tapped his cane on the floor for a moment. "This house is part of the Hilliard Street Legal Block. They don't like the fact I own the house but do not live in it."

"What difference does that make?"

Monty sighed. "It's a Legal Block."

"I don't understand."

"Yes." Monty paused a moment, thinking. "Legal Blocks were invented in the last days before the Die-Back—actually in the *beginning* of the Die-Back but no one recognized it then for what it was. They only realized that all those deaths were having a terrible impact on social systems. Legal Blocks were invented to empower small geographical locations with self-governing powers. To police themselves. Dispense justice. Have trials. Distribute medical supplies—all those things that were generally the province of the government but which the government was in too much difficulty to do. Some Legal Blocks survived the Die-Back. Their cohesiveness gave them enough stability to survive." Monty waved to the windows. "Hilliard Block had a few hundred people entering the Die-Back. Most of them died. Survivors in other parts of Cambridge came in and replaced them. Hilliard left the Die-Back with about the same number of people they entered with. Different people. Different families. But all people who had fought, died, and survived the Die-Back together. They're a tight-knit bunch."

"Yet someone sold this house to you?"

Monty looked around the room. "Yes. The Smiths were motivated sellers. The Block needed the money and I had it. So, I got a foothold here. I wanted a place deep in Cambridge where I could stash things. No one knew if the Restoration would take and I was creating insurance. Twenty years later, the Block is unhappy with their decision. Maybe I'll sell it back to them one day." He snapped his cane down on the floor. "But not quite *yet*. I dislike being pushed."

"I could have stayed with you."

"Extenuating circumstances, as I said." Monty nodded to himself. "You'll do better here. Besides, Carroll collects curiosities."

"Curiosities?"

"Human-faced dogs. Chicken eggs bearing the face of Jesus. I didn't want your presence distracting him from his work. He even collects pronouncements from Sister Andina down in New York. He's been down there to see her three times. Complete with recording equipment." Monty turned back to Lethias. "He doesn't bring her home, of course. Nor the dogs. He keeps the eggs in his lab."

"What for?"

"Because Carroll is a physicist, for God's sake, and that's what physicists do. One of the best, too." Monty nodded to himself and looked around the room. "Do you like it? It has a nice, quiet atmosphere even though it's only a few blocks from the Square. "

"I just got here a couple of months ago." Lethias sat down in the middle of the floor, rocking. The rooms were small and the glass was rippled with age. Lethias enjoyed the light through the beveled windows. If he couldn't see Harvard Square through them, he could hear it at night, a dim muffled party roar.

"Yet, you have no furniture." Monty gestured around the room. "I left you instructions on how to order what you need. How to order deliveries."

"I ordered deliveries."

"Only food." Monty gestured again. "You could fill this place with everything you need." He leaned forward and whispered theatrically. "There's a piano on the third floor."

Lethias looked at Monty. "What do I do now?"

Monty turned and gradually eased himself down the wall to the floor. He waved to the room." You get some furniture. You arrange it how you like it. You play the piano. You partake of the world." Monty released Lethias and reached into his jacket. "Here's your passport proving your name is Piotr Abramovitch. It took me a while to get it." Monty tossed him the passport and a card. "I put more money into your account. You can now access it with that."

"Really." Lethias examined the card. It was small,

no bigger than the ancient cards handed between past noblemen for no other reason than courtesy. He reached over and put it in the pocket of the overcoat.

"Yes." Monty sighed, looking at the overcoat. "Pity you don't have a Russian accent. This charade allows you to move freely. Don't get put in jail."

"Why not?"

"They use DNA identification in jails." Monty spread his hands. "The DNA on the card and your own match, of course. But I'd be willing to bet that a forensic identification system would choke on gorilla DNA even on a simple matching scan."

"What should I do?"

"You asked me that already" Monty pointed at him with his cane. "Dance with the ladies. Flirt with the men. Shop with abandon. Get drunk below a full moon. Take a class or three. You're here to see what's what, aren't you?"

"I don't know *what* I'm here for," said Lethias miserably and huddled against the wall.

"Come over here," said Monty softly. "I'm too old to come over to you."

Lethias slid across the floor next to the old man. Monty took his hand affectionately. "You are a catalyst, Lethias. Marcus was a genius to send you out. You could sit here and do nothing for a century and the rest of them would still be off their butt and figuring out their place in the world."

"It's not enough to just sit here. I feel like I have to act." Lethias looked at Monty.

Monty shrugged. "You'll think of something."

Monty left him to his own devices a bit later and Lethias sat under the moon in the small grass yard out back. He thought that Monty had probably hired someone to watch him, though Lethias didn't feel any safer. Absently, he ate a piece of the grass. The backyard lawn had a metallic, dusky flavor he wasn't sure he liked. He wasn't eating because he was hungry, but because he felt empty.

He had to *do* something. A human, Lethias reasoned, would have an agenda. Perhaps, a political goal or the pursuit of financial success in the complex world of technology or finance. Lethias had no political ambition. Now, he only wished to gather Catherine and other potential future wives close to himself to raise a family. His technological grasp of the world was limited by his experience. His life up to this point had been actively pursuing the intricate social politics of the apes, maintaining friendships, playing with children, studying the piano. From his vantage point here, he could think of no earthly reason why any of it could be considered meaningful. He had followed the discrete and circumscribed pattern of small-town life. Now, he had come to the big city.

Technologically, he, along with most of the apes, had remained passive. The apes did not tend to enjoy technology for technology's sake. When new games were available on the island, only a few apes were interested. They used the displays, both informative and virtual, to learn but did not appreciate them as recreation. Like most things, this varied considerably between individuals and grouped along species boundaries. The chimps were the most interested in devices, tracking information, and mechanical knowledge. The gorillas less so. The orangs' interest was almost non-existent. Their needs were different from humans.

Although, everyone loved *King Kong.*

Perhaps, thought Lethias, human beings are informed by the two great forces of their intelligence: their ability to use tools to change the world around them and their ability to interact with others of their kind. The apes, too, were so informed, but the proportions were different. The wild ape brain, enhanced by the addition of the human cortex like an intelligent bag on the side of the central device, had a greatly enhanced understanding and capabilities. But the older ape brain was in control. Humans long ago evolved the ability to make their technological ability part of their social display. Apes had never had the opportunity and remained largely concerned with social and emotional needs.

Lethias tried to reach Catherine again. There was no answer. He called Marcus.

"Yeah," said the old ape. "How is it in the outside world?"

Lethias signed: ==I have no idea==but added the sign for the scuttling crab, referencing an island joke: *the crab goes nowhere special with great intention.*

Marcus laughed. "I bet." He sobered. "How are you, boy? I expect it seems pretty odd out there."

Lethias nodded. "Unreal. Very unreal." He stared at the ground for a moment, then told Marcus about the trip, the change of the seasons on the train, the smell of the harbor, the wild, fearful joy in the back of the courier's boat. "Monty left me here in *March*—two months ago Then, he just showed up today and left. I've been alone all this time. I didn't expect that."

"What did you expect? You *are* alone."

"That's the problem," said Lethias uncomfortably. "I don't have any idea what I expected. Just... not being left alone in a strange place. I tried to reach Catherine."

Marcus grunted. "She's still in Women's Country. I've been keeping track of her for you. I thought you'd like to know when she came out."

"What's she doing there now?" Lethias looked up. "If she's pregnant, she's not giving birth for months. She's not sick. Most females just cycle in and out."

Marcus shrugged. "And some are there for years.

I have no idea what they do. Likely, I never will. But this is what women do—female apes, I mean. I have no idea what human women do. You're in a better position to figure that out."

"I'm not in any bloody position at all!"

"Calmly, son."

After he spoke to Marcus, Lethias stared out the window for a long time. On impulse, he went to the front door and opened it. He stood in the doorway and listened to the roaring world. He wanted to go outside, to walk beneath the crisp night—he'd been closed up and fettered since he'd left the island. Dropped here in Cambridge and left to his own devices for far too long. The night outside seemed thick as crystal, as threatening as a shark. He wanted to mask himself, shield himself, cover black skin, hair, and sex from sight in a great, tweed fig leaf. To cover himself in some kind of human skin for protection.

Lethias took the coat and put it on. He looked in the mirror. It masked his size and shape well, leaving only his gorilla head visible. He spread the front of the coat wide, like wings to bring in the breeze. The effect made him laugh.

"Now I only need a top hat and cane."

This time would be different. *This* time he would interact with people. Talk, laugh, drink, dance—just like Monty had suggested. He was as ready as he would ever be.

Lethias walked down to Harvard Square at night amid the musicians, actors, and magicians. No one seemed to notice him—or rather, he seemed to attract no more attention than the performers. Once he'd gotten used to the crowds, Lethias found the magicians bored him: along with the audience, he kept trying to figure out their tricks. Still, the credit card and bowling ball juggling was fun to watch. Afterward, he listened for a long time to a man singing about the tractor farms of Connecticut.

No robots here. Like working with one hand.

Some think we're stupid to live alone here on the land.

After he left the singer, he found a street vendor selling cooked vegetables. He ate prodigious amounts even though cooked vegetables always seemed a bit tasteless to him. Fresh produce was preferable.

Later, full, he sat on a bench and spread out the coat to both cool himself and, in a risky act of defiance, show his gorilla belly to the crowd. The crowd did not notice and he listened, instead, to the music, forgetting that he was different.

Someone sat down next to him. Lethias glanced over and away, then turned to stare. It was a bull ape as large as he was.

"Nice makeover," commented the ape. "Where'd you get it?"

On a second look, Lethias realized it had to be a man: the skull was shaped too large and rounded and the muscles, large though they may be, had a sculpted look as if they were made of clay or rubber. The man's belly moved loosely, like a foam sack. And he smelled like a man, of talcum, solvents, and sweat.

"I beg your pardon?" Lethias shook his head.

"You sound like you're from down South. Is that where you got it?"

"Uh. Yes. Charleston. Got what?"

"The makeover—that's not a suit, is it?" He pinched Lethias' arm. "It feels real."

"It is." Lethias pushed his hands away. "It's all mine."

The man sighed. "Look." He pushed on his belly and it deflated with a sigh. He pulled his hand back and it refilled with a hiss. "Fungus ball, I think. It's light enough—and it's not too hot, but a makeover should make a statement, right? I wanted to say something about man and animals—the beast within. It's not cheap and it's not exactly legal, so it should mean something." He sighed again. "I was happy with mine, though. It was the best I could get until I saw yours. Who did it?"

"I can't say."

"I know how it is. You got to protect him, right?" He parted his skin on one side and brought a card from the resulting pocket. "Here. In case you change your mind." The card read, *Harry Thungomen Insurance.* "Insurance is just a sidelight, you understand," said Harry. He pointed to himself. "This kind of thing—this statement—is the real me."

"The real you?"

"It's performance art. My whole life as a performance in the service of a statement."

"What's the statement?"

"I'm still articulating it." Harry waved a black and wrinkled hand in the air. "People and animals are the same—we are all beasts. Beasts aren't evil like they are usually portrayed. An animal is itself, neither a noble savage nor an unthinking destroyer. Things like that. That's as far as I've gotten."

"How about the business?" Lethias leaned back against the bench. He stretched his hands and arms on the bench, realizing he had a sudden freedom in the world: he was anonymous.

"Not too damned good," said Harry morosely. "It's just prejudice. Nobody wants to buy insurance from an ape. It's been entertaining—I'll give it that. Instead of buying they ask me to beat on my chest. It makes me cough and it doesn't put bread on the table. What's your line?"

"I'm a student," Lethias lied. It bothered him to lie that easily. It should have come harder.

"You want to get a beer? The Idleman's got a new local brewmaster—"

"Not tonight," said Lethias hastily. "I'm meeting friends."

Harry shrugged elaborately, his sculpted muscles moving in mockery of his soft, actual muscles underneath. "You keep my card. Remember, you put me in contact with the doc that did you and I'd be grateful."

"It would be expensive." Lethias considered how much actual money must be involved in the upkeep of the island and the apes.

Harry looked at him, appearing offended. "I can afford it," he said shortly.

"Sorry. No offense meant."

"Right." Harry stood. "Remember what I said." He shambled off.

Thinking about it, Harry's sudden offense and obscure motive, made Lethias insecure. Remembering who, what, and where he was, he was again struck by how little he knew. He stood and, huddled in his coat, walked through the crowd on Brattle Street until the night was quieter and the individual sounds of the crowd had faded into a dull monotone.

‹ 2: Wash, 5/30 ›

Wash received another message from Quinote a few days later asking the same question: would he be a bodyguard for Piotr Abramovitch? Wash told Rocco to give him the same reply. It made him suspicious about the courier job. Wash didn't want to have anything to do with Piotr Abramovitch.

The third time, Wash lost patience. "Tell him I'm onto him. Abramovitch isn't the problem. It's whoever Quinote is fronting for."

"Sir?"

"Quinote's a front. Maybe he's a front for

Monsanto or something." Wash reluctantly mulled it over again. "Some new kind of product, I bet. Quinote's not the business but somebody is. Maybe Abramovitch is supposed to digest plants and excrete gold—like those pangolins."

"Pangolins, sir?"

"Yeah. Like those. Gives me an idea: take a poem." Wash recited:

A man that's ape in essence
is digesting an excrescence
emitting olfactory unpleasance
and producing lots of gold.

"What do you think, Rocco?" asked Wash eagerly.

"I'm no critic, sir. I'm not competent to say. It does scan."

"Yeah. Send it to Poetry Review. And tell Quinote I want to meet who he's fronting for before I'll do anything. In person. That ought to keep him out of my hair."

The condors in New Hampshire had built a new nest. Three eggs had been laid and hatched. A group from the Summit Ave Block—including Wash—took several days to photograph them using antique film. The condors, hand-reared since hatching, did not deign to notice them but obeying hormones and instructions encoded by both man and nature, they gracefully regurgitated food into the mouths of their young. Every second so blessed was recorded.

As he listened to the shudder and whir of old, precise mechanisms, Wash kept thinking about Piotr: speaking in that low, careful voice of his, the long silences between words. Odd, he thought, that I would remember his voice and words more clearly than I remember his body. But then, the smell of Piotr came back to him. A dull, warm smell, like that of a bull or a goat, mixed with a sharp, pungent, and utterly unfamiliar odor. Like tasting cinnamon in banana or lemon in white bread.

This made him think of Carmine the Flying Boy. Holding the two together in his mind, he thought, oddly, there might be a connection. Wash and Carmine had spent a pleasant afternoon talking about birds. Wash wondered what Carmine had thought about being mistaken for a condor; Carmine had not volunteered much but mostly listened to Wash. Damn, he thought. He should have invited Carmine on this trip. Wash resolved to make a present of the photographs. He wondered if Carmine would ever fly with the condors.

Simon Peters was standing next to him, his neighbor from downstairs. Peters was not the most friendly of people, but he did follow the condors avidly—he'd been the one to organize this trip.

"Simon?" Wash asked tentatively.

"Hm?" Peters took another picture, the sounds delicate as the crackling on china. "You just can't beat silver nitrate, eh? Pictures don't look the same as electronics."

"Yeah. Look—"

"For stills, at least."

"Have any of the birds made it south?" Wash asked quickly before Peters could continue.

"South?" Peters rubbed his cheek, reminding Wash for a moment of Ichabod Crane. "Not far. Let's see—there was a sighting down as far as Manchester, I think. Manchester, New Hampshire. About a week ago. Little guy—first generation, I think. Flew back over Waterville. They're staying pretty much in the mountains, so far. 'Course, that may change."

"You're sure?"

"As sure as I can get without calling the Department of the Interior." He pointed to his left. "Can you move over a bit, Wash? I want to get another picture of the chicks being fed."

Perhaps someone, someday, would build really big birds. *Argentavis* or *Pelagornis*, maybe. On the train back, Wash fell asleep in the evening twilight, dreaming of broad, majestic birds flying over the sky, covered in iridescent feathers, catching the last rays of the sun.

The image was so strong that when he did awake, in the dark as the train slid along the river into North Station, he felt lost, looking for the light. He felt numb, stumbling, and tongue-tied as he caught the green line home. The strobe effect of the lights passing over the trolleys in the tunnels, the longer flashes of light as the stations passed, then the roaring eruption of the trolley above ground and the reduced noise did nothing to relieve the nagging disquiet. It was night now, in Brookline, and the fresh air that seeped in through the seams of the trolley dispelled the tunnel smell of moldy earth, urine, and decay.

The smells, and their subsequent diffusion, reminded him of his poetry and he grew depressed. As the trolley proceeded up Beacon Street, he watched the street lights and thought about how they stored up the power of the sun and presented it at the onset of evening, the harsh light of day transformed into night's pale moonlight. He remembered a conversation he'd had with Rocco.

"A poet should be dangerous," Wash said softly, repeating himself, then looked around to see if anyone had heard. The other inhabitants of the car were safely ensconced in their own activities: watching the street, reading books or papers, continuing work on the active surfaces in the trolley windows, sleeping.

What had he meant? *A poet is most dangerous to himself*, Wash thought. Had he heard that somewhere? Made it up? He would have liked to think it was original with him, but surely someone else must have thought it as well. Instead of pushing it away, as he had done with Rocco, Wash thought about what he'd done. There was the assassination in Guatemala—that had been a tricky piece of work. It had been the basis of *Blood on the Sand.* That, and when he was caught up in the fight between the California Republican Army and the San Francisco Liberators when he was a teenager. Fighting over water was always desperate.

Wash shook his head. The past was passed.

Bad as the book had been—and it had been bad. The reviewer had said so—he *had* attempted to make something out of what he had seen. Maybe he had no talent. After all, listen to his teachers. Listen to the reviewers. That's what they were saying. Was he afraid of that?

It was what he wanted to do, he realized. To make meaning out of the things he knew. "...a poem should not mean, but be." Perhaps in his blind pursuit of being a poet, he was missing the point of poetry entirely.

He stood up in the swaying car. Sitting seemed suddenly uncomfortable. Danger. He needed danger—not violence or death. He knew them both so intimately they did not challenge him. Some other kind of danger. Something to make him move.

For a moment, a thin slice of a remembered dream returned to him and he saw a *Pelagornis* flying over him, looking down, opening his mouth so the teeth in its beak glittered. Wash felt like opening his arms to it.

Then, it was his stop, and, startled, he called to the car to open the doors again. Outside, the dark air was brisk and he walked quickly up the hill. The stars were barely visible against the street lights but still shining like glass slivers on an obsidian wall. He felt raw as if freshly skinned. As he felt things, heard things, they came to him as if echoed: once to experience, once to keep, savor, and remember.

The texture of the sidewalk: remember it. The flaking paint on the door. The dull, pointed feeling of the crystal doorknob, like holding a hard, cold fist. The sharp and painful light from the apartment. Remember it.

A man was sitting at his table.

For a moment, Wash couldn't let go of the sensations he'd held in his mind. A voice cried out, blowing away his introspection and replacing it with striking clarity: it was a trap.

He leaped to one side, rolled over the floor, and came to his feet, crouched, behind the partition separating the kitchen and the dining room. "Rocco!" he yelled. "Scenario four! Now!"

Silence.

Shit! Rocco was out. No electronics on his side. He had his hidden guns and his skills. What the hell did they have? What would *he* have brought? They would have been at least as smart. An inductor? Christ. They could fry him through the wall. He scuttled through the kitchen into the shielded bedroom—*get to the manual controls.* Inside now, he kicked the door shut and opened the closet, placed his hand on the recognizer. Nothing.

"Shit!" He pounded on it, gave up, looked out of the closet towards the kitchen, grabbed his antique .45 from its display on the wall. The table where the man had been sitting was not in view from here. But he couldn't hear anything. Could he smell anything? He remembered Buddy Howe said he could smell an attack—hadn't helped him smell a landmine. He sniffed the air. Talcum powder. The smell of pesto. Wash looked towards the counter and saw the blinking ready light on the pasta maker: dinner.

"Mister Sunshine? Are you all right?" The voice was low and pleasant but with a faint old man's quaver.

"I'm fine! What do you want?"

Should he throw a grenade? Blast out of here and set up somewhere else.

"I'm LeRoy Parkin. You said you wanted to speak with me in person. I'm here."

No, damn it! The arsenal was under the main weapons control. One gated the other. He was stuck. He'd gotten soft in the last few years. Going to Harvard would do that to you.

"Mister Sunshine?"

Okay, then.

He stepped out of the bedroom pointing the gun across the room.

Parkin was a thin black man, older than sixty or so, but it was hard to say how much older.

"What do you want?" The gun felt slick in his hands.

Parkin glanced at the gun with some interest, then met Wash's gaze. "As I said, you wanted to speak with me."

"Pleased to meet you. What did I want with you?"

Parkin spread his hands. "From what I can tell at this point, it's to shoot me. *I* thought I wanted to offer you a job. But what do I know?"

"How did you get in here?"

"Amanda let me in."

"Who's Amanda?"

Parkin crossed his arms and rubbed his nose. "She works for me. I suppose this is a bad time. I'll just come back later—" He made as if to stand up.

"Don't move." Wash checked the rest of the apartment, keeping his gun on Parkin. There was nobody there. That didn't mean much.

Wash approached Parkin. "What do you mean I

wanted to speak with you? What happened to Rocco?"

"It's about the bodyguard position with, uh, Piotr Abramovitch. Doctor Quinote said he'd talked about it with your proxy—oh. Is Rocco your proxy?"

Wash looked at him. "You're Quinote's backer?" He let down the gun.

"LeRoy Parkin, LifeWorks, Incorporated." Parkin stood up and shook his hand. "It's a pleasure, sir. Though your reaction seems to me a bit extreme. I don't judge."

"It's just you here?"

"If there's someone else, I don't know about them. May I sit down?"

Wash looked at him. "Sure." He put the gun on the table slowly. "I know you. You're LeRoy Parkin. LifeWorks."

"Nothing gets by you, does it?"

"I figured Monsanto."

"I'm insulted."

Wash shrugged. "You remade Piotr, then." The adrenaline was wearing off and he felt a little tired. "Turn Rocco back on if we're going to talk. I'll feel much easier."

There was a squawk and Rocco's voice, uncomfortably loud. "Sir! I have to report an integrity breach—"

"Save it, Rocco." Wash smiled warily, staring at Parkin. Somebody was clearly listening. "We have a visitor."

"Sir—"

"Save it until later."

Parkin held his hands in his lap. "Mister Abramovitch would be quite happy with your services—"

"I want to know what's going on with him. I can't protect anybody unless I know the score." Wash smiled again. "So cut the shit, okay?"

Parkin smiled thinly in return. "I'd heard you were bright but more sophisticated."

"It's my upbringing. Sometimes it just comes out." Wash bit his lip and studied Parkin. "Why did you choose me for the courier job?"

"Let's say that there was a short list and you were on the top."

"That's not much of an answer." Wash glanced around the room idly, hand near the gun.

Parkin shrugged. "It's not much of a question."

"I do a quick courier job," said Wash thoughtfully. "Then, Quinote offers me this gig—which I refuse, having figured out there's something smelly. He won't give up and finally, you come." He shook his head. "I don't like it."

"You're very good at what you do."

"So is the IRS. It doesn't answer my question."

LeRoy held the palms of his hands together. "You believe in contract loyalty. It is hard to find an honest assassin."

Wash didn't speak for a moment. "I'm not an assassin."

"You terminate public figures for hire." LeRoy nodded towards Wash. "Let's at least be honest about it."

"Even if that were true—which I do not admit—it doesn't qualify me for being a bodyguard."

"You've been a bodyguard before. It's one of your many talents. Piotr needs protection."

"From what?"

"He's a foreign national with powerful friends—me for one. I'd like to make sure he stays intact."

"And you'll pay handsomely, right?" Wash shook his head. "I didn't like the deal before. I like it less now. What are you protecting?"

"I told you—"

"You told me exactly nothing." Wash swore. "I

don't pick up food left on the table. I don't fuck a woman I don't know. And I don't take money I haven't earned. Tell me what it is I'm trying to protect and I'll think about it. Is he a vector for some new disease? Is there some new infoparasite wrapped around his liver that someone wants? Is he really General Ibn Titus in disguise? Tell me or get the fuck out of my house!"

LeRoy stared at him for a long time. "His name's Lethias. You could call him my ward. He's a gorilla."

"I saw him. Nice makeover. Now, tell me what makes him so valuable."

"I did. He's a *gorilla*."

Wash opened his mouth to tell LeRoy to leave and stopped. He remembered to close his mouth. "He's really a gorilla? An intelligent gorilla?"

LeRoy nodded. "Yes."

"You've smuggled him into Cambridge. For God's sake, why?"

"It's his wish. He wants to understand human beings. He's here disguised as a Russian national."

"Son-of-a-bitch."

"Good," LeRoy said decisively. "It's settled. When can you start?"

"Wait a minute!" Wash leaned back in his chair. "We haven't discussed payment—or if I'll even take the job."

Parkin reached into his jacket pocket and placed a gold block the size of a soda bottle on the table with a heavy sound.

The glitter of the gold mesmerized Wash for a minute. "That's an illegal payment. Gold's been a controlled substance for three years. Resource Conservation Act."

"I'm sure you can adapt."

Wash reached for it and it wriggled away. "What?"

The gold bar bent and stood unsteadily on one end. Its shape changed enough that arms and legs were pudgily suggested. It staggered a moment, pushed out a head from the top, and shook it.

Wash had his gun out in a moment, trained on Parkin.

Parkin held his hand to his forehead as if he had a headache.

"Look—"

Parkin waved him silent. "I don't want to talk about it."

"You better."

"He doesn't have to if he doesn't want to," said the gold. Its voice was tinny.

Wash reached cautiously for the gold and it danced clumsily away across the table.

"Watch it," cried Wash. Little dents appeared with every footstep. "Christ! This table's an antique. It's a Chippendale."

"Oh, boy!" The gold began jumping up and down.

"Stop it!" shouted Parkin.

"Sorry," said the gold in a small voice. "I'll be good."

"I'm not angry. Just be still." Parkin reached over and petted the gold until it preened and smiled.

"What's going on?" Wash rubbed the dents in the table woefully. "This is not going to further our good employer-employee relations."

Parkin barked a short laugh. "You do have a brute sort of humor, don't you?"

"Not at all. I'm going to Harvard. If it's not in the curriculum, it doesn't exist. Explain, please."

"It's too long a story," said Parkin. "Let's just say I have a rambunctious employee. This is her idea of a joke."

"Is this the 'Amanda' person?"

"Exactly."

Wash held the tip of the gun against his forehead as he thought, realized what he was doing, and put it back on the table. "She turned off Rocco, didn't she?"

"Yes."

"Damned good work. Too good. I don't think I'll take the job."

"Oh, poo!" pouted the gold.

"Shut up," said Parkin. "I thought you might have more courage."

"Eh?"

"You know what Lethias is and what he means," said Parkin coldly. "I thought poets were supposed to be dangerous."

"Who told you that?" Wash said mildly. He held the gun ready in his lap.

Parkin glared at him with contempt. "Courage from the mouth of a gun."

Wash ignored him. "Did you get that from Rocco?" He looked around the room.

"Of course, I got it from Rocco." Parkin slapped his hand on the table. The gold jumped. Both men ignored it. "Don't be stupid. I know about the Guatemala assassination. Your role in the Quito disaster. The Portrait Gallery affair. I've read *Blood on the Sand* and *A Taste of Metal*. I've got your transcript from Harvard. I know how you spend your time, who you love, and the contents of your diaries. Don't you think I know you're tough? Do you think I'd be sitting here, unarmed, staring down your gun without knowing exactly who you are?"

Wash put the pistol on the table.

"Good." Parkin crossed his legs. "The best pre-employment interviews are executed without firearms."

"What do you want?"

"Exactly what you were originally told: I need a bodyguard and companion for Lethias. You and he get along. I know what you are capable of—he'll be safe in your hands." Parkin spread his hands.

"Besides, Lethias likes you. Do we have a deal?"

Wash barked a short laugh. "He likes me, eh?"

"How many cold-blooded killers can say that, eh? Do we have a deal?"

"I don't know. Did you like my books?"

LeRoy didn't answer immediately. "No."

"Why not?"

"Is that important?"

"Yes. Very." Wash brought the gun back to LeRoy. "Very. Answer honestly. Rocco's listening."

"You'd kill me for literary criticism?"

"I might kill you for trying to manipulate me by lying about my work."

LeRoy stared back. "There was no consistent narrative voice. Just a series of images tied together— mostly badly—but I'm not interested in images. I'm interested in the perspective that shares the images."

Wash watched him thoughtfully a moment, laid the gun back on the table and, continuing to stare at LeRoy, took his hands off it. "Funny thing about guns. You bring them into the conversation and they kind of dominate. Did he tell the truth, Rocco?"

"As far as I can tell."

Wash half smiled at LeRoy. "Are you going to try to blackmail me if I don't take the job? You think you know a great deal about me." He idly reached for the gold in the same manner a distracted man might pick up a salt shaker.

"Not yet!" cried the gold, dancing away on heavy, golden feet.

"Not the fucking table again," groaned Wash.

"Be still, I said." Parkin pointed at the gold and it nodded. He turned back to Wash. "No extortion. I'm sure you're well enough protected with identities and escape routes." He leaned forward, elbows on knees. "I need someone who takes this personally. Someone for whom Lethias means something."

"Something dangerous."

"Something that might make you a better poet."

Wash barked a short laugh. He didn't say anything for a moment. "First, I want to know how this 'Amanda' penetrated my system. And I want to know how she did it, the channels she built, the backdoors she left. I want her to tell me how to make Rocco tight enough that even she can't get in."

"Done."

"I'll need to set up my own crew. I can't watch him twenty-four hours a day. I need someone reliable." Armand Luka. Stan Hardy. Mary Laurel. They'd be the best. They could watch in overlapping shifts.

"You'll have to vouch for them."

"I can give you any background data you need."

"Done."

"And the gold. And any expenses—and I don't want to haggle about them. Carte blanch. If you have to ask me how much it's going to cost, you don't want me for this particular job."

"Done again."

"I'll need your Amanda watching over my identity. I need some measure of anonymity because of past... employment."

LeRoy looked at the gold. The gold nodded. "Done," said LeRoy.

Wash looked at the gold, thinking. "I'll take the job."

"Oh!" cried the gold and stiffened. The gold steamed and glowed red hot for a moment. Smoke came out from under it.

"Shit! The table!" Wash slapped the gold bar to the floor, then howled and ran to the sink to run water over his hand.

"Oops," said Parkin, and gave him an embarrassed smile. "It's only a superficial burn. The table I mean. Are you all right?"

"I'm going to regret this."

Parkin rose. "Well, I'll leave you. Contracts will follow today."

"And who's going to pay for my Goddamned table!"

Parkin stopped in the doorway. "Bill me," he said and shut the door.

‹ 3: Lethias, 6/1 ›

When Lethias awoke, there was a demon in his bowels, something red and rending, black-edged with hands tipped in talons and a human face. It reached deep inside him and pulled.

Lethias howled.

The demon spoke: "Christ, he's loud! Look how strong he is. Can't you sedate him?"

The demon leered at him. "Talk to me, Lethias. Come on, talk to me!"

Lethias signed ==*Beware!*== at it, lost the signing for a moment—where was he?

The demon reached inside his belly, pulled out his entrails, and began wrapping them around his hand like yarn. "Don't you know me?" said the demon. "Talk to me." The demon wrapped Lethias' hands in thick ropes and held him down, held a cloth to his face so that he coughed.

"Talk to me, eh?"

Lethias moaned and the demon opened his mouth—forced it open until the hinges cracked and reached down through his throat until he could hook his stomach with a hot nail, then, centimeter by centimeter, he brought out Lethias' stomach to dangle it outside in front of him.

"Come on, Lethias. You remember me?"

Lethias heaved against the ropes and they gave way. He reached up and took the demon by the shoulders. Tried to hold him but Lethias was weak.

"I could have picked a better way to die, eh?" said the demon.

Lethias released him. Looked around for Catherine, for Marcus. He was alone except for the demon. He felt so tired.

The demon looked at him kindly and bared his breast. "Here. Drink this." And held out his breast. Lethias suckled at it, and a soothing coolness flowed through him.

Lethias looked up at the demon. "Take me home."

"Hush, now. We'll take care of you."

The demon's face was white, pale with blue eyes. Lethias knew the face, even though it was the wrong color.

When Lethias awoke, the sun was shining in his window and he could hear the birds sing. There was a smell to the room he couldn't identify but didn't like. He felt too weak to move—breathing was an effort. The weakness was so strong and pervasive, it was as if a deep, sluggish ocean flowed through him, weighing him down with geologic strata of sand. For all of that, it was, oddly, not unpleasant. He wondered if he was dying. He looked around the room, thinking: if this is my last few moments, I should see clearly. The room was bare but for the mattress where he lay. There were gaping holes in the walls and built into the door frame was a gargoyle on one corner and a standing Christ on the other.

He wondered if either held any hope for him and suspected not. This struck him as funny and he tried to laugh but his throat was so dry he only croaked.

"I could have picked a better way to die, eh?" Lethias said to the figures.

The door opened and the courier that had brought him into Boston stepped in with a bowl in his hands. His face was bruised and swollen.

"You're feeling better, Lethias?" he asked as he sat

down next to him.

"Piotr," Lethias mumbled. It was important but he couldn't quite remember why.

"Lethias. If I'm going to be staying with you, I really ought to use your real name. I'm Washington Sunshine, of the San Francisco Sunshines." Wash reached into the bowl and pulled out a wad of straw. "Hungry?"

The smell of the straw was dry and austere and seemed to Lethias at that moment ambrosial. His stomach growled. "Yes."

"Sit up. You're too heavy for me to lift you."

Wash fed it to him carefully. "Don't eat too quick. You've had a tough time of it."

"What happened?"

"You got sick, friend. The standard twenty-four-hour bug that most people get when they come to a new place. Except for you, it was delirium plus. Did you eat anything the night before last?"

"Night before last?"

"You've been in the ozone for a bit."

Lethias looked around the room, unable to make his mind work. "I did eat something."

"There you are."

Lethias saw Wash's neck was swollen, too. "What happened to you?"

"Wrestling a sick ape that doesn't recognize friend from foe has its cost."

"I did that?"

"Yes, you did." Wash shrugged.

"I'm sorry."

"I was lucky you were weak. Next time I'll be more careful." Wash reached behind the mattress and pulled out a squeeze bottle. "Drink this."

It tasted salty. "I was sick?"

"Oh, yeah. Worse than I would have expected—usually getting used to a place just means diarrhea and nausea. You ran a good, solid fever as well. Doctor Quinote seemed to think you would handle it, eventually." Wash retrieved the squeeze bottle when Lethias dropped it.

Lethias looked at Wash as if seeing him for the first time. "Why are *you* here?"

Wash grinned. "I'm your new friend and companion, nurse and confidant, Damon to your Pythias. Mister Parkin decided you needed a bodyguard. The nursing was extra. You can pay me later."

"Oh." Lethias leaned back down, chewing contentedly on the straw. "You know who I am."

"You should have gotten that from me using your real name." Wash nodded. "But, yes."

The tone of his reply told Lethias how much he knew. Lethias listened to the birds out the window. "What kind of birds are they?"

"Starlings, mostly." Wash listened a moment. "That's a cardinal. That—the trill? Hear that?—that's a thrush. And, let's see..."

His voice faded and Lethias fell asleep, dreaming of birds dancing between the branches of a huge tree. Catherine was there—white face, tattoo and all— waiting for him. They climbed so high there were stars among the branches.

Wakefulness, the third time, came in darkness with the salt smell of the sea wafting in the open window. He felt stronger now. He stood, still remembering the smell and feel of Catherine on the corn-shuck mattress.

Lethias leaned outside the window, looking down to the ground from the third floor. He had a sudden, powerful urge for height. He looked up. The window was just below the peak of the house. He grabbed it and swung over to the plane of the roof. He carefully climbed to the crown of the house. He breathed hard from the exertion for a few minutes, leaning against the chimney. The days of sickness had taken it out of him.

Below, he heard a clatter and saw a dark hand feeling along the edge. Lethias eased down and squatted next to him. "Do you need help?"

"Sure," gasped Wash.

Holding on to the roof edge with one hand, Lethias reached out with the other and grasped him under the shoulder. Then, swung him onto the roof. Together, they returned to the chimney.

"I made the marks around your neck." Lethias reached over and touched them. Wash didn't move.

"Yeah."

Lethias thought about that for a few minutes. "I thought you were some kind of demon."

Wash shrugged.

"Why didn't I hurt you more?"

Wash scratched his cheek a moment. "You know, I'm not sure. You grabbed me with one hand—you're Godawful strong, you know that?"

"I feel weak."

"Hm. That's something I'll have to think about. Anyway, you grabbed me and I thought you were going to kill me. I said something stupid—one of those things you would never think of saying at any other time. And then you let me go."

"I could have picked a better way to die."

"That's the one."

Lethias nodded. "Maybe I trust you," he said. "I don't know why."

Wash laughed in the darkness. "I don't either."

Lethias edged over towards Wash so that they were touching. At first, Wash was stiff, but after a moment, he relaxed and put an arm around the gorilla. Despite Wash's small size, Lethias felt safer.

The smell of the sea was strong but the house was

set near the river. It was tall enough that Lethias could see a bit of the Boston skyline. He could hear the city's breath and smell its exhalations: sour, pungent, musky. The sea must be beyond it, the wind blowing it to them. For a long time, from a distance, he watched the city lights.

‹ 4: Marcus, 6/1 ›

Ape-Time flows differently from Man-Time.

If there was a single quality that delineated the difference between the apes on the island and the humans that observed them from the mainland, it was this salient fact: Time moves differently.

Marcus had built himself a summer nest next to the beach and the baboons. In one way, he resented how things turned out; if it hadn't been for everything had begun when he described the dream—the Council of Old Men, the baboons, and Lethias—he would have been able to resume his more or less contented life of sleeping and eating. But in the weeks since Lethias had left, things had changed. There was now a continuing agitation in the main building as apes discussed and re-discussed Lethias' move to the mainland, the significance of Pearl's suicide, and their own destiny. Factions grew and disintegrated too quickly to be of much account save to increase the general level of anxiety.

Politics was part of their ape biology, embedded in them back when they were living off the land in Africa and Indonesia—generations before any of them had language or intelligence. It was somewhat simpler since politics without language lacked a certain subtext. But the striving for mating rights, food access, and domestic peace predated the coming of genus *Homo*.

The clandestine meetings between Marcus, Lao-Tzu, and Maxwell had only served to confuse Marcus.

He had a feeling deep in his rumbling gut that there was an underlying principle to which they all were reacting. For him, the strangeness started not with the decision to send Lethias to the mainland, but with the precognition of the baboons. He began watching them more and more as island society became more disorganized.

Then, Jefferson moved to Women's Country permanently and he felt abandoned for the first time in decades. Jefferson was older than Marcus, second generation. But Marcus was third generation and felt old enough.

First generation had full language understanding but malformed vocal cords. They could sign slowly and understood language but could not speak. The brains were there. Joan's Disease was rampant. There was a risk of stillbirths and deformities with every child. They walked stooped over and were prone to hip dysplasia and arthritis; their hands were not as strong as a wild ape's and were graceless with crippled thumbs. Second generation gave grace to the hands, straightened the back, and improved the vocal cords but many seconds—like Jefferson—preferred sign. The hand, pelvis, and foot modifications were finalized in the third generation. Marcus' generation was the first to be fully committed to speech.

Marcus' grandfather, Joey, had been one of the last of the first generation to die and be buried in the bamboo grove. Marcus had childhood memories of him: hair almost entirely gray, nearly always silent. Joey had signed him the story of the first fumblings by the first Council of Old Men—the apes' first attempt to figure out their place in a human world. The apes themselves had insisted on changes for the next generation. What that meant nearly led to a civil war but did serve as a model for the second Council that formed after Pearl died.

A different conflict began when the third generation apes reached maturity. It had been expected that the second-generation apes would pair together, third with third, and so on. It had not worked out that way: some women preferred older apes, as did some males. Marcus, himself, had wanted Jefferson, a second generation ape some twenty years his senior. The chaos had not truly died down until most of the second generation had died of old age. Jefferson was one of the last.

But now, Marcus' children were grown and had bands and children of their own. His other wives had died or left him for another ape. Only Jefferson had remained with him and now she had gone, telling him only that he should not expect her back anytime soon.

Marcus had decided to out of the main dorm the night he was visited by Maxwell and Lao-Tzu. He moved first to his summer nest to watch the baboons. It was unsatisfactory: he was missing too much. Marcus was convinced there was a key here to understanding. He moved into the baboon band and ate what they ate as best he could. Gorillas are obligate herbivores. Baboons are omnivorous. Still, Marcus ate what he could when they ate, slept when they slept, spent long, idle hours staring at the hurricane trees that surrounded the island.

After a few days, the chaos of the island seemed to withdraw from him and he spent an empty time, foraging among the marsh grasses, helping the baboons fish, and watching—always watching—the sea. Whether from the gradual ease of familiarity or for some disposition of their own, the baboons seemed to change character in front of him and transit from animals just above beasts to insightful and even poetic beings. He also found that the regular bathings in the Atlantic eased the itching on his shoulder.

The baboons did not give him a name—among themselves, most did not seem to have true names but only descriptions made up on the spur of the moment. One day, an old black female was called "Dark-Female-With-Withered-Breasts." The next, she caught a striped bass and was known all that day as, "Found-The-Big-Meal." They had no coherent history in and of themselves. Their history was preserved in those that actually had names. Runs-From-Water's name came from being saved from drowning. At one point, he told the entire story to Marcus. The story was no mere occurrence, but a tale filled with sharks and visions and the best way to fish. After he'd heard it twice, somewhat different each time, Marcus realized that Runs-From-Water was a book of sorts, a history, a song. It made him wonder more than ever the significance of giving Lethias the name Comes-At-Noon. He asked Runs-From-Water about it.

==Tell me about Comes-At-Noon.== signed Marcus.

==Ah.== signed Runs-From-Water, nodding. ==A good story. Once there was a young gorilla who was not worth much. He could not fish. He could not dream well. He could not even watch the sea properly. He lived an unimportant life. He ate, slept, and defecated and no more could be said of him. Yet, one day, it came to him the opportunity to be singular.==

==Singular? I don't understand.==

==Ah. Most are transitory. They are strong or cowardly, languid or driven, enlightened or filled with evil glee. They cannot be fixed in nature. Comes-At-Noon had the chance to become singular: to always be one thing.==

==You mean he would never change?== Marcus shook his head. This didn't fit with his picture of Lethias at all.

==No. Comes-At-Noon would be of one *substance*.== Crooked forefinger for emphasis. ==Knowing one place, the next place could be seen. He would be fixed by a moment of unique importance.== Runs-From-Water watched Marcus until Marcus showed he understood. Marcus didn't but signified understanding anyway.

Runs-From-Water continued: ==Comes-At-Noon only knew the chance was his, not what the chance was or what it meant. He searched all over the island but did not find it. Finally, he came to my people who could see in him this chance. As it was noon, so we named him. He went from this world to the next and took up residence. There, he faced sickness and death, friendship, treacherous lust, forgiveness, sorrow, and betrayal. He returned to cast this island into the sea.==

==I don't understand,== said Marcus, frightened. ==I don't understand.==

Runs-From-Water brushed it aside easily. ==You will. And you will go now.==

Runs-From-Water turned from him and began digging in the sand.

"Marcus, is that you?"

Marcus looked around, bewildered. He saw the ferry had docked while he had been intently following Runs-From-Water's story. Carroll Sims was walking towards him.

"Sims?" Marcus shook his head.

"Outstanding," said Sims. "How are you?" He pulled Marcus' hand into a hug. Marcus hugged him back, thinking *there is too much here for me to understand.*

‹ 5: Jefferson, 6/4 ›

"Hm," said Sister Hanna, examining the painting. "I can't detect any change." She leaned back and looked around the clearing in which they sat. "I can't see anything at all."

Jefferson agreed. Jezebel stared the longest as if trying to wrest meaning from the sand painting by strength of will. Finally, she sighed and nodded herself. The Deadly Woman had not been deflected.

==What's that?== asked Jefferson, pointing to a shadow in the background. It was nebulous. One moment, it looked like a man. Another, it looked like a smudge.

"I'm not sure," said Jezebel. "I've been thinking it's an approaching opportunity."

==Opportunity?==

Jezebel shrugged. "I don't know. Maybe something's coming? Or maybe it represents a collection of dark forces arrayed against it."

Jefferson laughed.

Catherine watched the painting from behind the other three, deferring in attitude and manner to their seniority. This irritated Jefferson. She would have wanted someone with a little more *spark* to be Lethias' wife. A little more *gumption.* Jefferson shrugged. Things rarely happen as planned.

"Look here," Catherine said suddenly and pointed at the painting. The winged shape they had sought to contact had moved towards the Lethias-figure. "Doesn't this mean something?"

"What should it mean?" asked Sister Hanna grumpily. "The damned thing is about to shit on Lethias. This is like examining mates in the dark." She nodded towards Catherine. "Or like picking a mate at random."

Catherine glared at her. "I'm trying to help my husband. That is more than you can say."

"I don't care about your husband, missy. I care about *all of us!*" Sister Hanna leaped up and stalked away. When she was far enough for the painting to be safe, she began to dance, flinging dirt, sand, and sticks across the clearing.

Catherine looked down and rubbed her belly. It had barely begun to swell. She would bear in mid-December if all went well.

==Pregnant eyes have perspective,== signed Jefferson. ==I think this might be important.==

"The bird has moved but not the woman," said Jezebel thoughtfully. "It's hard to separate the actual from the metaphorical."

==It's all metaphorical,== signed Jefferson.

Sister Hanna stopped, looking distracted. "He's here."

"Who?" demanded Jezebel. "Lethias?"

"No," said Sister Hanna slowly. She came back to the painting and searched it. She pointed. "Here. The Snake."

Worked into the fabric of the painting and buried in the pattern almost to invisibility was a crooked snake, twisting below both the Deadly Woman, the bird, the Lethias figure, and above the sea.

"Here? Now?" asked Jezebel.

Sister Hanna nodded. "Now." She pointed back towards the main buildings as the ferry horn blew. "On the ferry. On the *unscheduled* ferry."

Possible passengers on an unscheduled ferry would fit on a very short list. There was Parkin, of course. Quinote. Lethias, himself. Some of the staff.

Jefferson looked at them, stricken. Her stomach hurt—that heartburn again. She made the sign of wet feet.

"Old *Walks-On-Water?*" said Sister Hanna, her voice rising. "Here? He's *back?*"

"*Walks-On-Water?*" asked Catherine.

Jezebel had already begun destroying the painting. "*Walks-On-Water. Sees-Too-Much. Run-Away-Man,*" she sang. Jezebel spit on the place where the painting had been and danced on it. "Carroll Sims. Come on. Help me dance it away."

Catherine rose and followed them in a Congo line down towards the water. A multicolored dust cloud followed them. "Isn't he our friend? Like Quinote and Parkin?"

"What we do, girl," panted Sister Hanna as she brought the end of the line to the water. "Is our own business."

They stopped, breathing hard.

"Sims can see into your soul." Jezebel shuddered. "He probably could have seen Catherine was pregnant before we did." She looked at them. "He sees things in eggs." She shuddered again.

"*I* think he can be two places at once," declared Sister Hanna. "Or three, maybe. That's how he learns so much about us. I spoke with him one time and he seemed to take the thread of my thoughts out of my head. He knew things I never told him." She shook her head. "He's been gone for months. I thought he would never return."

==Hanna, all you're good for is mouthing,== signed Jefferson. ==The best that would be is a hope. Now, he's back.==

"Are you trying to tell me there *isn't* something downright *supernatural* about Sims?" Sister Hanna glared at Jefferson. "Maybe he's the devil himself."

==He plays good poker,== signed Jefferson reluctantly. ==And he's damned smart. Too damned smart for our purposes, anyway. I say we put Catherine deep in the grove so he doesn't see her. She won't be able to hide anything.==

"I *can* keep a secret," said Catherine with quiet dignity.

The other three looked at her.

Jefferson sighed. ==No, you can't. Not at this time and not from him. Go with Hanna. Jezebel, you scour

Women's Country of any clues.==

"What will you do?" asked Catherine.

Jefferson grinned. ==I'm going to meet Sims.==

She found Sims sitting with Marcus on the beach. He looked up when she came to him.

"Ah, there you are," he said as if Jefferson had been expected.

==Good to see you.== she signed.

"Hi, Jefferson," said Marcus, looking away.

She went over to Marcus. He took his head and pressed it against her chest. Jefferson held it. She *had* missed him.

Marcus relaxed and patted her arm affectionately.

Sims stood and dusted the sand off his trousers. He hoisted on his backpack.

Still comfortably touching Marcus, Jefferson signed to Sims: ==You're going somewhere? ==

"Not exactly," Sims said as he adjusted the weight of the pack. "*We* are going to my lab near Women's Country. South end of the island, remember? Near the bamboo and the honey locust." He frowned. "Never liked honey locusts. The thorns were too damned big."

"Women's country?" Marcus stared at him. "What about the *baboons!*"

==Baboons? == Jefferson signed, trying to distract Sims. *What does he know?* Only Sims could do this to her, this mental rechecking of everything she'd done since last she had seen him. It was like talking to somebody you couldn't see, to some ancient dark god that did not have your own best interests at heart and still knew more than you did.

"Marcus has observed some interesting things about the baboons." Sims brushed it away. "But at the moment, I'm more interested in what's going on in your end of the island and my lab. Let's be going."

==You can't——==

He stopped and looked down at her. "Why not?"

"Come on, Sims," Marcus drawled after him. "That's the girls' place down there."

Sims ignored him.

==It's Women's Country.== signed Jefferson desperately.

"Ah. Because I'm a man, eh?" Sims looked at her with a smile and for the life of her, Jefferson had no idea what he was thinking. "My lab is next door and you'd prefer me not to intrude. Of course, my lab was there before there *was* a Women's Country, eh?" He thought for a moment. "Tell you what," he finally said. "I'll try to keep my work from disturbing you so you can make an exception." He started off again towards the south.

Jefferson ran ahead of him and stopped. ==You can't.==

His gaze had no smile in it now. It was dark, his wide eyes were suddenly huge and she felt as if she were drowning. *He was going to do something to her. Something terrible.* Terrified, she looked away. Jefferson felt the fear in her body. She rubbed her chest to make the pain go away.

"Jefferson," Sims said softly. "Lead me into Women's Country. It's time I went there."

Numb and helpless, Jefferson nodded and began to walk slowly back up the trail. She was silent and morose. She didn't even sign.

Sims brought out a small hand instrument. He chatted to her quietly, talking inconsequentially, checking the device every few steps. Gradually, her spirits lifted as he spoke until she was actually listening.

"Instrumentation has always been my central interest. Metrics. If you can measure something— sprinkle the salt on the bird's tail, so to speak—you can understand it." Sims grinned at her. He checked the instrument again.

When Sims saw he had finally gotten her attention, his tone changed and grew softer, comforting. "Jefferson, I have no interest in corrupting your environment. I will just take measurements for a while."

==A while? ==

"A week or two at most." He patted his pack. "I'll stay in my lab. You won't even know I'm there."

==This is my *country!* You *can't* stay here! == She felt enraged, ready to tear him apart.

Sims didn't seem to notice the sign. "This is a good spot. Let me do some measurements here." Sims dropped his pack and stretched.

Jefferson looked around. It was the same clearing where the four of them had been reading the painting. The beach where they had danced was just beyond the trees. *Maybe he does know things.* She realized why Sims had been called *Run-Away-Man.* Her anger melted into fear.

"No," Sims said looking at her with a small smile on his face. "You won't even know I'm around."

‹ 6: Monty, 6/5 ›

"So," began Monty, sitting back in his chair. The display showed Sims standing on the beach in shorts. "What have you found out?"

"Not much."

"Ever loquacious, eh? Can you go into a *little* bit more detail?"

Sims shrugged. "Look, we have an island full of undisciplined and essentially uncivilized aborigines here. It's like an island of sighted men who don't know they can see being managed by the blind. Of *course,* there's going to be Cori Phenomena here. How could it be otherwise?"

Monty bit at his thumb. "How much and what

kind?"

"I don't know."

Sims was lying. Monty had been living with the man for better than fifty years. He had never seen Sims lie before—certainly, the man did it well. But Monty could tell the difference. What Monty found troubling was that Sims had found something important enough down there to lie *about*. That was the scary thing.

"Do *they* know what they're doing?" Monty said slowly, pondering the enormity of what Sims was doing.

"I doubt it." Sims pursed his lips.

Another lie. The apes were knowledgeably attempting Cori Phenomena and succeeding—whether or not they knew it was called Cori Phenomena.

"Let me take that back," said Sims. "Whatever they're doing, they're doing it on their own. They're not using any of the Cori equations or model to do it."

Alright, maybe not a lie, exactly. For a long moment, Monty deeply regretted that he had ever let LeRoy talk him into continuing the project. *Maybe we should have destroyed them years ago when we had the chance.* If, at that moment, he could have gone back in time and strangled Pearl at birth, Monty would have cheerfully done so. Or so he told himself.

Whatever they apes were doing, the question was how much and what kind? The Cori Model allowed the execution of the fantastic. However, usually, the scale of the intervention was minuscule. Low energy and microscopic intervention. LifeWorks used Cori-talented Hopi to effect small changes in the structures of cell nuclei and genes directly, with a certainty built in by direct observation using Cori-based techniques. Monty's lab used those same techniques in his own work in Boston. Carmine had

290 • Steven Popkes   Brother to Jackals

been repaired that way. Chemical and viral methods were stiff and clumsy in comparison.

But there was always lurking in the equations and algorithms of the Cori Model the power to do *big* things. High energy, massive actions—Cori had hinted it had happened to him. The power to change a gene or effect a rain of frogs was the same: it was only a difference in scale.

"I've returned to my laboratory there," said Sims.

"What?"

"Well, not the whole lab. Just the Cori work. Not even all of that. Joanne is staying in Boston. I'm moving the detector instruments and some of the stimulator systems. I'm hoping the apes will give me some subject time." Sims looked at Monty. "I won't hurt them. Not at all. Completely non-invasive."

"You'll tell me what you find out?"

"Of course."

"Well, then," said Monty sweetly. "Tell me when you have something." He broke the connection and swore wretchedly. A public ape is one thing. A public ape capable of performing miracles was something entirely different.

‹ 7: LeRoy, 6/10 ›

It had been nearly three months since he had seen Malcom Luther. At first, LeRoy had Amanda give him reports hourly on the murky operations of Congress. There had been no news. The committee had met, discussed, recessed without report, and had not met again. It drove LeRoy crazy.

The Southern spring had given way to the Southern summer and Charleston grew hot. The June air was already thick as blood and LeRoy knew—as any native walking the streets knew—that by August the air would have the vitality and consistency of hot gelatin. The heat outside made one slow and stupid. Even inside, within the cool protection of air conditioning, the heat penetrated the walls and into the mind. Though one's skin was cool, the mind knew that the heat lurked outside so there was little psychological difference.

LeRoy grew short-tempered. He yelled at Amanda and indulged in the traditional ancient and formidable wrath reserved only for the very old. Amanda, in return, humored him somewhat and acted as a conduit of information. LeRoy knew from long association that this patience would not last forever and, in fact, he would come to regret his behavior. But it was not in him to stop. The two of them danced together and LeRoy listened to Amanda's digest of the net's cornucopia of information. To LeRoy's relief, there were no new biotech pranks from her. The lizard, teapot, and Molly disappeared. LeRoy hoped the best for Molly and the lizard. The teapot could go to Hell.

There were, of course, no certified reports of the state of the Biotech Regulation Renewal Bill, save the dull itemization of the committee tabling it until later in the session. The bonded net didn't even have that and Amanda's sifting the unbonded reports yielded nothing more than the sand of legislation. Through this he could see the deft hand of Monica Shuman doing exactly what she had promised; no more, no less. Malcolm responded only obliquely when LeRoy pressed him. LeRoy had the distinct impression that the Senator did not like the President's interest in a "piss-ant amendment to a two-bit bill" and blamed LeRoy.

LeRoy didn't care as long as the bill passed and passed before Lethias, and the other apes became public knowledge.

He had finally concluded that the public exposure of the apes could be done judiciously if the timing was right. With the addition of Sunshine to the team, he had more confidence that Lethias' existence could stay secret in the short term. The man had significant resources.

LeRoy began making discreet inquiries on two purchases. The first was VirungaLand: hiding the modified apes among VirungaLand's unmodified apes had definite possibilities. He could buy Herman Winebitter out, keep it operational, and relocate the ape colony there. After a moment of investigation, LeRoy realized it wouldn't work. VirungaLand was just too small—a few bands of gorillas. No chimps. No orangutans. No baboons. Expanding the operation to include more species was prohibitively expensive and too obvious. Increasing the size by a factor of ten invited scrutiny.

The second inquiry was on the purchase of the desecrated and denuded Virunga plateau in Rwanda. It would cost to reforest it with heat-resistant trees and defend it but the cost would be less than what he was already spending keeping up the island. Compared to the Amazon project, it was minimal. And there was a certain poetic justice to repatriating the apes to the home of at least one of the original species. It left the other three groups as strangers in a strange land but they would have more opportunities. Though Rwanda was half its original size—eaten up by Burundi during the wars of the Die-Back—the ownership of the Virunga plateau was not disputed. This was due more to its having been gutted and destroyed rather than any particular sensitivity to its past zoological glories. Like other wild members of the genus, *Gorilla*, the mountain gorillas were extinct there, an unfortunate casualty of war and human starvation. But the Die-Back had left few humans in the area. It was unlikely the apes would be disturbed.

The resemblance of LeRoy's idea of restoring the

apes to Virunga to the attempted repatriation of the slaves to Liberia two centuries before was not lost on him. Amanda made sure to remind him.

But the more he investigated, the less he thought he could make it work. He would have to transport not only all of the apes across the ocean and into the interior of Africa but all of the necessary technology and supplies they would require. Every step of the way was a possible breach of security culminating with them living with humans nearby. They'd be better off staying on the island. Not to mention, with the twenty-second-century climate, the Virunga plateau was not as hospitable as it had been. It was nearly on the equator and somewhat cooler than the lowlands but that meant it wasn't *excruciatingly* hot, just *painfully* hot. Besides, some of those few remaining people had decided being a little cooler was a good thing and moved uphill. They would have to be moved.

It came to him, as he listened to a presentation on the marketing of pangolin shell extract as a hair restorative agent, that he wanted to see Monica again. Something about the coldness and fear he had felt when he had seen her made him worry now. *I should have been honest with her*, he thought, then chided himself. Tell the President of the United States that she had a new species as a constituency? He shook his head. Still, he found himself uncharacteristically wanting to see her and reassure himself.

Widnergog stopped in the middle of his presentation. "Sir?"

"Never mind." LeRoy waved him on.

That afternoon, he sent a bouquet of roses to an ancient shopwoman in Florissant, Missouri. The shopwoman would, in turn, send the order on to Monica. This had been their secret code for years. LeRoy did not know who the woman was; only that it was a means to Monica and it was no one who had any public connection to her. For all LeRoy knew, the woman was an autonomous proxy owned by the Department of Defense.

A day passed. Then, a second. There was no answer.

‹ 8: Wash, 6/18 ›

Wash didn't know Lethias had a secret until the ape approached him.

Like many twenty-second-century Americans, Wash took Solstice fairly seriously. On Solstice, certain customs, rites, and excesses were traditionally performed. These required preparation. Wash was preoccupied in the kitchen when Lethias came in.

"Got some new greens in the fridge. Ever have bok-choy?" Wash measured out some oregano and added it to the dough. One of his favorite things to do each year was to make Solstice Bread.

"It's like cabbage, isn't it?" Lethias sat at the counter across from him.

"Exactly like cabbage. Except it isn't." Wash tasted the dough. More cayenne pepper.

"I'd like to get myself a present," began Lethias slowly.

"Big or little?"

"I don't know."

Wash nodded. "It *is* Solstice. It's time for a little excess. What is it?"

"I'll have to show you."

On the third floor, in a corner room, beneath a sagging ceiling and under a cold and drafty attic, lay an ancient and abused piano.

"Can it be fixed?" asked Lethias.

Wash looked at the ape's face and saw, not for the first time but for the first time with *significance*, the crossed humanity and alien in its expression. "Can you play?"

"Yes," said Lethias, and smiled. He sat carefully at the bench and made a few runs up and down the keys. The piano was badly out of tune and some of the keys were stuck. But Wash could tell that Lethias knew what he was doing. Then, the piano bench broke and Lethias fell to the floor.

"First things first," commented Wash as he looked down at Lethias. There was a sudden warmth in him and he knew at that moment why Parkin had hired *him* and not some man with the same skills. Wash, for reasons beyond his understanding, liked Lethias, and cared for him partly as adult to child, partly as adult to animal, partly as adult to adult. It was a giddy mix of roles and feelings and Wash found he liked it—though he did resent Parkin for finding him so predictable. "First, we get you a new bench. Then, maybe we consider a *new* piano."

"That would be nice."

Thus, two days later, and only a day before Solstice, while Wash was finishing the last of a dozen loaves of Solstice bread, he found himself whistling along with the music upstairs. *Chopin*, Lethias had said. Followed by Beethoven by way of Liszt. It was beautiful.

Its beauty was an underserved gift, reflected Wash. The wonder of music is not how well it is made, but that music is made at all.

End of Book 1.
Book 2, Women's Country, is to be released
12/17/2025

Read a Sample from *Women's Country, Brother to Jackals, Book 2*

Chapter 2.1

‹ 1: Solstice, 6/21 ›

Now we come to Summer Solstice.

Two hundred years before, the holiday was barely existent: a few pagan souls celebrating a half-understood moment of astronomic time: the longest day of the year. However, as the air, the water, and the ground grew more precious, and as people grew fewer, the celebration expanded and changed. Now, it was forged from several different holidays, changed wholly from its original intent.

This is how it always is with any ritual celebration. The first Fourth of July was marked with some celebration, but those who marked it had just gone through a long and bloody war and remembered those who lost, those who won, and those who had attempted to remain neutral. Later celebrants could not know what the original holiday meant since they did not have that experience. Mardi Gras—Fat Tuesday—is the last day before the fasts of Lent. Its excesses are celebrated but the Lenten fasts that follow are not. Similarly, the ancient Armistice Day was first observed by frightened, gaunt men with hacking coughs or lost limbs, who saw through the speeches to the battlefields populated with broken bodies. It could never mean the same to anyone else ever again. Christmas, that metropolitan, mercantile wonder, used to be a religious celebration. Gifts were often not exchanged at all. The later celebrants had no experience of that first miraculous night, which may have only existed in the transcendent, inarticulate imagination of drunken shepherds watching their flock. They celebrated what they knew, for themselves, for that day.

So it was with Solstice. The civil disturbances and wars of the Die-Back made celebrating the Fourth seem unseemly, tasteless, and a source of shame. Perhaps the Fourth had seemed the same in the South during Reconstruction. Solstice had no such extra baggage. Those who watched their own families die from disease, starvation, or war, saw the land shattered by the same forces that were killing them and had a desperate urge to save what was left. In this, perhaps, they were akin to the ancient peoples of pre-history, who might have felt a nameless dread when they first discovered the relentless sameness of Solstice: this is the longest day of the year; winter always comes. It was, perhaps, no accident that the winter solstice in ancient times reflected the summer solstice. This was not the case now—winter solstice was neglected in favor of the light of Christmas. In Solstice, there was only the joy of summer. There was only the sun. Eternal solstice was the dream. Let the dark pass us by.

‹ 2: Carmine, 6/21 ›

Solstice started at sunrise all across the city.

Sunrise, Sunday, June 21, broke a gray, wet light across the city. A cold and scratchy rain flooded the alleys and narrow streets of the North End. In Cambridge, the Massachusetts Avenue Canal was a dimpled mosaic where it emptied into the Charles River. A few lonely crews were drawing their sculls resolutely across the river in solitary preparation for the August races. A few boats near the Canal were fishing, picking up nets and laying them down, then bringing up from the water a sodden mass of perch or alewives.

In Brookline, the trolley lines ran against the rain on a weekday schedule. Empty because of the rain and the Solstice, they proceeded eerily up and down Beacon Street, preceded by a clatter and a clang, and leaving behind the sharp smell of ozone.

In Boston, there grew a great tree.

Its roots reached deep below the Trinity Church, growing down into the earth, concrete, and the broken, pre-historic fishing weirs of Back Bay. The thick main trunk began between the Prudential Building and the Hancock Tower. Three great side branches came from the main trunk. One spread from the main trunk and surrounded Trinity Church, limning the balconies and buttresses with an ivy-like filigree to support the aging stone from falling. The green leaves were beautiful against the architecture of the sanctuary but the resident organist said they ruined the acoustics.

Another grew to the west—solid, straight, an unyielding trunk—rising through Hancock Tower to erupt through the roof of the building. The eastern branch similarly pierced the Prudential Building. The three branches and the trunk mingled and interconnected in a vast canopy. The tree supported the buildings and their offices, fed power to them, and kept the air circulating and clean. The buildings had long since been modified to accommodate the tree.

The convolutions of the roots throughout the square were used by children for play and by couples and the elderly as benches. Beneath the square, they helped house the subways. The canopy was too high for pigeons—and the populace was therefore spared their indignities—though they still strutted on the ledges and other structures. But the larger, stronger, fiercer birds used the middle branches for their nests. Eagles, ospreys—perhaps someday, condors—were seen. They struck carp in the river. The lower branches were occupied by the smaller falcons and hawks. Often, these raptors would silently fall on an unaware pigeon in a mid-air explosion of feathers, claws, and blood.

Carmine rode the Prudential updraft up over the tree and slipped to one side towards the nearest opening in the canopy. These portals were designed to allow sunlight to illuminate the square. However, with the updrafts from heat generated by the buildings, they made for treacherous flying. In this, the tree was no different from anywhere else in Cambridge, Boston, or Brookline. Not for the first time, Carmine envied the birds that shared with him this eyrie. Born to this over a hundred million years, they had abilities he lacked, along with popular acceptance and anonymity. No one broke *their* bones for flying. He banked through the opening, giving a wide berth to the nest of a raven that had attacked him in April of last year. He caught its black and empty eyes as he passed. Carmine saw the gleam of recognition along with its intent gaze but the raven made no move.

Carmine was not even naked. He could not feel the wind across his open thighs. It was too cold. He had not regained the strength to generate sufficient heat and instead wore a tight leotard. It made him feel bound and wretched.

He brought himself to light on a thick trunk. Breathing heavily, he held himself there for a long time.

"It has been too damned long," he shouted suddenly. Weeks since those Godforsaken, spoon-brained, thick-fisted, ball-busted *cops* had broken his body. It wasn't the healing of bones that was so difficult—though *that* had been quite difficult enough, thank you very fucking *much!*—but the evil, lice-infested *physical therapy* that had kept him earthbound until he was strong.

Barely strong enough. Reaching the tree had winded him.

Carmine eased himself to sit on the branch and let his wings droop behind and below him in the sun. The warmth eased the growing stiffness he felt in them—*which requires even more physical therapy*, he thought bitterly.

"You're here," came a voice below him. "I wasn't sure you'd come."

"I said I would, Joanne," he snarled and gingerly eased himself down from the branch to the larger trunk where she was standing. Small monkeys, no bigger than the palm of his hand, watched him from the shadows of the tree. They made him uneasy.

Joanne helped him drape his wings out of the way of the foliage. She seemed unaffected by the hundreds of meters of empty air between her and the ground and stood casually in her jumpsuit and backpack as if she were standing on some hiking trail.

"What a place to meet me! Aren't you scared this high?" Carmine asked admiringly.

"I take my lunchtime constitutional out here." She gestured to the trunk. "Wide as a street—I could get in more trouble in the park."

"It's a bit obvious, isn't it? How many people hold clandestine meetings in a place like this?"

"You should see it at night. No one comes here but the monkeys and the night birds."

"I thought monkeys didn't like the dark."

"This is Copley Square. It's never dark." Joanne leaned towards him, her face a centimeter from his. "Are you a bird?"

"Hardly."

"Someday, my friend. Someday." She stood up and leaned casually against the trunk. "Did you meet him?"

"His name is Washington Sunshine. He's interesting. He's told me of a friend who is even more interesting."

Joanne raised an eyebrow. "Oh?"

"Isn't that what you wanted?"

She sighed. "I suggested you would be contacted and you should be receptive. That's all."

"Why?"

"I don't know." Joanne shrugged. "It's not at all clear why. Just that it might be useful."

"Useful how?"

Joanne didn't answer.

"I will be seeing them later today. I will make contact then." Carmine shook his head. "I do not like the idea of falsely pursuing friendship."

"Carmine, that's not my intention."

"You said to meet this person."

"I did." Joanne thought for a moment. "Isn't Mister Sunshine someone you want to befriend?"

"Possibly," admitted Carmine. "I find I like him— something I did not expect. Perhaps I will like being his friend, too." He would accede to her judgment for the moment. "Or was Tamar the person you thought I should reveal myself to? Someone I should talk to? Your details were not specific." Now in the shade, Carmine felt cold. The leotard wasn't enough.

"I just thought you should open yourself up to someone. A woman. Now, a man." Joanne smiled at him. "You have opened yourself to me. I can't be the only person you talk to." Joanne pulled off her backpack and squatted on the trunk, pulled out a blanket and handed it to him.

Carmine wrapped it around his chest.

Joanne smiled at him. "You did more than talk to her."

"And stopped, as I told you."

Joanne lost her smile and stared at him without

expression. "I know." She leaned against a branch of the tree and stared down into the square.

Carmine's anger and frustration gave way to apprehension as he waited for her to say something. "What are we going to do?"

She laughed. "'We'? Carmine! I have given you so very little and yet you trust me. "

"No one's like you," he mumbled and looked down.

She leaned down, tipped his chin up, and kissed him full on the mouth. "I do enjoy you."

"You could enjoy me further," said Carmine in a low voice, meeting her gaze.

Joanne ruffled his hair. "Why, Carmine," she said gently. "What a compliment. We have to get you a woman we can trust not to hurt you."

"I was serious."

"Don't entertain the thought overlong, dear," she said, standing straight again. "I'm *much* rougher than Tamar."

"I bet you are." He looked up at her. What *did* he want from Joanne? Sex? Love? Something more? What more could there be? "Bless me?" he said suddenly, surprising them both.

Joanne touched his forehead and his eyes closed and face relaxed. Her voice was gentle when she spoke: "May all your dreams come true."

Acknowledgments

It's a little odd to put Acknowledgements at the end of volume one of a trilogy.

But here it goes.

The usual suspects are all the same: the Cambridge SF Workshop and my son Ben. Little of my work would be here if it weren't for them.

Another shout goes to the lovely writer John Dos Passos, who inspired the structure of this trilogy. Any failures of implementation are purely my own and do not reflect on the master. If you're interested in his work, I suggest trying *Manhattan Transfer* or *Chosen Country*.

Finally, I want to pay homage to my wife, Wendy. I had given up on this book for the longest time. She insisted it had to be finished. Lethias and all the rest would be just a vague regret in my life if it weren't for her.

Thank you all.

Credits

Descending from the Moon.
Brother to Jackals, Book 1
Steven Popkes

Published by Walking Rock Publications in association with Book View Café Publishing Cooperative.

ISBN: 978-1-63632-326-8

Production Team:
Cover Design: Wendy Zimmerman
Proofreader: Rachel Neumeier
Beta Reader: Paul Piper
Formatter: Steven Popkes

Some AI imagery was used in the creation of the cover and illustration.

About the Author

Steven Popkes' work has been nominated for a Nebula Award and collected in severl Best of Year anthologies. He lives in Massachusetts on two acres where he and his wife raise bananas, persimmons, and turtles.

He works in aerospace making sure rockets continue to go where they are pointed. He insists he is not a rocket scientist.

He is a rocket engineer.

For updates, notional entries, subscription to the newsletter, blog, and all-around interesting things, look on his website:

www.stevenpopkes.com

About Book View Café

Book View Café Publishing Cooperative (BVC) is an author-owned cooperative of over fifty professional writers, publishing in a variety of genres such as fantasy, romance, mystery, and science fiction.

BVC authors include New York Times and USA Today bestsellers; Nebula, Hugo, and Philip K. Dick Award winners; World Fantasy Award, Campbell Award, and RITA Award nominees; and winners and nominees of many other publishing awards.

Since its debut in 2008, BVC has gained a reputation for producing high-quality ebooks and is now bringing that same quality to its print editions.

www.bookviewcafe.com
Book View Café Publishing Cooperative

www.ingramcontent.com/pod-product-compliance
Lightning Source LLC
Chambersburg PA
CBHW060359260626
47160CB00006B/2371